Prologue

Mathias was high up in the mountain reaches of Manthripur, looking down upon ranks upon ranks of enemy forces gathering below. He was tired to his core of all the death and destruction.

That morning he had been summoned to the war council room. In front of him were some of the most powerful beings alive. They had told him that he was needed for a special mission. Mathias had told them he wasn't the man for the job, that he wasn't worthy. Falling to his knees with tears in his eyes. He was just a crafter with no magic to speak of. The god Knowledge had helped him to his feet. An actual god had helped him to his feet!

"I want you to listen, Mathias Assai. You have been chosen exactly because your abilities are different. It is time for magic to evolve. My advisors say you speak to the elements while you are crafting, and you see them in your mind; do you not?"

"I suppose I do."

"Then it is settled! How is your singing voice?"

"S-s-sire, I do not understand?"

"It would seem you understand more than you know.

Have you named them?"

Confusion and doubt plagued Mathias' mind, and he had started to hyperventilate. That was when the god had reached out and touched his brow. A feeling of calm washed over him and understood what he must to do.

"We must stay and bear witness, but yours is a different path, your time is yet to come. They will need crafters in the new world. When the time is right, use the portal stone on the southern face. I have given you the gift of creation and the words you must sing as you enter the portal stone outside of time. I want you to add the names of the elements you use in your crafting to the song as you pass through."

"I know the words and what I must do, but how will I know when?"

"You will know, now go!"

Hours later sat alone on stone battlements that ran along the southern side of the mountain, waiting for a sign. A cold wind battered the mountains. A final refuge from the Dread armies of the god, Instinct. His evil horde had relentlessly waged war and destruction on all that was good.

Once there had been seven great realms, each a creation of its god. Now the world of gods and mortals hung in tatters. The first realm to fall had been the lands of the goddess Faith. The Fenn had fallen without a fight, maybe a few hundred or so refugees remained alive on these mountains. There were other species and races here too, all forged together by a singular purpose. To survive!

Manthripur was the last realm left standing. The lands of the giant Anunnaki and the god Knowledge. Here they were safe at least for the moment against the vast legion of darkness surrounding them. The giant Anunnaki had fought valiantly to protect their lands, but even they had given up the continent and fallen back to the mountain range.

This morning facing a god, Mathias was sure about what he had to do, but knowing a thing and doing a thing are two completely different things. For now, they were safe behind the shield.

Mathias had been awaiting a signal for hours. The enemy had hit the barrier with everything they had. The shield had held unbelievably, attack after attack, after attack. Through his tears, he had to admit the explosions and lightning that impacted the shield's invisible surface almost looked pretty.

Mathias had lost everyone he had ever loved, his homeland had been wiped out, and his family were dead or worse. For all, he knew they could be part of the mindless force attacking in the valleys below. Wiping tears from his eyes; he had moped for long enough.

That was when he noticed something strange. One of the fireballs he had been watching did not impact on anything. Instead, it seemed to be heading straight for him.

Panic welled up in Mathias. He was not some all-powerful warrior mage that could just bat the attack away! He began yelling a warning. Setting off at a run, he noticed the horror appear on people's faces as they saw what was heading their way. Those living in the homes built on the side of the mountain had no warning as the enormous fireball hit. The explosion had landed just above a makeshift settlement of refugees.

The fireball hit with such impact the very mountain shook. Fire and molten debris cascaded down onto the homes below. Mathias watched in shock as someone ran from one of the homes engulfed in flames and leapt clear from the battlements screaming.

A thunderous cracking and crunching noise echoed through the mountain range. Mathias looked on in horror as a large chunk of the mountainside came loose in a gigantic landslide. The walkway, the homes, everything was gone, including the spot he had been sat on only moments ago.

He had no idea what just happened to break the protective shield, but it didn't bode well, he needed to get to the Portal Stone. Survivors and refugees, countless dirty, dishevelled faces bore a look of loss and fear as he ran past them. It was the children that broke his heart though regardless of species, to see that innocence taken away filled him with rage.

With no time to stop, he scooped up one of the Fenn children as she ran over to him, a young girl called Lyssa.

"Are you ok, Assai?" she asked with a worried look on her face "The mountain shook!" she weighed next to nothing in his arms.

"I am okay little one, we are safe!" he reassured her as best he could, wishing he believed his own words. Like all the Fenn, she had developed feint short fur from head to toe, her eyes more fox-like than human, and her ears had small points. Lyssa was probably physically stronger than him despite her childlike size.

Lyssa was bereft when she arrived on the mountain, distrustful and distant, but she had imprinted on him like a baby bird, and he could not resist her, he found Lyssa adorable. The field had failed, and he didn't think he was ready for what he must do next. Was that the sign? Arriving at the portal stone, he put the girl down and caught his breath. The moment was short-lived.

Lyssa screamed. Mathias turned to see another giant fireball was coming their way and another hundred behind that one. Well, it was now or never. Picking the girl up again, he activated the portal stone and sprinted for all he was worth, carrying Lyssa in his arms as they passed into the portal stone.

There was a lot more power than there should have been. Mathias was floating above the earth, all the lines of magical energy laid out below, and the instructions the god had given him echoed through his mind. He began to sing the Song of Morning, a verse to each of the five elements used in crafting.

The words took on a life of their own as he sang their names, he could not see them so far below, but he felt them now, a subtle heartbeat on the wind. As the song came to an end, Mathias watched in wonder as all the lines of power slowly re-directed. Floating above the earth, he watched as it turned faster and faster, and then it stopped. Lines of power that had crisscrossed the land now flowed to the five new elemental entities, sleeping beneath the ice but still there.

Then suddenly, he was through the portal. Lyssa still clung to him tightly. He could feel the power pulsating through the stone under his feet. The mountain slowly began to glow. At first, the larger rocks closest to them, then the light spread from stone to stone. It had not stopped at the mountain top; the light was spreading across the lower reaches as well until the whole mountain range had become so bright he could not look at it, and the earth shook. There was a silence that hung in the air, followed by a high-pitched ringing in their ears.

When Mathias opened his eyes, he was confronted by the majestic beauty of a clear starry night. The plan had worked, they had escaped. He stood and looked down over the planes below to see the army of darkness was no longer there. The vast legion had been left in another time, long dead. The Dread Army was gone!

At least that was what he had thought. He jumped as a blood-curdling scream echoed across the range. Rushing to the battlement, he looked down upon the lower valleys. His nightmare had come true; they had brought some of the enemies with them. Panic welled up inside him. This was not the plan! Unable to do anything, he looked on in despair. That was until he noticed the enemy had found themselves outnumbered and fighting an uphill battle alone. The magic that had fed their blood lust was gone, and what remained of the enemy army turned and ran.

"Go on, run!" Yelled Lyssa, shaking her tiny fist at them.

*

There was an Oracle in the mountains from the before time; no one knew how long she had been there. The giant Anunaki had found her while scouting and Mathias had gone to see her.

At first, it was flattering. He entered the room, and

Kairos had bowed to him and named him the Breaker of Chains and Allfather. She had then told him he would live an extended life and bear witness to many sorrows. His sacrifice would turn the war! Then it seemed she drifted from reality, mumbling, that "he must give his arm..." and this was the best bit... "all for the dragon that shared its sandwich." Mathias had laughed.

It all sounded too unreal for Mathias, who dismissed the prophecy as the ravings of a mad hermit woman. A remnant of a time long gone. Although there was power here, Mathias didn't know how, but he could feel the magic tying her to this place. Even sense the danger inside the mountain.

"You will do great things, Mathias Assai! You need not heed my words yet, not while I live."

"What can you tell me Kairos about how to proceed. I have been told you demand we stay away from the back of the mountain and inside."

"There is still a portal stone in the remains of Kalistiel.

You should be able to sense it."

She was right, he could feel it.

"The portal stones still span this land, it's how to use them that has been forgotten, but I doubt that would be a problem for you Allfather."

"Why do you call me Allfather?"

"Are you not the one who named the elements a millennia ago?"

Mathias stayed silent.

"Here the magic that once flowed freely through man was transferred out of reach for all those that didn't know the names of the new gods, and for millennia the five elements you named, have slept and evolved. New beings the likes of which you have never seen before walk the realm, be sure not to make the wrong enemies."

"So are you the right friend... or the wrong enemy?"

"Most of the west is uninhabited. The ruins of Kishar are extensive and easily accessed with the portal stone. I tell you this as a gesture of goodwill and friendship."

"We shall see." Mathias bowed slightly and left. If Kishar was even slightly intact, it could provide them all a home. He had been surprised to find the portal stone still working and investigated Kishar. It was perfect, and Kairos had more than proven her friendship.

The Council had decreed that this would be a time of new counting and celebration. Year one after the gods or 1AG, a time of celebration.

The Forgotten

Index

Awakening
Chapter one 600 AG

Bishop stood in front of the battered and broken body of Aleator Darkwing. Emotions tore at him, but he had to keep himself calm. After three years of searching for this man, he was shocked to find him within the belly of the vilest of cults. The Oracle told him of his mission, and he was to free the prisoner from his bonds and direct him to a rendezvous and no more. There Rekhaert Stone would take charge of his care.

The man in front of him was a far cry from the one he remembered. Bishop doubted Aleator could stand, let alone escape.

The Oracle had been adamant the prisoner must escape on his own. "You can open the cage, but he must walk out alone or not at all!"

The Oracle had raised him, and he knew better than to doubt her word. He had flown in over the walls as a Griffin and landed inside the compound, changing into his diminutive human form and sneaked through the grounds without alerting anyone to his presence.

Maybe he could give Aleator some strength. Sitting down in a recess against a wall facing the shadow of a man he once knew, visualizing a wave of energy coming off himself, this was the trade-off with elemental magic, Bishop sacrificed what strength he could and sent it washing over his tortured friend. In this form, he had some elemental ability, but even this small transference had him gasping for air.

*

The prisoner's eyes snapped open, and his stomach cramped. He was unsure where he was or how long he'd been there. He was sure he would die here on the floor.

Unable to even remember how he had gotten here, wherever here was?

He remembered catching a rat. It had tasted good at the time, or that's what the man had told him as he ripped the small creature apart with his teeth. Today he was vomiting and sweating from a fever. He wanted to die, but every time the end was near, he was healed by his torturer, a man he had come to know as Mandrake. He had begged for death many times under his torturers' ministrations, but It never came. He was suddenly ashamed at the pride he had shown in catching the rat for his dinner.

Mandrake had patted his head and called him a good dog. Waves of disgust and nausea flowed through his battered and scarred body at the memory. Head spinning as he tried to gather his wits, he decided to focus on his surroundings. It was like something was calling to him from the other side of the room. Maybe he had gone insane. A cold realisation suddenly hit him. He couldn't recall his name just his time in this dungeon.

Heart pounding so hard it felt as if it would burst through his chest. The reality of his situation crept in on him, suffocating him. 'Breath, man, breathe,' he thought. Instantly he knew he had to regain control if he was ever to understand how he got into this predicament and more importantly, how to get out of it.

The dark and dank dungeon was lit by a couple of fading firebrands that didn't cast much light. The door was a thick reinforced timber with what looked like wrought iron hinges and a keyhole for a lock that was no doubt as formidable as the door itself. The straw he was laying on was dirty with what he could only guess was his vomit and defecation.

There was nothing else to see, just damp walls and chains. The far side of the room was where Mandrake kept what he called his tools.

The torturer's voice echoed in his mind "A tool for every job... dog!"

The chained man shook himself from his memories and decided to check himself for injury. Maybe he'd been harmed. It would explain why he was so bereft of identity. He ran his hands over his face and head. His hair was long, but his stubble was no older than a couple of days. He could feel there was one scar that ran just above his right eye. The injury felt old and healed. He moved onto his body, removing the old, stained robe so he could take a better look. He gently removed it wincing as it reopened some wounds on his back, pulling off scabs that had joined him to the filthy garment.

Under the robe he was well defined and bore a lot more scars, unlike the scar above his eye, these seemed to be varying in age, becoming frustrated at his lack of answers he wanted to scream out in anger. Closing his eyes for just a moment as the weight of despair tumbled down on him.

That's when it happened; a small naked older man with hair as red as fire seemingly appeared from nowhere!

Aleator double-checked his head for any bumps but found only short, coarse hair. "Okay, I'm crazy, and this must be my nuthouse. It's all making sense now."

"Don't worry laddie. I am no figment of yer imagination and ye ain't crazy as ye think. Let's just say ye have some mighty powerful friends who want you out of here, myself included!"

"Look where I am. I have no friends?" The older man's accent was familiar and somehow trustworthy, yet he had been tricked before.

"I'm here to help ye, but we dinnee have long. If your captors find ye awake, ye'll never escape." "But th-the door," he stuttered.

"I have already unlocked the door, and the path is clear to the stables."

"Why are you helping me?"

"You dinnee recognise me, Aleator? If I had known I would've come sooner and rooted out this cult. I'm sorry, my friend." From the blank stare he was getting, his tortured friend truly had forgotten him.

"I am Bishop, Spymaster and hand of the one true

King Leander. You are a captain in the Athanatos, The Kings' private army. I have trained the last three generations of men from the Darkwing lineage. It will all come back to you in time. I can only direct ye away from here, and your escape willnee be easy, but I will have to meet you down the road. Listen carefully, Tor." The little old man proceeded to tell him where he needed to go.

Aleator Darkwing was still ruminating over his revelation of a name and was trying his best to take it all in, while at the same time, he couldn't help wondering if all this was real. I mean who was this Bishop and why was he naked. He had a memory of a fantastical creature, a giant flying feline of immense power, lost in thought Tor had stopped listening.

The little man stopped his instructions, giving Tor a fierce stare, then walked over to him and slapped him full in the face. He sat slack-jawed in shock.

"Now, ye know I'm real, ye can stop yer daydreaming. Listen carefully!" He growled. It was an oddly deep and resonant growl echoing briefly throughout the dungeon room. It was said with a slight mischievous smirk. The naked man proceeded with his directions from where he left off. Once he had finished, he placed a hand on the chain that bound Tor, which clicked and fell from his ankle. Bishop smiled as Tor absently stroked the area where the chain had been attached.

Bishop hadn't noticed before. There was a warding spell of some kind around Aleator. It was probably some kind of warning if Tor stepped out of it. Bishop wasn't strong in the elements and giving some of his strength to Tor had been taxing, but he had some power left, certainly enough to crack some rocks.

*

Bishop had stopped talking and stuck what looked like a fighting style called Horse stance. Tor smiled. He had recognised the man's Horse stance. He didn't get to finish the thought as Bishop raised and brought down his barefoot with more force than Tor could have dreamed. The impact had left spider web cracks throughout the solid stone floor, and a cloud of dust hung in the dank cellar air.

Aleator cowered away from the blow. It was like he was waking from a foggy dream all at once. Before Tor could even gather his thoughts to thank Bishop, the name sparked something, and it was coming back to him, Bishop was his father's friend. Bishop walked over to the heavy door that was now open, and just as he had appeared, the naked red-haired man that had freed him, disappeared once more, leaving the door open.

Aleator sat there, momentarily stunned. Whatever the reason for his imprisonment, it had eluded him, and he had no wish to stay in such squalor or wait for Mandrake to return. He could always figure out how he had come to be in this place later, preferably on his way out of this accursed place.

He had to remind himself that he was no longer chained. His legs did not want to obey at first. He felt bone-weary. It took everything he had. It was sheer willpower alone that drove him to his feet. Telling himself time and again, "I will not die in this place!"

It was strange he could swear he heard another voice in unison with his own, deep and resonant in his mind. Giving him strength, he continued to whisper those seven words to himself like a mantra. It was like some of his pains had just fallen away, his stomach growled bringing him from his reverie, his head had stopped spinning. Taking the closest lit brand from its bracket on the wall, he began to search. Mandrake often left food just out of reach. He knew he needed to get out of there, but rage had begun to simmer, and maybe he could find something that would help him later. Walking to the darkened side of the dungeon lighting other brands as he went, he continued to search.

Bishop had broken the runes, running in concentric rings across the room, Tor wondered why he hadn't noticed them before. He knew there was a Rack at the far end of the room and a large open fire where Mandrake liked to cook. He never shared the food; the same could not be said for his tools. His torturer seemed to get a perverse thrill from tormenting Tor. Mandrake liked to sit and watch him begging for scraps as he ate, often throwing things just out of his chains' reach. That's when the rats would come, sniffing at the food unrestrained by chains. Tor had begun to hate them more than his keeper. His tormentor had enjoyed torturing him.

Tor could see there was an apple on the fire's mantelpiece. He took a bite and felt his teeth move as they pierced the surprisingly fresh skin. Juice dribbled from his mouth down his chin. It was divine. He didn't know the last time he had eaten let alone enjoyed the sweet taste of an apple.

The rush had ignited a memory of stealing fruit with a friend. He just couldn't remember who. He blinked, and the memory was gone. It took a moment to realize where he was stood and involuntarily began to shake in front of the rack. Tor had spent time on that Rack, sometimes for hours, other times days. He knew Mandrake kept his tools nearby, although he had never been able to investigate them before.

Starting the mantra again, he turned from the Rack and walked over to the other side, lighting several more wall mounted brands as he passed. The extra light illuminated a well-organised workspace of books and papers. There were several weapons displayed on the wall. On the desk was a brass bowl sat amidst hooks and knives, there were even a few implements he had no name for. Hanging on the wall was a coat. It was Mandrakes. Tor had seen it before. He took note of the initial L finely embroidered into the lining as he put on the jacket. It was lined with fur and soft against his skin. It was a lords coat decadent yet reserved. Taking it filled Tor with deep satisfaction. He was more than a coat; it was his pride he was taking back.

Part of him was curious about the runes; Bishop warned that he should hurry though. Looking over the desk, he pocketed a few more items, a small purse of gold, a notebook. The books collected here were dark lore, old books. He had already decided to set it all on fire as he left. First, he looked over the weapons. Usually, he would have taken a sword, but he was weak, and if he were in tight corridors, he would not be able to swing it. His eyes fastened on a short sword on the desk. He almost felt it called to him.

The Ib'ren Cohar
Chapter two

On the desk in a position of pride was one of the most intricately carved short swords Tor had ever seen, it was about the size of his forearm. It had a giant winged reptile carved into the hilt. Taking the blade from its sheath, it glinted even in the low light of the dungeon. It was like looking into a pool of water. His mismatched eyes stared back at him, and he shivered at the realisation that this blade was meant to kill him, Tor reminded himself he was not free yet. It was time to go.

Looking out the crack of the door, he could see stairs just like Bishop had described. Tor was about to leave when a voice in his head whispered

"Fire."

Without a second thought, he quickly gathered the brands from their brackets, placing them under the desk, lighting parchments and books. Satisfied with his handiwork, Tor was out the door and up the stairs with a new sense of urgency. Taking a right took him to a sizeable windowed corridor. Bishop had told him to go down to the door to the right, and not towards the curtain at the far end of the hallway. The door opened into a barn and stables "and dinnee dally", whatever that meant.

Tor heard voices chanting from behind the curtain at the end of the corridor. Before he could think he was at the curtain, creating the smallest opening possible in the bottom corner. He could see a sizeable pillared room adorned with giant beastial statues. A pale moon cast coloured light through the stained-glass window down onto a large hole. There were windows, but most were covered. What remained was not enough to light the room. He could make out at least thirty people kneeling in prostration.

They were chanting around a massive hole in the ground. Six creatures of nightmare, Tor did not know what else to call them, they appeared to have human bodies but wolves' heads, they were stood to attention joining in with the chanting, a horrible growling guttural sound mingled in with the harmony. The light appeared to be devoured by the shadows in the room. In the centre of the congregation was a creature that radiated evil. Tor thought he must be hallucinating. The large and muscled man had the head of a goat. This dark chimaera had runes carved into its horns that seemed to cast a freakish green light, matching the ones on a fierce-looking spear it carried, it was arcing green energy into the pit.

The Voice in his head spoke "Alal comes… Run!" Something was coming, and it was not good. Dropping the curtain, he padded his way quickly to the door at the other end of the corridor, opened it and exited into the stable. In one of the stalls, he could see a shape tending to the horses, saddling them for some journey. Whoever he was, if he was working with those things in the building, it was evil and other than being in his way he needed shoes and pants.

Bishop had told him that he would meet him a quarter mile North East of here. He needed to steal a horse and be away from here. Soon they would know he was missing, or the noticed fire, he mused with a smirk.

Tor pressed himself into the shadows. It was clear the stable hand hadn't seen him yet. Sneaking from recess to recess, he was the predator now, lying in wait for his victims. The shadows were his allies. All he had to do was wait for the right moment.

Another man had joined the first, and he crept closer.

"I hate this bloody job." moaned one of them. "I swear, Jeb, I'm gonna steal one of these horses and go get another captive for Azazel. Find a nice spot in the mountains to hunt in."

"Quit your moaning, Otis. Sick of hearing you go on with yourself. Maybe I should tell Azazel you're unhappy. Maybe he can twist you with a frog-like those villagers last week?"

"Haha, do you remember that strange noise they made?"

"Well that's what you sound like, now show me to my horse and quit your moaning, else I report you to the goat."

Otis didn't care about what was done to other people. One more captive and he would be rewarded with a blending and become one of the Va'nahual. Until then, he had to bow his head. He had a few of the Azazel's failed experiments caged around the stable, fit for nothing. If it were up to him, he would just kill them. If nothing else, it would save him cleaning their crap. Jeb's horse was behind the creature's cages.

Grabbing a torch, he marched forward with grim purpose towards the closest caged beast. His anger seemed to grow with each step, muttering as he drew near to the cage. He pulled back a tarp and rammed the burning torch through the bars into the beast's side. He liked to cause pain and causing it to howl always cheered him up. He was going to become half-wolf, a Sokar and become one of the masters. A Va'nahual. Then he would come back and teach Jeb some manners.

Instead of the satisfaction he had expected at the beast's cries, he was shocked to hear himself gasp for air as white-hot pain erupted across his chest.

*

Tor had watched in anticipation. The time had come to strike. He jumped from the shadows slashing out with the ornate blade. What happened next shocked Tor to his core. As he dealt the blow, the weapon's blade separated into five segments that appeared to be multiplying as he swung, each section held together by strands of light as it extended. Whipping out and slicing clean through the man's back and abdomen in a single graceful arc cutting the vile stable hand clean in half. It had been so fast. Tor hadn't realised he'd also disembowelled the second man.

A look of surprise frozen on the stable hands face as his torso slid sideways from his legs, unceremoniously thudding to the ground. The legs had remained standing on their own for a few seconds before falling over in time with the second man's intestines hitting the ground.

The dagger reformed into one smooth blade again, covered in viscous red blood. Aleator watched in awe as the blade seemed to absorb the blood, drinking it in. He tried to throw the cursed weapon away but found he could not drop it.

The inscribed serpents' eyes were glowing blue now. Panic swept through Tor. His hand was open, but the blade had stuck firmly to it. The handle began to swell and grow, extending up his arm. The base of the grip started to shrink, the finger guard began to form a serpentine head around his hand, and he was holding its tongue. He tried to throw it, but it was no use. The weapon was alive, writhing and extending onto his wrist. Newly formed jaws worked their way up his forearm. The serpents' head had entwined itself entirely around his arm in seconds, until it reached his elbow joint where it stopped, becoming some sort of brace.

The artistry was beyond anything he could remember, not that he could remember much of anything. Looking at the brace, he couldn't help but feel it was staring back at him. Suddenly, it sank its newly formed obsidian fangs deep into his arm and settled in place.

Pain, rage and pure power surged through his veins. Tor screamed out in agony and fell to his knees, panting in pain. Then something new, something powerful took hold of him. The pain was gone, and he felt suddenly at peace with himself, something had taken over the fight, he felt it assert itself and Tor was glad.

He was a passenger in his body which looked up to face a courtyard full of monstrosities akin to the ones inside. Still, he felt no fear and smiled as he rose to his feet, one of the Sokar stood snarling in front of him. It seemed impossible

Tor looked away in fear, but he was no longer in control. An almost sweet silence proceeded over them before absolute carnage erupted.

His newly formed brace came alive with gleeful violence. A blade shooting out from just above his wrist segmented as before, only this time like a serpent's scales, slicing and extending through flesh and bone. Ducking and weaving under claws and swords with ease, he let himself go and lost himself in a sea of death and blood.

It was like he had blacked out and something had taken over his body, that is until the fight was over, looking around he caught his breath, his heart was pumping like crazy. Bodies lay strewn across the ground everywhere. It was time to get out of this shit hole before the goat thing came. He scanned the area and saw at least fifteen twisted beasts' dead. Some were beheaded, others lay with their guts spilt to the floor. Kicking one of the monsters as he passed. Looking around, he found it hard to believe the bloody violence he had unleashed. It took a moment to find the dead stable hands legs and strip him of his surprisingly well-kept pants and shoes.

He had feared to look upon the brace at first, but his eyes drawn toward it. His senses had somehow heightened, and the world was bright with colour. The sword that was no longer a sword had become some strange metal brace had firmly bonded to his forearm.

It had an intricate design of wings down the sides, runes he did not recognise. A winged serpentine body slightly raised on the surface was coiled around the brace and continued halfway up his arm. The craftsmanship was unbelievable. The creature seemed to be breathing. While he had been inspecting what once had been a short sword, he couldn't help but feel that he too was being evaluated.

Tor shook himself off, taking one last look at the carnage he had wrought in the courtyard. Moving fast, he took what looked like a well-stocked saddle and an expensive-looking horse.

Mounting, he set off in the direction which Bishop gave him. The sun was rising as he rode hard toward the horizon and a new feeling of hope washed over him. He was free.

Rekhaert

Chapter three

Rekhaert Stone was a beast of a man. Years of drills in the Athanatos, the King's Guard had made him into a wall of muscle. A full head taller than most. Rek certainly struck an imposing figure in any crowd. He had lost his childhood friend, Aleator Darkwing and after years of searching had even been cast out from the Athanatos. The memory was still a bitter draught.

Growing up, he and his friend Tor, would always find trouble, but they had still stuck together, he missed those days. Even back then it was Tor who was the real troublemaker. Rek smiled and took another swig of ale as memories flowed freely through his mind. A bittersweet melancholy.

In the Athanatos Tor's father was a Captain of the King's guard. A tough man who rarely compromised with anyone they had had to work twice as hard to prove themselves. Despite that, or in spite of that, they had risen through the ranks quickly. Rek quickly earned a reputation as a fighter. He was known and respected throughout the realm.

Rek smiled at the memory of his friend, Aleator Darkwing. Tor had thrived on the edge, his captain enjoyed the game and enjoyed pushing people's buttons just to see what they would do. The man had instincts that were borderline supernatural.

They had fought side by side, Rek with his hammer and Tor with twin short swords. The memory weighed on him. It had been three long years since his captain and childhood friend had disappeared. He spent two years looking with force, but no matter how many people he questioned, it was like Tor had just vanished.

Up until this point the Athanatos had offered him all the things he loved, but he had been a raging bull for those last two years and gotten on almost everyone's last nerve. The cost of his attitude was a heavy one. The worst blow came when his commanding officer, a man he trusted and respected, deemed him unfit for service and discharged him from duty.

A few months later, he found himself making a living fighting for the entertainment of others on the backstreets of Sha'mack. He couldn't get over the not knowing what had happened to Tor, and the pits gave him somewhere to work off his rage.

Rek finished the last of his ale and stumbled out into the streets. Rain hammered down from the night sky as he stumbled down a cobbled back alley. With no money for a roof or beer to drown his sorrows, life seemed bleak indeed.

Exhausted, Rek collapsed into a small doorway and fell asleep. He was slipping in and out of consciousness, his body shaking from a fever that was blossoming. He knew even strong men died quickly from the shakes, but most died peacefully in their sleep, and sleep sounded nice to him.

He had gained more than his share of regrets. Though for the most part, he had little to no guilt. It had been a downward slope from the day his best friend had disappeared. "Should've died with you Tor, standing by your side, enduring the same fate." Rek admonished himself to the night sky. It was not that his companion was lost or dead that haunted him so. It was that he didn't know what had happened to him, and for all his strength, he could not let that go; would not let go. He had broken his word and should've rightfully died long ago.

The world seemed fuzzy, and time lost its meaning. The shakes were coming on strong now, only a matter of time before the warm embrace of death took him. Through blurry eyes, Rek saw a small man walk towards him.

"Yer time is not yet Mr Stone. Ye still have work ta be done." The little man spoke in an odd accent, and that was when the fever dreams must have kicked in. Beams of light momentarily streamed around him then all was dark.

He had awoken in the smallest bed he had ever slept in. Small shelves crammed with books and oddlooking trinkets dressed the walls. Then he saw the little, red-haired man sitting next to the bed watching him, a warm smile on his face.

Rek stopped himself from blurting an obscenity. After all, this little man was no less than the hand of the king, known only to a few. Rek was one such privileged to have met Bishop.

"Water," Rek croaked at his host.

Over the next few days, Bishop explained that he required Rek's services and had nursed him back to health. When his guest was feeling more energetic, Bishop had asked Rek to grant him a favour, and that's how Rek came to be standing in the pouring rain again.

Bishop had asked him to wait on the outskirts of Niveneh and give aid to anyone who looked to be fleeing for their lives. Rek had asked how he would know the right person, to which Bishop had said. "You'll be sure to know them Rekhaert Stone."

Rek had chuckled to himself at the how stupid the request was, but Bishop had saved his life, and the pragmatic Rek believed in honouring such debts, he would not refuse such a simple request. Bishop had also given him a bag of gold pieces to seal the deal. Once he had brought him this runaway, he could get back to drinking and whoring. The thought warmed him now as he waited for this mysterious stranger.

Rek was shocked to see a horse in the distance. He could hear its hooves pounding the earth, and maybe this wasn't a fool's errand after all. There was a cloaked figure leaning in the saddle. Rek snorted at the ridiculous nature of the situation he had found himself in.

For some reason, his instincts were on alert. Something felt off. Rek loosened his hammer in its holster. He had a strange feeling about the horseman heading his way. Even at this distance, Rek could sense danger. It seemed the land and wildlife had quietened at the stranger's approach. He was preparing for the worst. After all, his instincts had kept him alive, and he saw no reason to doubt them now.

Rek mounted his horse as the stranger got closer. A cold shiver ran up Rek's back. It couldn't be Aleator surely? Rek watched as a man he had thought dead for so long approached ever nearer. A ghost on horseback stopped opposite Rek.

It must be him thought Rek, but there was something different. "Captain... Tor, is that you?" Rek stumbled over every word. There was no denying it. This was the man that had commanded him, fought beside him. A man who had saved his life a hundred times and vice versa. This was Rek's commanding officer and best friend, Aleator Darkwing.

A tide of different emotions ran through Rek, trying to keep his poise as he studied his former captain. He could see that this was a very different man, but what he could not tell was just how different. Somehow Tor looked more dangerous than before. Rek noticed Tor's eyes. They had once been different colours, one blue and one green. Now both were a striking blue-grey, scanning Rek just as deeply as Rek's own.

"Tor?" Rek ventured

"Do I know you?" Tor responded coldly.

Rek's fury erupted, how dare he forget who he was. The arrogant shit, "You fucking arrogant..." was as far as Rek got.

In the blink of an eye, a weary-looking, almost ghost-like Tor leapt from his horse and knocked Rek clean from his saddle. Tor landed on top of him with a blade to his throat, Rek had not seen him pull a weapon. The two men remained motionless, but both poised to strike a blow if the other flinched.

The tension mounted until Rek started to laugh. "You weasel you! Still quicker than a Warg with a firework up its arse."

Rek's laughter caused a change in Tor, and his eyes softened somehow. Rek watched in amazement as the blade at his throat recoiled and disappeared back into a serpent brace.

"Don't you recognise me, Tor?" Rek saw the confusion in his eyes as he got off him slowly. Rek could see again the weary ghost that had initially approached him. "What the fuck happened to you Tor?" Was all he managed to say before Tor collapsed.

He looked on at his unconscious friend and muttered to no one in particular "Oh, I'm fine! Thanks for asking. Here, let me carry you. No, no. No need to thank me. You just rest yourself." And with that, Rek picked up his old friend, flung him over his horse and made his way back to the camp.

The Dragon's Den
Chapter four

Tor found himself standing in what seemed a deep dark void. He did not remember waking or how he came to be here, but there was an eerie, unnatural feel to the place. It was hard to focus on anything, but he could sense a presence in the distance.

"Hello?" he blurted out into the darkness.

No reply returned, yet he could feel something out there was watching him. The fear became overwhelming, but Tor was not one to stand and wait for fate. He took a step forward into the void.

"HALT!" A voice boomed from the darkness.

Tor immediately dropped to a crouch. From the void, a pair of plate-sized electric blue eyes appeared, staring intently at him.

The floor beneath Tor's feet rumbled and shook as if an earthquake was about to strike. Loud, cracking noises reverberated throughout the darkness. Magma began to flow from the cracks, eating it away until Tor was surrounded by molten lava, marooned on a singular rock.

In front of him was a beast of legend. A dragon so large that it towered above him, its eyes focused upon him.

"Who dares enter my realm!" the words shook every single bone in Aleators body. "Who are you, mortal?"

It was hard to find his words. This majestic creature awed him. At a rough estimate, this creature was as big as a barn with iridescent blue scales. The behemoth had eyes the size of Tors' head. Lightning danced in those slitted eyes. It was like the creature was in his head.

"My name is Aleator Darkwing. I do not know how I come to be here, and I mean you no disrespect or ill will." He replied as stoutly as he could.

The dragon roared, causing magma to erupt from the walls of the cavern. Tor ducked defensively, his instincts sharp. Lava flowed around him now, glowing and flaming menacingly close to his feet.

"Are you worthy or another vile creature trying to desecrate my prison for power? If so, you shall perish like the rest!" the dragon boomed, seemingly growing with each word.

Tors temper flared, and he roared back at the dragon, fists clenched and veins bulging from his neck. He screamed until his throat was sore, and his breath was ragged. Finally, He met the dragon's gaze, to see it staring at him, then laughter, or what he could only assume was laughter echoed around the cavern. When the dragon stopped laughing at him, it seemed to consider Tor a little closer.

The lava ebbed away until it was no longer there. The dragon leaned in close and sniffed at Tor. With a grunt, the beast seemed to relent. "You smell different; familiar.

What did you say your name was?"

"Darkwing. Aleator Darkwing." He stated without confidence.

"Do not worry yourself, Aleator Darkwing. I will not harm you."

"What are you?"

"I am a dragon, and you may call me Argento." The Dragon paused briefly and took another sniff of him. "I sense dark magic upon you, yet I do not see evil within you. What happened to you?"

"I am not sure, Argento. Truth be told, I cannot remember much beyond this morning. I'm not even sure how I've ended up here with you, or if you're even real?"

"Hmmm, strange." Argento pondered to himself. "You are the bearer of my Ib'ren Cohar, yet you did not seek it out?"

Tor just stared blankly back at the dragon.

"That brace upon your arm is called Ib'ren Cohar. It is my prison. Please look closer."

Tor lifted his arm and inspected the blade that had attached itself to his arm.

"The Ib'ren Cohar is a tool of powerful magic. When it attaches itself to a wearer, it takes the form of the soul to which it is attached. Yours appears to be a dragon. Curious?" mused Argento.

"What does that mean?"

"I am not sure, other than you have a better soul than the last wearers of my Ib'ren Cohar." The Dragon chuckled to itself. "Hmmm... maybe we can work together. I can help fill some of the gaps in your memory, but time is of the essence. I don't know how I came to be in your hands. We are now connected nonetheless. and for that, I am grateful beyond measure."

The Dragons' mouth hadn't moved, but he had been speaking aloud, it was like the words had just come to him. It was the same voice he had heard in his mind in the dungeon. Looking around, Tor asked "Where are we. How did I get here?"

Argento looked around before speaking, "This is nowhere and everywhere. This is my prison." The Dragon seemed forlorn. "For the moment you are with me in spirit inside the Ib'ren Cohar. The ground you stand upon is just a place I dreamed up to make intruders uncomfortable. You, like me, are now in my souls' prison within the brace upon your forearm." Argento paused briefly. "I needed to see you and ask a question of my own, knowing that you cannot lie to me here. In this place, I am everything." Those huge azure eyes brooked no deception. "Would you earn my loyalty or take it by force?"

Tor did not know what to say. He may not have known who he was, but he understood this creature was not something to be owned. If he could help, he would. "I would rather call you a friend than an enemy." He earnestly replied as he summoned up the courage to ask a question of his own. "You said we are bonded, what do you mean?"

"The Ib'ren Cohar you wear on your wrist has now sealed itself to your arm, and like it or not, until the day you die, I will be your companion and you mine. I want to make you a deal, Aleator. I will add my strength to yours, and you will become as powerful as a hundred warriors. I will give you your retribution, but will you promise to set me free when it is time."

Tor was dumbstruck. He felt like his brain couldn't take in all the information.

The dragon continued. "You will be the first human who has wielded the spirit of a dragon willingly. I have been a source of power and a curse to all those who have thought to enslave me. I have been passed down from one monster to another, all of them dark and cruel souls. With you, I feel a kinship. You are the first whose mind did not repulse me into driving the holder insane.

You will have noticed all your senses are sharper, and your body will become stronger than you could believe, over time, your wounds will also heal quicker. Already your eyes have changed colour to match mine. The cage you wear was made by servants of the dark to enslave me. The Ib'ren Cohar was created by an evil man called Khnumm." Argento almost spat the name out. "This prison is based on the designs of another man called Assai. His apprentice Khnumm corrupted what he had learned and used the knowledge for his dark purposes."

The dragon appeared to consider its words before continuing. "The bond is a sharing, and for you to be fully Dragonborn, we must accept each other, more than that, we must be as one. For now, we must get to know one another. You will benefit from my strength as did those that came before. When you empty your mind, you can visit me here. If you need me all you have to do is just think of me, we are linked so I will always be near." Tilting his head, Argento looked up as if listening for something.

"What is it, Argento?" asked Tor.

"Your body needs nourishment, and we both need rest. You must go back to the real world, go now, and we will speak a gain when you are stronger."

Camp Fire Tales
Chapter five

Waking up by a campfire, Tor stirred. He was sore from head to toe, and weariness plagued his mind, yet physically he felt stronger if hungry. Tor looked around to try and spot the giant of a man who he had encountered at the rendezvous. He wanted to apologise, but he could not see him. Though he was confident, he would be close.

Tor looked into the flames and ran through that last encounter. The reaction from the big man and the more worryingly, the dragon's response to a perceived threat and the sheer speed and force of that reaction. The dragon had been in control. It was the big mans' laugh that brought Tor back to himself, recognising Rek from a distant memory. The tension left him, and with it, the dragon and consciousness.

His memories were disjointed and distant, he had no recollection of his time in the dungeon and only fragments of his past were slowly starting to come back; including the formidable Rek. Where was that godforsaken magician Bishop? He had a mountain of questions. Tor Rubbed his temples to relieve the tension that was building there.

Rekhaert appeared from the woods with a rabbit slung over each shoulder, breaking Tor from his reverie.

"You will need to eat, Captain; we have a long journey ahead of us, and you look like shit."

"I see you're as eloquent as ever. I am sorry for before my friend."

"What the fuck happened, you just flattened me?"

"It was a reaction, and I'm sorry it won't happen again, I just didn't know you."

"You're serious Tor... you don't remember?"

"No."

"What is the last thing you do remember?"

"Just flashes, then Bishop was releasing me from my chains. I was confused as I escaped and managed to steal a horse. Then, meeting you on the road."

"Nothing else?"

"No." For some reason, he trusted this man, but not enough to tell him about the dragon.

"That damn midget Bishop owes us some answers. I don't know what his interest in you or me are old friend, but Bishop pulled me from the brink of death. He's an odd little fucker, to say the least, but I owe him my life. I trust most of what he says. I say most only because the rest of what he says I can barely understand."

Aleator took in the information as best he could. His mind felt like he was being assaulted. The sun was just rising on the horizon, and around the clearing, he could hear and see like never before, it was a struggle just to focus. "Rek, you seem to have me at a disadvantage, so how about you answer a couple of questions first?"

The big man nodded and began to prepare the rabbit.

"Bishop requested to speak with you as soon as you woke

Captain, said it was important."

"Well, he has no way of knowing I'm up yet, let's you and me have a talk first." Tor noticed Rek's eyes drop and a look of guilt plain as day crossed his face. "Tell me, Rek, why do you look so ashamed?"

Rek hesitated before answering, and his words came out as a whisper at first. "I wasn't there!"

"What do you mean?"

"I'm sorry I failed you, I should have been there. Can you ever forgive me?"

"To be honest, I don't know what happened that night myself. It's not your fault Rek, and it brings me strength just to be in your company again. You can repay me by filling in some of the blanks though. Like who I am?"

"You are Aleator Darkwing, Captain of the King's elite guard. The Athanatos feared in all of the realms, and I was your second in command, Rekhaert Stone master of arms."

Images flickered through Tors' mind at the mention of the Athanatos. Men and women of unparalleled fighting ability. Peacekeepers, protectors and judicators of the King.

He remembered Rek leading the charge, the man's favourite weapon was a double-handed hammer which he wielded in one hand and an axe in the other or any of the numerous weapons attached to his body that day.

In battle, above the typical clash of swords and screams would be a thud, thud, thud of that hammer falling like a blacksmith at a forge. A truth that came with the memory was that this man would walk through fire with him, swearing all the way. Even if he couldn't remember much else, it was a start. He had a name and a friend.

Guilt was etched across Rek's rugged features. "Captain, I need you to know how I spent the last three years trying to find you. I drove the Athanatos mad with my searching, I was dismissed from service in the end, and even then, I continued to search. As far as other people are concerned, you are dead. Shit, as far as I was concerned you were dead, I had finally given up. I've spent the last few months at the bottom of a bottle. If you give me a chance, I will help you find out where you've been or die trying."

Tor had too many gaps in his memory, but he knew this man could be trusted. "Well, Rek, there's still a lot I need to figure out, how I got to be in a cell ready for slaughter, is at the top of that list."

He knew he needed Reks help and what the answer would be, but he had to let this man know what they faced. "It will be dangerous. It could even be the death of me, and I'm prepared to roll the dice, but I cannot ask you to do the same. The choice is yours, Rekhaert Stone."

Rek's face lit up like a child with a cake. "Well, if it's up to me and there's fighting, and a strong chance of death ahead, I'll be fucked if I let you have all the fun."

Tor smiled, but his stomach growled. He couldn't remember when he'd eaten last. Rek tied the rabbit carcass to a makeshift spit he had made.

"Bishop still wants to talk to you alone. He's just behind those trees. Said he wanted some time to think." Rek shrugged. "Maybe he can fill some gaps. It'll give me a chance to cook up breakfast while you figure out our next step. I'll have it ready for when you get back."

Tor was so hungry he was close to pouncing on the rabbits and eating them raw. He shook his head to clear those thoughts, nodded to Rek in ascent before heading in the direction of the strange little man.

Bishop
Chapter six

Bishop was deep in thought. So much to do and so little time. He had walked some of the paths of the future with his foster mother, the Oracle of Manthripur. The future is ever-changing only giving a general idea of the possible outcomes, and even then, he felt his mother had kept things from him. Aleator being chief among those secrets.

Bishop hadn't seen or heard Tor arrive, which should not have been possible. When Aleator coughed behind him, Bishop had jumped and fallen off the tree stump he was sat on.

Trying to cover his shock, he stood up and brushed himself off, Aleator had smiled at his astonished look.

"So ye found me Aleator, and ye seem in bonny health. So I take it ye got away without incident?" He perched himself back on the stump. "Ha, ye still dinnee recognise me at all do ye? What did they do to you, laddie?" He asked with genuine concern.

Tor ignored the question and asked one of his own. "I don't have time for small talk, and I need to know what you know? And remind me why I should trust you?"

Bishop looked at Tor. "I am Bishop ye great lummox a name known to few and only friends. I've searched a long time for ye, and it brings a light of hope to an old man's heart to know yer not beaten, which means we still may have a chance to change what is to be,"

"You go too fast, old man. Can you tell me why I was in that place and who put me there?" Tor took a seat in front of the little man, so it was easier to see his face. "I'm not certain who kidnapped ye, Darkwing. I know the people who held ye, they go by the name of the Fidelus. A vile cult, so they be. Their sole purpose is to bring back the Dread Licht Alal."

"The who?" Tor asked as he struggled to keep up.

"The Dread. Powerful mages of evil from ancient times. Four were banished centuries ago during a war nearly forgotten. The Fidelus believe that Alal walks the halls of the dead and want to bring him back, so he can reverse the magic that banished the other Dread. Prophesy says they are destined to return and reclaim the world." Bishop paused for a second as he spotted the brace upon Tor's arm. "By the stars, what have ye got there?"

"Nothing, just something I picked up when I escaped.

Thought it might help me." Tor lied weakly.

Bishop cast a curious gaze under raised eyebrows. Whatever it was it radiated power. He had seen his share of elemental weapons in the Athanatos. This was something else, and it was changing Aleator. Whether that was a good thing or a bad one, would have to be seen. "I'm sure it will. Anyway, where was I?"

"Fidelus, Licht, end of the world." Tor snorted.

"Aye, end of the world," repeated the little man with little humour. "These are dangerous times, Darkwing. I dinnee joke. There are forces here that I do not fully understand, and if we dinnee react purposefully, our world will end.

"You still haven't said how this involves me?"

"Te be honest laddie, I was only told that the prisoner had to be set free and to do no more if we were to have a chance against what is coming."

"Who told you this?"

"Kairos the Oracle of Manthripur."

Tor sat down on the log, rubbing his temples.

"What de you remember Aleator? Do you know who took ye?"

"I'm sorry, but it's all still a blank. I only really remember waking up yesterday. I was hoping you could help me fill in the blanks, like what happened to me and why I remember so little? Maybe, if we start with how we know each other?"

Bishop gave Tor a sympathetic look. "Of course, laddie, how rude of me. Nice to see you haven't lost your questioning side. It seems events have gotten ahead of me. My name is Bishop, and I have been around for several generations. I have witnessed the rise and fall of great kings and queens, warlords and warlocks. I am a man of considerable talents, but my work must be done through others, such as yerself. You saw me when you were young, as I met with your father in my duty as spymaster and hand to King Leander."

None of this sparked any memories for him. Tor noticed that Bishop was looking at the Ib'ren Cohar. "You know what this is, don't you?"

"Not exactly laddie. It is old and powerful. I can feel its power." Bishop motioned for Tor to show him the brace and reluctantly he offered Bishop his arm.

"The markings name it the Ib'ren Cohar. I can tell ye it was forged by a master. It is of the old tongue and roughly translates to Soul cage. I know not of its origin or who its creator was, but from what I can see, they must have been truly gifted." Bishop was caressing the brace as he explained which started to disturb Tor. Pulling his arm away from Bishop, he gave the half-man a stern look.

Bishop turned his attention to the fire when he spoke next. "The brace is fused ta ye arm. It would seem it is a part of you now. Has anything strange happened since it joined with ye?"

Tor felt uncomfortable with how the conversation was going. He didn't know if he could trust this man yet. Despite the help in freeing him, the half-man had given him little to trust, especially with the way he had left him back at the dungeon. Bishop was clearly a man of many secrets and plans. Tor wouldn't be an unwitting pawn in a game he knew nothing about and decided to conceal the truth.

"Nothing as of yet, Bishop, but I shall inform you of anything if it does. Changing the subject, Tor asked, so what's the plan?"

"We go to see the Oracle."

Tor nodded and started to walk away. Bishop smiled in return "I saw what ye did outside the church of the Fidelus, Aleator, the corpses of a full pack of Sokar strewn all over the stables. I was assured the way would be clear and that I should focus on the road. I decided to circle to check your progress. I have seen ye in battle before, and as skilled as you are, you were no match for so many. How you killed the Fidelus and Sokar is a story I would love ta hear."

Aleator seemed to think about that a moment before excusing himself. "Please forgive me but I have not eaten for some time, and Rek's rabbits will be cooked by now.

Will you join us?"

"No, go, eat and rest. We shall talk when yer more up

to it."

Tor stopped mid-stride and turned to the half-man. Before he could say anything in reply, Bishop continued, "I realise that there is a lot for ye to understand Darkwing but know this. I am a friend. I need your help just as you will need mine.

Time, however, is not on our side. There are forces beyond your understanding at work, and they will not wait for you to figure it all out. Now go an eat with Rekhaert and regain your strength as we have a long journey ahead of us." Bishop turned his gaze back to the fire.

After staring at Bishop's back for a short while, Tor turned on his heel and set off back to Rek.

Bishop sat contemplating everything he knew and decided some rabbit might not be a bad idea, joining Rek and Tor at their fire. Rek was dutifully answering questions from Aleator. They had been laughing, which was a good sign.

Bishop's attention was drawn to the flames of the fire. He was more worried than ever. Tor was not the same man. It was clear he had been tortured by the Fidelus, evidenced by the sheer number of new scars that laced his body. They had broken him by the time Bishop found him in that cell. Tor's mind was shattered, his very soul beaten into his body's darkest corner. It had broken Bishop's heart to see the son of his old friend lying in his own filth.

Bishop had watched from the shadows as Tor's senses came back.

Looking over the fire into those now pale blue eyes, he knew something had changed and would guess it had something to do with the Ib'ren Cohar. He sighed, and suddenly feeling old and tired, he wished he knew more about the brace.

The craftsmanship was that of Assai, but it did not bear his mark, which left few others capable of such weapon-craft. Khnumm, the apprentice of Assai, was one such smith, a man who had unleashed a swathe of cursed weapons on High Garden. All his creations had been inherently evil, granting great powers, but eventually driving the bearer's mad. They turned sane people into raging maniacs. After seeing the carnage Tor had wrought escaping, Bishop was rightly nervous about this revelation, the risk was high. Bishop also knew for there to be any success, Aleator Darkwing was fated to find the Ib'ren Cohar.

Once again, Bishop found himself sitting there, staring into the flames. A chill came over the camp. Closing his eyes and opening his senses, he could feel Tor and Rek on the other side of the fire, but there was something else too, much closer. Opening his eyes, amongst the flames and burning wood, hidden amongst the embers was something that didn't belong, something cold.

Smouldering, coal-black eyes, stared back at him from the fire. Devoid of life, Bishop gasped at the depth of evil contained in those eyes, fearsome and pitiless.

"You will burn for your interference wizard!" the creature screeched from the fire.

Bishop instinctually shielded the group, drawing on the life of the land around him. As the fire they had been sitting around exploded with enough force that it shattered the stump Bishop was sitting on sending him flying skyward. When he eventually came to a standstill, he saw the power of the explosion had also flattened the trees that surrounded the camp, and many of them were on fire. Fear grew in Bishop's heart. The creature that had attacked him was a Djinn, and they were supposed to be extinct since the world had fallen into an ice age, and yet here one had marked him for death.

The wizard's heart was pumping with adrenaline. The attack meant he was doing something right.

He laughed and yelled at the sky, "Ye'll have te try harder than that!" but the Djinn was gone.

No sooner had the words left his mouth; he heard the howls of Wargs. A cold chill ran down his spine. They were close, too close. He needed to draw the Wargs away to give Rek and Tor a head start.

The enemy knew where they were. It was rare for a Djinn to make itself known, preferring to slowly twist its prey to its will and finally absorb the soul of the enthralled. This one was strong too, the devastation wrought from such a distance would have taken immense amounts of energy. It would be a while before such an attack could be attempted again.

Bishop picked himself up and stretched as he stood removing his clothes, a resolute look in his eyes. He had a secret known to only a few. Most saw him as the diminutive Jaden, or half-man, not something powerful. It was time to show them an apex predator. Two giant wings unfurled momentarily covering Bishop, his body flexing and rippling as bones formed and changed under his now furred skin. Then with a flap of those powerful limbs, he revealed his true self, a Griffin.

Bishop briefly inspected himself with glittering feline eyes flexing his newly formed muscles, outsized claws biting deep into the earth. Then he roared long and loud in his exultation, terrifying yet majestic. This time his enemy had missed. If it weren't for his shield, they would be Warg meat now. He laughed, but it came out more like a deep purr, bounding forward, mighty wings launching his newly formed bulk into the air. It was time to take the fight to them.

*

Tor and Rek were thrown from the exploding campfire. The sheer force of it sent them flying into some nearby trees. Tor had hit a tree with such force. The impact had shattered it. Around them, smoke was everywhere. Dazed and confused, Rek saw Tor was unconscious, not too far from himself. Moving toward his friend as best he could, he exclaimed to no one in particular, "What the fuck was that!" and instinctually loosened his weapons in sheaths. Tor was out of it, and Rek was worried but was glad when he found a pulse.

It only seemed seconds after that howls filled with hunger and menace sounded nearby. It was the unmistakable sound of Wargs on the hunt.

Rek was understandably disturbed. He had fought against a warg and was lucky to survive. Alone, they were dangerous, as a pack, staying where they were would be assisted suicide. Whatever they did next, they would have to be quick. Rek was thinking about moving to some high ground he had seen when he scouted the area.

Tor was still staggered from the explosion, and the tree that had broken his fall must have at least have also broken a few of his ribs. The impact appeared to have demolished the tree.

They had been in many situations like this in the past, with backs against a wall, wishing to be anywhere else. "Captain, we need to move." Rek shook his friend.

Tor showed no response. Rek looked in the face of his captain and, for a moment, lost himself in those blue eyes, lightning danced in them, but he was unresponsive. There was another terrifying sound the roar of an animal Rek couldn't place. Rek shook his head. They needed to move.

*

Tor shouted the dragon's name for what felt like ten minutes before Argento appeared out of nowhere. He had looked in one direction, and when he turned back around, he nearly had a heart attack, as the dragon was snout to face with him.

"Why am I here?" he asked the dragon, exasperated at the timing.

"You are hurt, Aleator. You have a Djinn tracking your group, our enemies are powerful beyond mortal measure, and you have taken a great prize from them. They hunt you now, but you are wounded, and it will take me some time to heal you. We must trust in Rek."

Tor had held his tongue for long enough, and if it weren't for the Dragon's indomitable presence, he would have shouted. Instead, he just interrupted. "Dragon, my camp is under attack. My friends could be in trouble.

Damn, I could be in trouble! Return me!"

"As you wish, but you are wounded, and I am healing you. Be warned, do not to push yourself too far or you will blackout."

Back in the clearing, Tor came back to himself. A Warg cry filled with hunger could be heard in the distance. His friend was saying his name repeatedly while gently shaking him.

"Rek, let go of me."

"You okay, captain? You seemed lost for a moment.

We need to move. We got Wargs coming this way."

Tor stood, but his legs failed him. Turning to Rek to seek his friend's help but instead, his vision began to tunnel, and his head swam. Tor was assaulted with the flashbacks from his three-year torture under the unrelenting ministrations of that evil son of a bitch, Mandrake. It was his laughing face he saw again and again as he floated away into a sea of pain and blackness.

Rek watched incredulously as Tor collapsed once more writhing and screaming as if attacked by an invisible assailant. He pulled him into his arms and tried to calm him. That was until Rek saw two wargs loping through the brush and head towards them.

With Tor in this vulnerable state, he would be torn apart in seconds. Rek rose and reached for his hand axe that rested at his hip. He would have to time this just right. He was no stranger to battle and knew he would only have one shot at this. Taking a deep breath, he stepped over his friend's prone body and with every ounce of his strength, aimed and let fly the axe at the lead Warg.

It thudded into the beast's ribs, knocking it from its feet and causing the Warg to tumble into its partner. Rek knew when he threw the axe that it would not stop the powerful predators. It would, however, buy him precious seconds. He took out his war hammer and positioned himself between the carnivorous predators and Tor.

The lead Warg had regained its feet, and the second was now padding more cautiously toward the duo, splitting up as they got closer, slowly approaching from two sides at once. The wounded beast in front was snarling as it approached, saliva dripping from its massive jaws.

Rek closed the gap quickly for a big man, bringing the full force of his war hammer down on the Warg. He caught the beast just behind its muscular neck. With a sickening crunch and yelp, as the hellish hound's spine was crushed beneath the impact of Rek's hammer. He turned his attentions to the beast's partner. It had circled and seemed to be focused on Tor's prone body. As the Warg pounced, its massive fetid jaws opened wide and ready to snap around its victim's neck. Rek turned on his heel, bringing the war hammer spinning round with his full force. The weapon caught the beast full in the mouth, smashing its teeth and jaw and leaving it dangling at a disturbing angle. Rek finished the job with a swift, crushing blow to the Warg's head. He was lucky they weren't fully grown, but from the howls in the distance, he knew more would be on their way.

Rek hurriedly approached the still form of Tor. "Captain?" Rek shouted as he shook Tor.

Tor gasped a breath, and his eyes momentarily came into focus, but where Rek had earlier seen danger and magic, only terror and pain remained. Tor began to scream and flail his arms. It seemed as if he had lost his mind. In the distance, Rek heard the growls and howls of the Warg pack. They had to leave quickly. Rek didn't like his choices, but he was a pragmatist, and he did not have time to nurse his old friend.

"Sorry, captain." Slamming his massive fist into Tor's temple, knocking him senseless. He picked Tor up and threw him over his shoulder. "Sorry, Captain, but we need to go."

Placing the unconscious Tor over his horse's saddle and fastening him into place. Mounting his horse, he knew he would have to push them hard. Rek heeled the horses and galloped away from the sound of the oncoming wargs.

The Enemy
Chapter seven

In camp a few miles from them, there was a hunting pack of Va'Nahual. Lead by one of Alal's favourite assassins, The Spider. It was a creature born of pain and suffering. The Spider was once a child with dreams and hopes, not that it could remember those now.

The Va'Nahual was a blending of man and beast. It was a dark magic of the worst kind. Those unlucky enough to have lived through the process fell into three distinct sects of abominations, this particular Va'Nahual was something out of the darkest nightmare; a Dren.

Children could be blended multiple times due to their bone structures not having fully formed yet, but the transition did something to them. To call them insane would be close, but incorrect. Something about the brain in a child still forming allowed for human intelligence. A bastardized version of it, smart enough to understand the need for a pack, but unlike the adult Sokar, they were not sheep to be lead. Clear lines had to be drawn if you wanted control of the pack.

He was one of the Dren and, as such, guarded fiercely by the Sokar. Adults could only survive one blending, and they were the Sokar. They had a primal need to protect the Dren, and to procreate were probably the only attributes that you could associate with humanity; everything else was burned away. If your village was taken by the Va'Nahual, pray you're eaten as far worse fates befell any captives. After all, if you were killed, you could not be made into one of them.

The most feared of them all were hybrids, giants towering over the Sokar by a couple of feet in most cases. These monstrosities were the result of Sokar raping their human captives. Va'Nahual offspring were rare from these couplings, and it would be unusual for the victim to live through the ordeal of pregnancy.

If you were unlucky enough to live through it, stillbirth was common, and the bearer almost always died in childbirth. A human born Sokar could take a second blending. These twice tortured beings were referred to as the Soulless. They had size and strength and were surprisingly smart. They were imbued with dark magic in the womb. Capable of great violence and even a little dark magic.

On this occasion, The Spider had been put to the task by the First of the Soulless, Azazel himself. He was to find Tor alive and bring him and the Ib'ren Cohar back to their master Alal alive.

Dren feared little. Power was to be respected, but Alal was worshipped by the Va'Nahual as a god, and all would follow his commands or feel his wrath.

The Spider had no legs to speak of. In their place were arms, six in all. He was able to walk on two hands or all six and even climb. Plates had formed an armour-like skin. A night-black body with solid bone chest plates which held eight eyes inset within the bones, they watched its subordinates malevolently. Most disturbingly was where there should have been a face was a single head-sized armoured eye.

He was given command of a hunting pack and some wargs to accomplish his mission and a warning, Alal would not tolerate failure. There would be a sign that would guide him to his target and to stay alert.

When two Wargs had not come back, he climbed up a nearby tree to get a better vantage point. Careful not to tangle the two swords on his back as he went. The Spider had taken them from the corpses of supposed masters he'd killed. They had posed little to no challenge for his swordsmanship.

Once he had climbed to the top of the tree, he looked for the promised sign and was not disappointed. In the distance, he saw a giant fireball leap into the sky, shortly followed by a shock wave, which made the tree he was perched on sway as it passed.

The Spiders giant eye blinked. He would be rewarded if he succeeded. Looking down from his vantage point, he could hear two Sokar arguing about his order to bring the human in alive. The pack hadn't eaten in a while, and tempers were flaring. The Spider couldn't afford to risk a Sokar going and killing first and thinking too late. All killing would be by his direct order only. The pain inflicted by his god for failure was a horror he did not wish to contemplate.

Launching himself from the tree at the un-expecting creature below. If it wanted death, then it was time. As The Spider fell, a horizontal line split the giant eye revealing three rows of razor-sharp teeth in a mouth that opened in a rictus snarl. His mouth could open wide enough that he could crush a skull with his bite.

Landing perfectly on the back of the overloud Sokar, The Spider's jaws sank deep into its shoulder. Bones could be heard breaking by the other Sokar in the clearing, even over the howling cries of pain. The Spider jumped from the stunned beast in a graceful pirouette unsheathing his swords in mid-air and landing ready to strike.

The next words he spoke aloud so all could hear, "Any killing done without my direct order will result in death." His two swords snapped forward in a scissor-like motion beheading the wounded Sokar. A gory smile broke upon the middle of that enormous eye. Blood from the mauled Sokar had run into the eye, making the bottom half glow red. "No one feeds until I say so. This is not the time to lose your heads! Lose your heads... Haha." The Spider laughed long and loud at his genius before cartwheeling to where the head had landed. He grabbed it and turned to face the remaining Sokar. "Remember, if you must get ahead, haha, a head, hahaha." The Spider threw it at the pack and continued, "In life, listen while you have ears. The prey we hunt is mine, and anyone who cannot control themselves will join your dinner."

Dren didn't suffer from the same sort of attachment that the Sokar felt towards the Dren. Most were devoid of it. Random acts of cruelty and violence were what made you the pack master. The Dren commanded through fear. Now he had the pack's attention. The Spider let out a feral roar. His two Night Wargs ran over, one to either side of him. It was time to go. He jumped onto the back of the ferocious beasts.

Dark as night and at least three and a half feet tall, with jet black hair that seemed to pull in the light. The Spider was balancing his body weight, in between the two wargs as they ran in perfect synchronicity with each other. The Spider kept himself low between both their backs as he set off, a living war machine. The Pack followed.

He wanted to be one of the first there, to make sure nothing went wrong. The Sokar wouldn't remain far behind. He needed to get a lead on the pack, while they ate the beheaded pile of flesh, he had left bleeding on the grass.

Arriving at the campsite which was still smouldering, The Spider reined his Warg and dismounted, two Warg whelps sprawled dead before him, their heads caved in. The Spider reined in his temper, taking in the scene in front of him. Taking in every detail in his mind, The Spider replayed the events as they took place again. It was one of many gifts Alal had bestowed upon him.

Closing the mouth that broke the giant eye, he took in the scene. He was able to envision what had happened even days or weeks after an event. Making him the best tracker in his lords' dark army and invaluable as a consequence. It had ensured his survival against the wrath of his masters' anger at him more than once.

A scene unfolded in his mind, and The Spider watched as the Warg pups attacked the humans. He smiled as he saw the one known as Tor rolling on the ground in pain. It appeared the Djinn had done some damage. It would not be long before he caught them.

The Spider watched as the wargs were dispatched by the second bigger man. This disconcerted him. Even as pups, wargs were ferocious creatures, and no human should be able to kill them so quickly. Something or someone else was in play here, possibly the wizard they were reported to be with had put a protection spell on him. From what he could see, they should be dead. The Spider pushed the thought away. He would prove a much more demanding test for his prey. The Spider watched them race off to the northeast not moments ago.

During the Spider's trance, the pack had caught up. The Spider spat orders at the Sokar. Grabbing the young warg corpse in front of him and threw it in anger at the waiting Sokar pack that had just caught up. The Warg corpse slammed into two of the Sokar, flooring them instantly.

The Spider let out a terrifying screech and hissed his warning at the moronic pack. He wouldn't waste his words on the imbeciles, but his warning was clear. The next freak to step out of line would suffer horrifically. The Spiders' patience was running thin now. Calling his wargs, he raced off in pursuit of his quarry.

*

Rek had decided to leave the main road for the forest path in order to make it more difficult to be tracked, but every now and then Rek noticed a shadow in his periphery. He could not quite make out what it was, but he was reasonably sure it was big and that it had been following them since they had left the camp. Whatever it was, he had more pressing matters.

Rek stole a glance down at Tor and saw that he still looked ill. He had seen his captain take some mighty wounds from battle and even suffering heavy blood loss, while still being able to fight. To see him go down so badly worried him but then the tree should've snapped Tor in half, not the other way around.

Somewhere in the distance, the sound of growling and howls of the wargs getting closer added to his worries. They had his scent now, and he knew they were relentless. Hoping his luck would remain long enough for them to escape. Listening to the noise of what was coming, it sounded as if there was at least a dozen or so and they sounded fully grown this time.

Spurring on the horses, he redirected his thoughts toward the prevalent danger and escaping what would no doubt be certain death at the jaws of the ensuing Warg.

Warg were known as speedy hunters and would be closing the distance between them. Even at the breakneck speed, he was pushing the horses at now. Death would be biting at their heels soon enough.

His horse was healthy, although it was not bred for endurance, its stamina was already at breaking point. Nevertheless, he spurred his mount for all it was worth. Trying furiously to figure out a plan of escape, but only one idea kept coming to him. The problem was, it had just as much chance of killing them as being successful.

Something flashed past Rek's ear. Glancing back Reks' breath caught in his throat as he laid eyes upon the most horrific creature he had ever seen. A creature of darkest nightmare was riding abreast two Wargs. It was a monstrosity that only the most twisted of minds could fathom. Black as night and covered in what he thought were eyes. Behind that hideous thing came more than just wargs, lots more wargs! What followed them could only be described as monsters of his worst nightmares.

They were now in full flight as they sensed the predators right behind them. Rek harrumphed and decided he was left with no choice now. He cut loose the spare horses hoping they would provide enough distraction to give him time to enact his crazy idea.

With all his might, Rek reined his panicking horse to the right. He would only get one chance at this and could not afford to lose control over the animal. The Wargs that were not devouring the spare horses were now nipping at his horse's hind legs, and that nightmarish beast with the eyes was almost riding alongside him. As Rek looked on the head-sized eye that sat atop the creature's body, it split open to reveal razor-sharp teeth in a wicked smile. Rek answered with a demented smile of his own and pointed his chin at the oncoming opening.

"Can those fucking eyes of yours see what's coming up, you ugly fuck!" Rek shouted.

The creature turned and looked ahead, instantly bringing his wargs to a standstill.

As Rek's horse cleared the opening in the treeline, it noticed the sheer cliff drop suddenly beneath it. Instinctively it tried to pull up as it struggled to save its own life, but it was too late having leapt from the cliff.

Rek had scouted the area before setting camp to get a lay of the land. He had almost gone over the cliff then and ironically remembered the relief he had felt looking down a sheer drop into the frothing white rapids below. This time he had taken the leap voluntarily. It was the only option, that is, if they survived the fall.

They fell to what would be a watery death. Rek heard a gruesome shriek of frustration from the creature still up on the clifftop. As man and horse fell, Rek knew that the only way to survive would be to let the horse take the brunt of the impact. Using all his strength to manoeuvre the horse while holding firm to his unconscious friend. As they finally hit the water, Rek felt the horse's ribs snap and crunch beneath him, and then he felt his breath get punched from his body. The impact took its toll. The world went cold and black as the torrent of water swallowed them whole.

Rek awoke coughing up water. Panic and pain rushed through his body as he sat up. Where was Tor? 'Please, not again!' How could he lose his friend again after only just finding him? He lifted his bruised and battered body. It was more through sheer willpower than ability, as the agony of his ordeal and losing his friend again wracked his body.

It was to his surprise and relief to see Tor standing a little further downstream. Rek laughed so hard that pain enflamed his ribs. Not only had his they survived the fall, but it also seemed to have knocked Tor out of his stupor. Rek approached him, amazed at being alive, he smiled.

Between them, his dead horse had washed up a short distance from him. The saddle packs still appeared intact which he threw over his shoulder. He also found his beloved weapon. A battle hammer which he used with devastating results he had strapped to his pack which he now holstered on his back. Moving upstream closer to Tor, he found something much more valuable; a half-filled gourd of Keshian wine. Approaching his captain, he took a swig of wine in celebration of being alive and then offered the flask to Tor. His friend seemed lost in thought and appeared to be scanning the horizon.

"We need to go Oracle, Rek" Tor stated as if they had not been involved in a life and death chase.

Rek coughed and spat. He felt like a horse had trampled over him, and he had drunk most of the river. He watched his old friend closely as there was something strange about him, a light behind his eyes. Offering him the drink again and giving his friend a look of amusement and bewilderment at their luck, he spoke up. "It's okay buddy, no need to thank old Rekhaert for saving your lazy arse while you took a nap?"

Rek met Tors eyes, and he knew it wasn't his friend. Lightening danced in those slitted eyes. Tor suddenly seemed to tower over him in that moment and in a cold tone that brooked no argument

"We must be gone from here; the enemy still hunts us, and I must heal your friend. Take me to the Oracle of

Manthripur." He ordered

Rek noticed that the blue lightning was fading behind those pale eyes and then Tor passed out. Fucking typical! Rek thought as he caught his friend mid-fall. From here

Idrienne would be a much closer place to get supplies and a boat if they were to travel to Manthripur. Gathering his thoughts, he muttered some profanity and threw his friend over his shoulder, before setting off for Idrienne.

Death from Above
Chapter eight

The dark creature which had chased them off the cliff had a malevolence that made Rek nervous. He had bought them a couple of days head start and was just glad they didn't die in the process. It would be a day's ride from atop the bluff, and even if that pack of monsters came, he would be gone.

Still, the one creature with the giant eye that had opened revealing rows of teeth, barking what had seemed like commands, had made his blood run cold. It had been riding across the top of the two fiercest looking Wargs imaginable. Never had he seen anything like those Wargs, fully grown and black as night, they seemed the size of small horses in the moment. They had moved in perfect unison. He knew the image would haunt his mind more than once on this journey.

*

Helplessly Bishop watched high above the scene. Too far away to Intercede and too slow to help, he was mortified as Rek and Tor raced over the cliff. Flying high above, he was relieved as the two came into view and seemed to be alive if a little beaten up. If they died, his plans would fail. His relief at seeing the two down below, alive, had been immense. He would show these creatures no mercy.

Circling back, he could not allow this hunting pack to catch them up. Starting at the rear of the pursuing group, flying in with unimaginable speed and ferocity, two Wargs had died in an instant as his claws ripped through their skulls spraying brains into the air. Then he was gone, climbing back into the air.

The pack hadn't seemed to notice his attack yet. He spotted a small group of three Sokar who had fallen behind. In this form, he was the predator. Wings of glorious white billowed on the wind propelling the immense feline bulk, all muscle and grace, higher and higher. Unfurling his wings at the last moment, he floated momentarily before dipping his wings and letting gravity take hold, faster and faster he sped toward his targets. Bishop landed on two of the Sokar with a massive kinetic force. Claws biting into the backs of the unsuspecting creatures, tearing into flesh and bone while simultaneously driving them into the ground with tremendous momentum. Bishop felt their rib cages cracking under his sheer bulk.

The last of the Sokar in the group, a wolf-headed perversion of a man looked back at what had befallen its companions. Its fetid breath quickened. Bishop could see the Va'Nahual wanted to run, death was approaching, and all it could do was watch, frozen, helpless, as Bishop stalked closer and closer.

When Bishop was within a foot of the Sokar that paralysed with fear, the creature cried out, its eyes darting about looking for any salvation. There was none. The filthy beast emptied its bladder as Bishop's giant claw ripped away its throat and most of the Sokar's lower jaw. Blood sprayed from the gaping wound, colouring the nearby flora red.

Bishop didn't stay to hear the body drop. Two leaps and he was in the air again. He had killed several more of their pack before they had realized what they were facing, he managed to pick off another five as they organised.

The remaining Sokar and warg had grouped together watching the sky, trying to form a defence against the death descending from above. Bishop wanted to find the leader but couldn't seem to spot him. He knew by killing the leader he could render the pack inert. Where was that thing? He would kill it!

Bishop hated the Va'Nahual. They had been absent for nearly three hundred years and had been presumed to be dying out. In the last ten years, more and more sightings had been made. He did not know how or why they had become active again. Whatever the reason, Bishop knew that with attacks this far North, it would mean there was a larger force to the south.

Some of the Wargs must have caught his scent, growling in his direction. The enemy was clearly afraid as they brandished their weapons at the sky. Wargs stood to attention, sniffing the air, pawing and barking in fear.

Bishop charged from his hiding place straight at the pack. A Warg bit at his side as he passed. Ignoring them, he knocked two more out of his way as he launched himself at the Sokar. With claws like daggers, he ripped into their ranks. They were outmatched. Two died, guts hitting the floor as they were disembowelled by a single ferocious swipe. Bishop picked up another one of the smaller

Va'Nahual in his jaws; they didn't stand a chance. He shook the offending creature and threw its dead body back into the pack.

A bear-like Sokar attacked with a giant club studded with nails, missing by mere inches planting itself firmly in the ground with a colossal thump. The bear only had time to swing once before its forearms had been severed from its hands by a fast and vicious mauling. Its hands were still clenched to the club in a death grip. It seemed to take the creature a minute to realize its lower arms were no longer there. Blood began spurting in all directions from the dismembered and gesticulating creature as it died screaming.

It hadn`t taken him long to despatch the Va'Nahual pack. Looking at the carnage he had wrought, it gave the griffin in Bishop an enormous feeling of satisfaction. Bishop roared triumphantly.

He started to preen his wings and inspect his minor wounds. Nothing serious. He watched which direction the few remaining Wargs ran. Hopefully, they would lead him to the pack master. It took a while, but finally, he spotted it in the tree line. It had been watching him from the trees overlooking the horror he had wrought. The time had come for Bishop to kill this abomination!

A sibilant voice emanated from the darkness ahead of him. "Here kitty, kitty... Here kitty."

Bishops resonating growl filled the grove.

Once more, the creature taunted, "if you want me dead, you'll have to come closer."

Most living things would fear that sibilant voice, and if that wasn't enough, the maniacal laugh that followed was dripping with menace.

Bishop raged, how dare this creature try to goad him! Padding into the shadow of the woods, looking for this insect to crush. He sniffed the air, but there was no scent, only a deathly silence in the shadows.

*

The Spider had watched the slaughter of the pack unfold from the shadow of the trees. He would not fight this animal on open ground. Pulling his swords from their sheaths on his back, he waited. The Spider had watched the Griffin enter and waited high in the trees above the unsuspecting prey, jumping from the tree The Spider spun and landed perfectly on his new enemies back. Before the Griffin could react, the Spider opened its one-eyed maw and sank its jaws into the base of the wing. The beast jumped and spun, trying to dislodge him. The Spider only intensified its bite, and the Griffin roared in fury.

The Spider released his hold of the wing. He had drawn first blood, perfectly pirouetting from the Griffin, he landed at Bishop's hindquarters, slashing at his rear leg before disappearing behind a tree. The Spider's weapons had barely left a mark. If only he had some of the Soulless in his ranks. Minos would've cut this cat in half. He jumped onto a tree and ran up its side, swords back in their sheaths.

*

Bishop's claw missed by inches, gouging a head-sized chunk out of the tree where the creature had been mere seconds ago. He would kill this abomination. Spreading his wings, a tidal wave of pain crashed over him. Roaring his agony at the shadows in the branches high above.

Bishop was worried for the first time during this extermination. The creature had shown much more cunning than its companions and was a definite threat that needed removing. The bite must have been poisonous and a potent toxin at that. Pain clouded his mind as the venom spread into his system. Torn between a need for a cure and the necessity of killing the Dren but he knew he needed a cure more.

He would come back for this tick and bite off its head. Bishop could not afford to die here. Summoning every ounce of power, he spread his wings and bounded from the grove. There were healing springs behind the mountains of Manthripur. He only hoped he could make it. A lot of legends had Griffins as immortal beings. The truth was they were mostly indomitable, with skin three to six inches thick, solid muscled bodies, and claws sharper than most blacksmiths could replicate.

This creature shouldn't have been able to hurt him, but nevertheless, something was seriously wrong. Flying for all he was worth, he left the clearing and the despicable little Dren behind, taking flight and heading for Manthripur.

The Spider had watched in amazement as his tormentor turned and flew away. It looked in terrible pain which caused the Spider to smile a toothy one-eyed grin. He hadn't thought his venom had gotten through the Griffins hide, but it was hurt. He had hurt it! And on the upside, he no longer had a pack slowing him down.

He couldn't resist yelling after it, "Don't go kitty. Here kitty, kitty. I PROMISE I WON'T BITE, KITTY KITTY! Hahahahahah." When he caught his breath from laughing, he called out to his night Wargs. Leaping onto their backs, he continued the pursuit of his original prey.

Even though The Spider knew he had to catch Tor, he still wanted to follow and watch the pussy cat die in agony.

The thought of it brought him joy. He had never tasted Griffin, but the vessel was getting further and further away, and if he didn't bring it to Azazel alive, he could inflict worse punishments than death; death would be a release. He could not afford diversions.

Kirk

Chapter nine

Mariana had lived her whole 57 years in the town of Kirk, and she loved her home. She had watched it grow from a tiny settlement on the river Ouroborus into the bustling trade centre it was now.

A town in which she had become the mayor. Situated north Uxmal, Kirk had thrived with trade from nearby ports.

Mariana now stood upon the small balcony of her mayor's villa overlooking the marketplace upon which the town had flourished. She sat here every morning, taking in the noise of the traders hawking their goods. She loved the hubbub of the open market square. It reminded her of her own childhood, so many summers ago now.

She smiled contentedly to herself and sipped her tea, breathing in the aromatic fragrance. The morning smells as unique and pleasant as any town in the land. The aroma of baking bread merged with the scent of her roses and exotic spices sold at the marketplace. It was safe to say that there was no place that Mariana would rather be… Except for when the Va'Nahual came to town.

The first she saw of the attack was when her teacup began to shake violently before spilling its contents across the table. Mariana stood at the balcony edge to see where the low rumbling was coming from. She was greeted by a vision from her worst childhood stories.

Mariana had thought them myths used to make her behave, tales of monsters, and hideous creatures that stole naughty children away in the night. The people who were taken had fallen into sin and became the souls of the Va'Nahual. The forgotten and the damned which the dark ones had twisted and manipulated until they formed the very faces of fear and torment that would be forced upon them.

Fear struck through her as the Va'nahual slashed and clawed at her citizens. A helpless witness as her people fled the horrific onslaught, Mariana was transfixed upon the destruction and bile rose from her stomach, she had never witnessed such horror in her life, but she could not look away. She watched on as hideous creatures attacked and maimed at will.

One monster sliced a grown man clean in half with a giant sword. Another beast ripped out the throat of an old woman with its fangs. Several of the smaller creatures that were no bigger than children themselves brought down a large man. One of those little nightmares gouged out the man's eyes and began to urinate on his face as the others laughed and followed suit.

*

Minos had known as soon as he had seen the town, it would be nothing to take it. Azazel had made it clear Alal wanted him to guard the land bridge at Uxmal. Minos felt like he deserved a chance to give in to his bloodlust and reasoned that if he got prisoners and transformed them into Sokar. Alal might overlook his transgression.

Minos walked through the burning carcass of the town and felt satisfied that his pack had destroyed it so thoroughly. Blood and viscera pooled on the ground at every turn. The years of watching this miserable race prosper as he and his kind hid in the shadows, but now he was free, and he would take pleasure in every ounce of pain and suffering that he and his pack could inflict.

Minos stood in the centre of the carnage that his pack had reaped and breathed in deeply, savouring the pain and despair all around him. He smelled the sweet aroma of spilt blood, fear and adrenaline floating on the air. This was the smell of violence, and it made Minos feel alive for the first time in a long time.

From the corner of his eye, he spotted something. Turning his massive frame towards the movement, on a balcony of a large stood the lone figure of an old human female, she was wailing as she watched the slaughter of the town's inhabitants. A cruel smile curled Minos' lip. It was time for him to have some fun.

*

Mariana was watched her town being ripped apart, hypnotized by the violence and destruction, when a low thudding sound caught her attention. She turned towards the noise and saw an image from her worst nightmares charging towards her home. The beast was huge and grotesquely formed with the head of a bull. It ran at her home, knocking man and beast, friend and foe, out of its way.

Turning to run, sprinting indoors, hoping against hope she had not been seen. Once on the ground floor, she ran for her front door, but she was too late. The wall of her kitchen exploded inwards, sending timber and bricks flying everywhere. Something hard caught Mariana on the side of her head and sent her sprawling to the floor. Her world spun, and blackness threatened to engulf her.

Mariana somehow managed to hold onto consciousness. As the dust settled, she wished that she had passed out. In front of her stood an immense beast towering over her. Its features were that of a bull, and large fangs lined a ferocious smile in a twisted maniacal grin.

She looked up into the beast's eyes which were black as pitch, highlighted with blood-red irises. The monster let out a threatening snort from its bull-like nostrils and charged at Mariana.

*

Minos could smell the fear emanating from the woman. His blood fired with excitement as he charged.

He was about to smash into the old woman when his senses picked something else up. The excitement was replaced by pure fear, and his blood ran cold. His red eyes fixed upon the female, and his worst fears were realized. Alal had found him! Minos' momentum was too much for him to stop. His cloven hoofs found no purchase on the stone floor, and he slid into what was once a feeble woman. That woman existed no more.

Alal had possessed her, his insidious form burning away at her from within. The Vessels face began to rip, and its cheeks were blistering and tearing into a demonic smile. There was a hunger in those eyes that was not there before. A need to inflict pain. Alal struck the charging Minos across his chest with unbelievable force, sending him reeling across the room.

Minos watched Alal stroll towards him. Placing two fingers under his chin and lifting him as if he weighed nothing. Alal smiled a wicked grin and tilted her head peering at Minos. "Why are you wasting my time here Minos?" she asked in a voice dripping with menace "You were ordered to hold Uxmal ready for the invasion. Instead, I find you indulging yourself here like the pitiful fool you are." Alal's voice had started to rise with fury as his temper became more apparent. Minos' fear rose alongside Alal's rage. He had made a great mistake giving in to his bloodlust, and he was about to pay the price.

The arm that held Minos up had begun to scorch and burn before Minos' very eyes. Alal effortlessly threw him aside. He landed heavily, and as he looked up, the hosts face began to blister.

"You are fortunate on this occasion, Minos. My host's vessel is not strong enough to sustain me. This is your last chance. Fail me again, and I will peel the skin from your bones and cook your meat for the Sokar to feast upon! Now go and ready the army and stand down until I command. Do not disobey again!" Flames began to breach the body of Alal's host. "Do not dare to disobey me again, now GO!"

With those words, Mariana's body began to blaze brightly. Flames swirled and danced intensely around her. A loud piercing scream escaped the inferno just before the fire finally engulfed her withering body. For a moment she burned so intensely that it temporarily blinded Minos. When his vision came back, Mariana's body stood there, burnt into ash and cinder, frozen momentarily in a pose filled with pain. Then a breeze hit, and she collapsed into a pile of ash.

Minos knew he had escaped his punishment. Dusting himself off, he called the pack and set off back to Uxmal, before his master returned and killed him.

Kiva
Chapter ten

Kiva had been surviving alone for a long time, that was until she came to Idrienne. The town was a large fishing village, built down one side of a sinuous river that was its namesake. The village was a prosperous one and was becoming a regular trading post. Some of the new buildings were even being built in stone, like the Blacksmith's and Baker's. Soon it would become a proper town.

Two years ago, Kiva had fled the city of Sha'mack. The journey here had been long and dangerous. On more than one occasion, she had thought she was going to die. When she finally stumbled upon Idrienne, half-starved. The smell of bread cooking in the morning air as she arrived. That was her first memory of Idrienne. Looking at the village with a renewed sense of hope and wonder.

She had come to love this little village. Kiva was thirteen when she arrived here, travel-stained and worn. Surprisingly, her aunt Marin had recognized her, even under the dirt and rags.

"My God! you must be Valena's child?" Her aunt had fussed over her, grabbing her chin, yanking her face this way and that. Taking pity on the child, Marin had brought her niece into her home. Kiva remembered her aunt mumbling to herself "This will never do!" again and again. It was like getting caught in a storm, her aunt was a force of nature, and she didn't have the strength to protest.

Her aunt burned the clothes she had worn as a disguise for too many years. Over the next few weeks, she had sulked at their loss, but her Aunt did not give up on her. Kiva smiled at the memory. It had been impossibly hard for her to lower her guard, but her aunt persisted no matter what she did.

Kiva barely remembered what it was to trust or be loved until now. She considered it a miracle that on that first day, she had found the bravery to knock on what could've been a stranger's door. It had been a place from a distant memory, a dream almost. It had not been her first choice to make the journey or even her second. That this place was real or that she would be welcomed with open arms had been a long shot at best.

Two years later, the dream and the reality were starting to trade places. It had taken months for the nightmares to fade and only more recently had she begun to put the past behind her. Even now she would occasionally wake up in the middle of the night, sweat dripping from her brow and back, gasping for air, heart beating with fear from losing her brother. On these nights Kiva would sneak out to watch the stars.

A new town hall had been erected that year. She had figured out a way to climb up the grand building. The first two floors to a balcony were easy, but the central hall had been built with a third floor. Balancing her way across the balcony ledge and getting to the next set of handholds. There was another floor of tricky climbing around a stained-glass window and over the crenulation. It was worth it, though. From here you could see the whole village and look upon the beauty of the night sky while listening to the river flowing by. This was her safe place; a place to put things into perspective on nights like these.

From here, she watched the trees gently sway in the evening breeze, recalling the events that brought her to Idrienne. Kiva knew she wasn't always a thief. Hunger and fear could alter your opinion on right and wrong, especially if you had a hungry younger brother to feed. It had started with food, stealing from saddles, stalls, anywhere people weren't paying attention. At ten years old Kiva was using the rooftops as her personal highway, avoiding the dangerous streets below.

She and her brother had been noticed and taken in by the Guild of Thieves. Things were good for a while. She learned something she had not thought possible. As a thief in Sha'mack, she earned well, well enough to provide for herself and her brother. The problem had been she was coming of age, and at thirteen summers, she had started to draw the unwanted attention of men. That was enough to prompt anyone in her position to start thinking of the future.

Unfortunately, she hadn't paid enough attention, or things may have happened differently. A trusted member in the Guild called Chuin had offered her a once in a lifetime score. She remembered being excited by the prospect of moving up in the guild. This would set her and her brother up for years to come. As Kiva arrived, Chuin was talking to a stranger. Something was off, but she didn't want to risk the opportunity and seem scared, how foolish she had been.

The stranger had spoken first and asked, "So we have the girl, but where is the boy? I have the hundred gold for the Ishtar and the Adad." The man hefted a large purse. "What does he mean, where's the boy, Chuin?" Kiva had tried to sound commanding, but the slight tremor in her voice broke that illusion.

Chuin ignored her and gave a sharp whistle, and out of the shadows stepped some large men, Kiva tried to run, but a grip of iron held her in place, she hadn't even heard his approach. Panicked she kicked at her assailant. She had been captured easily. More men appeared from the shadows holding her brother Adam. Kiva's heart dropped, and she stopped fighting. That night they had been betrayed and sold to an evil man.

Thinking back on that night, tears welled in her eyes at the memory of her brother being taken. She had run through it all a thousand time before, and she could not shake her guilt. Even now in this safe place, her skin crawled at the memory. She was grateful for the skills she picked up in the Guild, and she would make good use of them later that night. The stranger's words echoed in her mind. "I will take the boy now. I will give you half and be back for the girl in a couple of hours." The evil-looking stranger coughed what looked like blood onto a clean hanky he had pulled from his inside pocket. She had noticed a bold embroidered L on the bloody hanky just before the man took her brother away. That was the last time she would see the stranger or her brother again.

Kiva was left with a tough looking thug for a guard, she had watched him drinking late into the evening and had waited for an opening, but her attempt had proved futile. With one blow, he had knocked her unconscious.

Kiva awoke tied to a bed and panic set in again. The brute had told her the night was just beginning, his stinking breath inches from her face.

"When I get back, you're going to wish you were a boy." He leered at her before he headed for the door. He called over his shoulder as if an afterthought, "We can start with a bed bath when I get back."

As soon as the door closed, Kiva began to study her surroundings. She had to be in a house in the wealthy quarter. Lush drapes lay against marble window ledges. Even the bed she was tied to was ornamental and even had a feather mattress.

The man hadn't taken her clothes off before tying her. Even more surprising, upon checking for hidden weapons, not all her throwing knives had been found. This man was evil, and she had to escape. It only took her a moment to slip her bonds. Making her way to the window, she jumped into pitch darkness. Brought up on the streets of Sha'mack you did not fear the dark; it was a place to hide.

Given the choice, she had chosen the unknown and fled. She was not proud of what she had done to stay alive.

Too much had been done to dwell on the past. It had been the hardest thing she had ever done; she had tried to search, but with enemies on every corner, she had to leave her brother behind. Besides, if she was captured, who would save them or even care? She had vowed to herself that she would come back and find her brother and kill Chuin.

The memory had filled her with pain, and Kiva tried to think of more recent events. Looking at the stars from the roof of the Great Hall. Idrienne had recently fallen into troubles. Rumours of yellow eyes in the night and disappearances. At first, it had just been livestock, but then people started to disappear. Some of the town's best hunters had gone into the woods and never came back!

Looking toward the dark forest, darker than the night. She saw the reality of the rumours, as yellow eyes began to appear in the blackness. They seemed a mockery of the stars, as hundreds of glowing eyes started watching the village. She saw no beauty there. What pushed through the trees caused her blood to run cold. She had to warn her aunt.

Jumping up had caused a roof tile to come loose under Kiva's feet. Falling face first and hitting her head on the roof wall, the world went black. That accident was probably the only reason she was still alive. That, and no doubt her location, unconscious on the third story roof, unseen by the creatures below.

Calls of scavenger birds awoke Kiva with their chattering mockery. She heard a loud cracking noise from inside the building that sent a shiver down her spine. From her vantage point on the roof, she could see the bloodstained streets, doors smashed, some even hanging on broken hinges. Near the well, in the centre of town, dead bodies lay in a grisly stack. The brutality of what had been done shook her to her core. Blood so much blood...

Kiva wanted to run to her aunt's and make sure she was alright, but as a child, her instincts were the only thing that had kept her alive. Every part of her screamed the danger was not gone. Looking around the village again, a movement in a doorway a few buildings down caught her eye and her breath caught in her throat, it was her aunt, but something was off hunched at an odd angle in the doorway, but then she noticed her aunt was moving ever so slightly. Then with an unnatural speed, her aunt's body disappeared into the doorway and was gone, dragged inside by some unseen thing into the shadow. Her aunt had not screamed or yelled, and Kiva's hands came up, covering her mouth and stifling her cry of anguish. She had never felt so alone as she did at that moment alone, on the roof of the sleepy little village town.

How long she had remained on the roof lost in despair; she was unsure. The death of her aunt nearly broke her. Forcing down her loss and pain, it was time to leave. Climbing back onto the balcony below that's when she heard the popping and crunching noises coming from inside. Worse still was the noise of people crying. She had to escape. Climbing down the rear of the building, ignoring the sounds of terror coming from inside as she scaled down past an open second-floor window, Kiva couldn't resist a look and regretted it. There was a time to run, and this was it.

Kiva leapt from the building. She had made larger drops in her time at Sha'mack. She hit the ground running toward the river. She ran for her life. All she could think about was a hope, a hope that the monsters feared the water like in the stories.

Idrienne
Chapter eleven

It had taken Rek longer than he thought it would to get to Idrienne, but he had been carrying Tor. Keeping to the river as the ground was more favourable. Even Reks famed endurance was waning though. Finally, Rek came across a small boathouse on the outskirts of town. A couple of four-person boats were moored to a small wooden quay that jutted into the river at an odd angle.

From here, the town seemed deserted. It was showing none of the usual comings and goings for a settlement of this size.

"Right yer kingship, you can wait here while I get us some supplies in town," Rek said as he put Tor down with his back against the boathouse.

It had been over a year since he visited Idrienne. It would be dark soon, and he would have to be quick. Rek jogged to the town not wanting to leave Tor alone for too long. He planned to be in and out.

He slowed as he approached the town. There was something wrong. An all too familiar smell of death hung in the air. It was too quiet. Death had come swiftly for the settlement.

He saw no bodies as he slipped through the town. He was making his way to the blacksmiths. He followed the northeast wall to the back of the building. Quietly opening the back door and letting himself in, straight away, he had a bad feeling. A feeling in his gut that there was something else inside the building still. Part of him hoped it was a survivor, someone who could tell him what had happened here.

Cautiously walking through the kitchen, Rek did a quick weapons check and headed on silent feet towards the door for the main living space. The noise he could hear was coming from the room ahead. Rek edged closer until a sound like whispering set his teeth on edge. Looking through the crack in the door, he couldn't see anything, although he had a nagging feeling.

Rek closed his eyes, took a deep breath and looked through the crack in the doorway, willing his eyes to focus in the darkness of the room. He started to make out a shape hanging from the rafters. The rope was gently creaking as it swayed ever so slightly. Nausea welled up in his gut from the size of the form it could only be a child. A child had been hoisted for the grisly task of feeding. A moment later, he understood what had befallen the village and how little time he had.

They had eaten the child's arm and face, probably while the boy was still alive. Swallowing back some bile and forging his intent. There was nothing he could do for the dead child. Drawing attention to his presence wouldn't help anyone. Shadows in the room started to take shape, even more so now he knew what he was looking for. One of the creatures seemed to stir. 'Ugly little fuckers!' thought Rek. He had come across Nightkin before, and it explained the panic he felt. Nightkin never travelled away from the mountain ranges. They were scavengers that lived in a symbiotic relationship with trolls.

How, or why they were in Idrienne was beyond him. They had very few weaknesses, though they did have a natural intolerance for any type of light, which was why they never left the shadowed safety of their mountain regions. It was all very confusing. What would bring them out and into a town? If they were roaming free, without restriction, this could be a big problem. They weren't afraid of anything as far as he was aware, not even death. Alone they were reasonably easy to kill, but they were never alone. Pain... Nightkin loved inflicting pain. Rek thought it was probably because they felt none.

Stories were told of how deadly these creatures were, travellers disappearing even from large groups, never to be found. He knew that most of the stories were exaggerated. Nightkin would feed on anything that ventured into their habitat at night though. Generally, that was vermin or birds. That was not to say they didn't take on bigger pray if it was stupid enough to enter the caves' they called home. Rek had seen one bite through solid plate armour once.

Not seeing any Nightkin present didn't mean much, it was light outside which meant most of the creatures would be sleeping in the buildings. A large window let the evening sunlight into the kitchen. Rek decided to scrounge around for supplies. He spotted some bread and cheese, an evening meal laid untouched, set out for a family that would never enjoy it. As quietly as he could he picked up the provisions, looking around, he needed to plug his ears to block out the sound of the Nightkin, reluctantly filling his ears with the soft cheese, which did a great job of blocking out the Nightkin. The sun was setting, and he would have to salvage what he could quickly, any horses he may have found would be dead or long gone, chased away by the Nightkin.

Backing out of the kitchen into the safety of the fading daylight outside, he silently closed the door behind him as soon as the sun went down Rek knew they would swarm from the buildings like angry ants.

Rek ran to the front of the blacksmiths. Eli had been the blacksmith's name. He had known the family. They had taken pity on him last winter, letting him work to pay for food and lodgings. He made his way to some cupboards at the back of the outdoor smithy. A place where the blacksmith had kept the best weapons. Rek walked to the forge and just as he remembered there was a spare key under a fake stone. He was a practical man. No one was left to use these weapons, and with night approaching, he may well need them.

He helped himself to varying weapons refilling his many sheaths about his person. He hadn't felt right since losing them in the jump from the cliff. He had felt naked even with his massive war hammer. Spotting a large ornate box, he found a beautifully crafted double crossbow. It must have taken Eli a long time to create such a beautiful piece. A memory flashed through his mind of a happy child at play running through the forge. The thought was like a blow as the image changed to the child swinging in the house. It brought a tear to his eye, and he had to remind himself time was slipping by. These had been good people. It would be dark soon, and he needed to be out of the area by then.

*

Kiva had followed the river down to the boatshed. On the trip down she rationalized her loss, dismissing the village in her mind as a hindrance. After all, it wasn't the first time she had been on her own and in her experience, thinking on the loss was a sure-fire way to get killed. Death lived in Idrienne now. Her best chance of survival would be a boat downstream.

When she got there, Kiva saw a couple of boats tethered to quay. Searching the area for supplies, she came across a man, asleep on a pack with what looked like a well-stuffed saddle.

She knew she'd be hungry soon and in need of a blanket. They say old habits die hard. Creeping over to the pack she rationalized quickly, anything she could find was more than she had. While she was borrowing some of the stranger's gear, Kiva noticed the man had some sort of golden armour strapped to his forearm. Tiptoeing to his side, she crept nearer. It was beautiful. Looking closer it appeared to have no discerning latches or straps. It was one solid piece. She involuntarily reached out while studying the runes on the brace.

*

It had been Tor's injuries that had brought him into the Ib'ren Cohar to find Argento. He had been here for what seemed like months processing his past. Sharing his pain as he shared the dragons. The dream the dragon had called it. They had built a bond. Of all his memories, the last few years were the hardest as he dwelled on his time in the dungeons. Tor didn't think he would have survived those memories without Argento's rage at what was done to him. He was also the beneficiary of the memory of how Argento got to be in the Ib'ren Cohar. The horror of it had filled him with a wave of furious anger. Everything after that seemed more manageable somehow.

Tor spent many an evening talking with Argento and training. Finally, he understood what was coming, and he was as ready as he could be. Practising the forms of the Fenn fighting style The Dance With Dragons using the Ib'ren Cohar.

His mind at rest Argento's voice echoed in his head, "It has been but a day in your world Aleator and you are healed enough to go back. Remember your training. You must focus. I won't always be here to help you. He will be coming for us, and he could be in anyone. We must stop

Alal. Seek the Oracle in Kadingir. We must forge our path."

Sensing someone stood over him, even in his unconscious state, Aleator's hand shot out and grabbed a small wrist.

*

Kiva was caught! She tried to drag her arm from his grip. The man was like stone, and when his eyes opened, they weren't human. Brilliant blue surrounded slitted eyes like foxes or reptiles. Lightning flashed dimly in those eyes. She froze, It was like he looked right through her.

"Let go of me," she yelled.

His next words brooked no argument. "Where am I, girl? I do not recognize this place."

"Not far from Idrienne." The girl replied, voice quaking with fear.

"I won't hurt you, child," he said as he released his grip on her. "Did you see a man with me?"

Kiva didn't know why she hadn't bolted already; taking a deep breath, she met those eyes as defiantly as possible, "No one in the village is alive!"

Concern briefly danced across the strange man's features as he spoke. It lasted for only a moment before it disappeared. "My name is Aleator, but my friends call me Tor. What is your name?"

"Kiva," she replied hesitantly.

"Well, Kiva, I have been asleep for some time and could do with food and drink. Would you like to share what I have?" He found some water and biscuits in the saddle and took a swig of water before offering it to Kiva. She took the water and drank as Tor watched her intently.

"Why are you looking at me like that?"

"You have a large bruise on your head, Kiva. You seem hurt."

Kiva knew she was barely holding herself together.

There was something about Tor that made her feel safe.

She relaxed when he offered her a biscuit, which she took gratefully.

"Please take a seat. Tell me, Kiva, what has happened?"

She hadn't eaten in nearly a day. She didn't know why she felt safe near this man. He radiated power and strength. She had known evil men and could usually get a sense for them. Aleator was something different.

Nibbling on the oatcake, she replied, "I remember the eyes in the night and a terrible chittering noise coming from the darkness. I saw them coming. I tried to warn the others." Her eyes filled with tears in the retelling.

As she spoke, she could feel Tor appraising her.

"Kiva you are safe nothing will hurt you. Tell me what happened next?"

Kiva pulled at the tattered corners of her dress, unsure of what she had seen. "I was sitting on the roof of the new town hall when they came. I slipped and banged my head. When I awoke, there was blood in the streets, bodies being dragged into shadowed buildings." Retelling the tale had caused a vision to flare in her mind of her aunt's body being brutally dragged into the darkness. She pushed it down as quickly as it appeared and exhaled a deep breath, regaining her composure.

"I saw something in the building when I climbed down. It was big, and it scared me, it was eating people!"

"What was?"

Ignoring the question, not wanting to remember anymore "We need to get out of here. The thing in the town hall is evil. We have boats, let's just go." She pleaded.

"I cannot go, my companion, Rek, will not go far. I must wait for a while. We'll be safe here. Let's load the boat with what we have, just in case we need to make a quick exit. No doubt Rek must have gone more supplies."

"He's probably dead, and we should go."

"There is another boat, Kiva. If you choose you may leave, or you can stay, and I will see if I can catch us something better to eat. Can you make a fire, Kiva?"

Keeping busy was precisely what she needed. Besides, she was still hungry and decided begrudgingly that she was probably safer with Aleator than alone.

*

Rek had managed to get most of what he wanted without entering the dwellings again. He needed to be away from here. The sun was nearing the horizon. The houses must hold hundreds of sleeping Nightkin. He should just leave, but he had heard crying coming from the newly built town hall.

A moment later he was at a front window. Peering through the stained-glass window. It was a disturbing scene. What remained of the townsfolk lay caged and battered. He couldn't see any Nightkin. "Fuck it," Rek muttered deciding against his better instincts to run.

Entering the town hall as quietly he could with his battle hammer in one hand and a newly acquired hand axe in the other. Except for the cries of the survivors, the hall seemed empty. Making his way to the cages, he found a group of women and children sitting in their own filth.

At his appearance, the townsfolk had become excited at the prospect of escape. Pleas for help began to echo the hall. He angrily signalled the prisoners to be quiet, before wedging his axe between the joints of the cage. He used it to wrench the door out of place. Once done, he was still surprised at the lack of attention he had drawn. Removing the makeshift door was tougher than he had thought it would be. The townsfolk nodded their heads and gave thanks as they exited out of the hall. Rek whispered as they passed to stay quiet and get out of town.

Moving as quickly as possible, he surveyed the room for threats and any more prisoners using what little light coming in from the large doorway and windows behind him. It occurred to Rek that it was strange there was no light coming in from the other side of the building. Just as the thought crossed his mind, he watched as the last of the prisoners left the building. Rek exhaled a deep breath. He had gotten them out. As he turned to follow them, he watched in horror as the last person to leave let the door swing shut. He watched in slow motion as the door closed with a loud resonant bang. Rek looked back into the darkness. "Don't be a troll. Don't be a troll. Don't be a troll."

That's when it opened its eyes, giant saucer-like eyes of gold, taking in the hall as it stretched its muscled limbs.

"Iiiiiit's a fucking troll!". Rek dejectedly exclaimed to himself, cursing his luck and watched as the abomination dislodged a dismembered hand that must have gotten stuck between its head-sized teeth. The troll tossed into its cavernous mouth. Then took time to stretch before unleashing the foulest of wet growling flatulence Rek had ever heard.

Rek had been slowly backing away from the horror. Its bulk was filling the whole back wall of the hall blocking all the windows. He was nearly at the front entrance as the troll took in its empty cage. The beasts face filled with loss and rage mangled together on a tombstone sized head. He was nearly out, just a few more paces.

"Where are my meats!" Screamed the troll.

Suddenly, the air seemed to thicken. A smell of rotten eggs and death hit Rek like a blow from his war hammer. He gagged; this time unable to hold down the contents of his stomach. He would wonder what it had been eating, but he already knew too well. The thought caused him to wretch again. It was only a couple of seconds before Rek looked up at the creature. A chill ran down his spine. The Troll was looking right back at him with a hungry gaze.

This was no time to try and hold ground, Rek turned and bolted for the door and the creature charged. It had short legs compared to its bulk. Rek felt every bound it made vibrate through the ground as he bolted out into a glorious and ever fading sunset.

*

Tor was starting to worry for his friend. He had an idea of what was hidden in the town and set about building a fire as the sun was setting. Most things that lived in the dark feared the light. He just told Kiva the fire was for cooking, but he could see she knew the real reason. He was surprised at the girl's resilience, she had even laughed when Tor caught a couple of fish, flicking them onto the shore and he had offered to teach her how to tickle the fish.

While she ate, Tor continued to add to the fire, even using the other boat. As the sun started to set, they had built a roaring bonfire. The light it cast would cover the retreat to the boat.

"It's time. Do you remember our deal?" Tor asked Kiva.

"I do, but do I have to put clay in my ears."

"The Nightkin have a very effective way to attack. The light burns them so they won't be able to get to you, but they make a chattering noise that fills people with sheer panic. One always runs into the darkness away from the safety of the light. They never come back. If you are to be in charge of the escape, I don't want you making decisions out of imagined fear."

"But you're not doing it."

"Don't worry about me Kiva I will stay in the light. We must wait until the last possible moment for my friend. "

Kiva seemed to think for a moment before agreeing and heading back to the boat.

The fire cast enough light to block the quay as well offering manoeuvring room around it. The shadows lengthened as night crept ever closer. Tor knew they were coming. More than that his newly trained senses had started kicking in. Argento's voice came into his mind. "They are here, Aleator. Will you let me help as we practised?"

"Yes, I am ready."

*

Kiva was still unsure about the plan. From the boat, she could barely see the tree line. The sun had set, and Tor looked like he was praying of all things. With the damn clay in her ears, she couldn't hear a damn thing. She could, however, see yellow eyes appearing all along the shadowed tree line. Yellow eyes filled with menace. Fear gripped her; they were coming again. Oddly, she did not feel as scared as she had the last time.

To start, there were only four or five sets of eyes that appeared in the dark. She stopped counting as more and more eyes came into view. None approached the light cast from the massive fire they had built. Tor stood and moved further into the dark, and the Nightkin closed in.

What came next was a thing of beauty and death. Something had extended from Aleator's wrist guard, whipping about like a ribbon caught in the wind. He seemed to go into some sort of fighting stance. Kiva was mesmerized as Tor spun into action, the blade from his wrist spinning in an arc around him as he attacked. Now there was a set of lightning blue eyes amongst the yellow.

*

Tor was in the void watching in awe as Argento took control. There was a rush of adrenaline as the power of the Dragon flowed through his veins. With new eyes, he could make out hundreds of Nightkin despite the darkness. His new senses lit up the scene as clear as day. Every sound of the tiny Nightkin feet as clear as charging horses. Argento had no fear though which reassured Tor. Further up the road, he could see a much larger enemy, and it was heading straight for them. Tor felt Argento was enjoying himself too much to notice the threat as he dispatched the Nightkin with ruthless efficiency, totally engrossed in his gruesome task.

"How dare these filthy creatures attack us..." Argento ranted during the slaughter.

Tor had learned a lot about the functions of the Ib'ren Cohar. He had been adept in the soul cage, but Argento was something else. He became one with the weapon. The blade whispered death as it sliced through the Nightkin with ease.

The Nightkin were around two feet tall. What they lost in strength they made up for with claws for hands, teeth like daggers, and skin thicker than leather. One after another, they threw themselves at their prey. They were no threat to a dragon.

*

Outside Idrienne's town hall, Rek was fleeing for his life. Nightkin poured from the windows and doors as the sun cast its last rays. The creatures were throwing themselves at the waning light their skin scorching and blistering as they tried to get at him. Hissing and chattering their fury, trying to overwhelm him with panic. Luckily the cheese he had stuffed in his ears earlier was working a treat and blocked the worst of the chittering.

Rek had faced many demons on the battlefield and wouldn't let something like panic sway his decisions. Ignoring the Nightkin, he ran from the town hall. Looking over his shoulder at the giant solid oak doors he had run through. The brickwork appeared to be a solid granite stone structure. It should at least slow the creature down.

The front of the town hall seemed to explode with earth-shattering force into the square, causing stones to rain down around Rek as he ran. Dust clouds erupting from the ground all around him. The troll stepped from the wreckage of the hall and roared its anger at the night sky. The Troll Picked up one of the giant oak doors and threw it at Rek. It must have had some force thought Rek, as he felt it fly overhead, smashing into one of the buildings ahead of him. The warrior had seen all he needed to see. Putting his head down, he ran for all he was worth.

*

Argento was enjoying himself immensely. He had not spread his wings in such a long time. These Nightkin were a plague on the land, and unfortunately for them, became the focus of generations of suppressed rage. He had killed dozens of the enemy already, and still, they were relentless in their attack as claws and teeth tried to take a bite out of him.

The Ib'ren Cohar reacted instantly to Argento's command. As he turned to face another enemy, the ribbonlike blade shot out in a graceful arc as interlocking scales glimmered in the moonlight. The creature seemed surprised as Argento ripped out its lower torso, its intestines spilling onto the ground. Argento jumped into a spinning back kick, launching the now gutless Nightkin into several of its oncoming kin. It slowed them for a moment as they fought and fed over the fallen corpses.

The Nightkin seemed to stop their attack. They were sniffing the air, and then they scattered in all directions.

The night suddenly became dark and eerily silent. The tree line seemed to tremble at something passing. Sounds of snapping branches broke the momentary silence. Argento saw Rek appear first entering the clearing.

"In the boat!" Rek yelled as he sprinted toward the boat.

*

Kiva watching from the keel of the boat and was awestruck by Aleator. At first, she had thought the stranger mad, but wherever his blue eyes shone in the dark, yellow eyes went out. The strange weapon on Tor's arm glittered when the moonlight hit it. It had seemed alive and able to go from nothing to a whip-like blade around six or seven feet long. Then the yellow eyes were gone, and Tor just stood there looking at the woods.

A moment later, another man emerged from the woods in the direction Tor had been looking. The man was running towards them, yelling and pointing behind him. Kiva thought she heard him yell Troll as he ran past Tor. The giant of a man hadn't stopped until he jumped into the boat, surprised to find her there.

"Who are you?" asked the man before looking to Tor standing his ground "What is he doing?" He asked her.

Kiva was still watching Tor. She just pointed and said, "Watch.

*

Tor could see the surprise on the trolls face; that the man-thing wasn't running away. He was running towards it Argento bunched Tor's legs using the trolls attacking arm like a springboard, landing gracefully on the giants lumbering shoulders. The blade whipped out of the Ib'ren Cohar and wrapped around the heavily muscled neck of the troll, the intersecting blades of the Ib'ren Cohar slowly tightening like a noose made of razor wire. The more the creature fought, the tighter its noose became, as the blades ripped through muscle and sinew of the troll's neck.

Tor spoke in Argento's mind. "Finish it. We must go!" Tor could see his Rek and the girl had started to drift from the quay.

"I will get us to the boat." Replied the Argento. The troll was starting to slump forward from blood loss. The dragon seemed to tense all Tor's muscles at once. It was an odd sensation watching his body wreak such havoc.

Balanced on the cave troll's shoulders, Argento pulled on the Ib'ren Cohar, giving one final yank while somersaulting from the troll and using his body weight to rip through what was left of its neck. The head landed with a thud behind him as he set off running. By the time the body dropped, he had sprinted to the shoreline and jumped to the boat.

The trio drifted away, the electricity in Tor's eyes dimmed. He was back in control and stretched his arms.

"So you're feeling rested then?"

"Much better Rek."

Rek's brow was edged with worry and the girl's with awe, as they proceeded to float downstream.

Down River
Chapter twelve

A chill night was upon the land. Kiva watched as the light from the fire they had built as they floated off into the distance. The flames lit the frame of the headless troll. Kiva could make out those dreadful yellow eyes of the creatures that had slaughtered her town. The Nightkin were dancing around the body of the dead troll. Kiva could not make out what they were doing, but just seeing those eyes again brought back the memory of her aunt's body dragged into the darkness. She shuddered and pushed down the memory.

Kiva took a glance at each of her new companions. She would not usually trust strange men, especially the big man that had come running from the troll, but considering what they had just escaped, being alone would not be wise at this time. Plus, she found herself strangely drawn to Aleator. The way he had danced around the horrid creatures as they tried to swarm over him like ants had been hypnotising.

Aleator had fought like no other with his strange blade, in one moment it was the size of a short sword and the next it would extend like a whip, slicing through flesh and bone as if it were butter. Kiva's most vivid memory was of the lightning in Tor's eyes that had shone brightly through the darkness, and it fascinated her. Was this a man or some sort of god? Kiva looked at Aleator now from the corner of her eye. The light had left his eyes now, and although his body gleamed with sweat, the man did not appear to be even winded, he looked entirely at ease with himself, and the scene they had barely escaped. She took a glance at the strange weapon on his arm. She had never seen anything like it before.

Recalling the first time she had seen brace. She had been drawn to it like a moth to a flame. It amazed her to see that it was perfectly fused to the man's arm. Kiva realized she was staring at it again. Aleator was staring back with an arched brow. Kiva quickly glanced away and found herself now looking at the big man that she had not been introduced to yet. He was still trying to catch his breath and was scowling across the boat at Tor. He was the biggest man she had ever seen. In fact, she had seen smaller bears. He sported a bald head and fearsome dark brown eyes, he had a square jawline hidden behind a thick beard. He reminded Kiva of someone from her past, but she could not quite place his face. Whatever that sliver of memory was, she would not be letting her guard down until it came back in full.

"So, now you're awake from your beauty sleep, Tor. Could you tell me why it is that since I found you the other day, I've been chased around the countryside by a horde of fucking monsters? How do you find it so easy to have a catnap at the most inconvenient times?" fumed the big man. Kiva noted how his voice became louder and more aggressive as the sentence finished.

Aleator returned the big man's stare and replied, "Sleep? Ha! How about the next time you decide to ditch me while I'm unconscious, you maybe try to wake me, or at least don't leave me next to a town full of fucking

Nightkin!"

Both men were now standing toe-to-toe in the boat, making it rock from side to side. As the tension rose between the two warriors, Kiva prepared to dive into the river.

As a means of escape, it did not offer much. The river would be deathly cold at this time of night, but she had a better chance of survival there then if she stayed in the boat with these men fighting. Both held the icy stare of the other. Just as Kiva was about to leap overboard, the two men laughed and embraced each other.

Kiva just sat there confused with the scene in front of her. She had been prepared to leap to the icy waters, so sure that the two warriors were about to slaughter each other. Now they were hugging and laughing with one another. Kiva seriously did not understand men.

"Ah, Tor my old friend, it is good to see you awake again. But I am serious. What the fuck is going on? Why are there Wargs and Nightkin so close to the towns? And what were those ugly fucking things that have been chasing us?"

"I'm sorry, Rek. My memories are still vague, but whatever is going on, I will remember. You must understand I have been through a lot, so much so that parts of my mind had to be blocked off. When I was caged, I hoped one day someone would set me free. That's what Bishop did when he found me back in the cell. While I have been... How did you put it? Getting my beauty sleep." The two men shared another quick smile. "I am in your debt Rek. I couldn't have escaped without you." Tor looked down to the floor.

Whatever he had been through, Kiva could see, he wasn't over it.

"My captors took me someplace that I have never seen before. It was dark and dead. No life would grow there. Even weeds would struggle in that desolate place. I remember seeing huge forges and wild screams of both men and animal. After we reached our destination, they shackled me and threw me into the dungeons. From there on in, I only saw one other face. His name was Mandrake." Tor's whole body shuddered at the name. Tor took a moment to compose himself and then began to tell his story again.

"Mandrake was my torturer. Day after day, he would burn me, or cut me, or half drown me. He remarked once that each punishment was a lesson. On occasion, he would make me swallow some awful potion which either made my skin burn or made me bleed so much that I would feel as if I was going to die."

Aleator took a deep breath to compose himself. Kiva saw he had visibly paled as he recalled his imprisonment. Nevertheless, he continued.

"As well as being my torturer, he was also my healer. When I was upon the cusp of death, he would stop torturing me and begin to care for me. That is until I was strong enough for him to restart my torment again. In the meantime, as I was healing, he would read to me about the days before the Great Emigration. He talked about the gods and how they had robbed us of magic. I would listen intently, knowing one day of learning would mean one less day of torture."

Aleator paused again. Kiva noticed that both of his fists were clenched so tightly they appeared bone white.

"If I failed to learn, the cycle of torture would restart until I was once again at death's door. I don't remember when, or how it happened, but I know Mandrake broke me. Once they had achieved it, I was lost. It was as if they had extinguished my soul. I became a walking corpse for all intents and purposes. I have no memory after that. Not at least until I woke the other day and found Bishop in my cell." There was some steel in Tor's voice now.

"I have since come to realise they had planned to kill me. I was to be used as a blood sacrifice to leash the power of the dragon called Argento, caged within this brace. I do not know much more than that, but if they had been successful, a plague like no other would've been visited upon the land, and I would most certainly be dead. Bishop may, or may not know it, but he saved High Garden that day."

Kiva did not doubt what he was telling Rek. It reminded her she was not the only one to face hardship.

"I stole the blade they were going to kill me with and used it on them as I escaped. They must be stopped at all costs, Rek."

Aleator turned towards his two companions "We are not free yet. The darkness follows me still, and I need information. Bishop told me that we need to go to Manthripur before our camp exploded. There is an Oracle there waiting for me. He thinks she can help with my memory or will have some answers that I need to defeat the things that now hunt us." Tor looked at his two companions, waiting on a response.

Rekhaert was unsurprisingly first to speak up. "So, let me get this right. You're supposed to be some sort of sacrifice for some old evil. Which then intends to bring back the old days of darkness and chaos. We are being chased by monsters and god knows what else, and you decide it's a good idea to bring a defenceless little girl along with us?" Rek asserted.

Kiva responded to the insult with a swift kick to the big man's shin.

"Ow! Why you little..." Rek did not finish the sentence but instead gave the little girl a wry smile.

"Okay, she's maybe not so defenceless after all," he acknowledged, chuckling. Even Tor let a smile break over that stoic face of his.

Drifting down the moonlit river, Kiva listened as the two men as they recapped on old war stories and funny tales of days gone by. She found herself laughing and smiling along at the anecdotes of the two men. By the time she had fallen asleep, she felt safe. Little did she know that their troubles had only just begun.

Kishar
Chapter thirteen

Gabriel, the leader of the Athanatos, he was an average looking man when he was out of uniform, today he was disguised as a merchant. Under his arm, he carried some maps from his private collection as part of the ruse.

He was on his way to meet the Spymaster Bishop, the other hand of the King, in the Royal Gardens. He had a secret meeting away from the council and prying ears. As the King's justice and right hand, he had been suspicious of the attacks coming from the south for some time now. He was hoping the information he would receive from the Spymaster would reveal that he was just paranoid.

The rumours of assaults amid sightings of creatures from the old world were becoming more regular. It was possible these stories, were just that, Gabriel believed they hid a strategy, what he saw as the first push from a hidden enemy in the south. It seemed to him that the reports from the south hid an enemy that had even managed to cross the land bridge at Uxmal, which would mean the Jaden had been beaten back by some unknown force.

He had reports of scouting parties attacking peaceful villages along the way. The most recent report was of some people escaping a town called Idrienne. The remains of a Troll had was found decapitated; it could only mean something was forcing the creatures from their mountain homes. Homes they would not leave of their own accord.

No one seemed to know what was happening in the south. He had already received approval to send a large contingent of the Athanatos south to investigate. Gabriel was worried it would not be enough. He'd had his trusted second in command, Raif, to arrange the assignments. In his opinion, they needed to send the army and quash any uprising before it achieved momentum. He would be approaching the King with this grave news at the next council meeting. It wasn't something he was looking forward too.

It was all just politics in the palace, and the consensus was that the farmers were telling tales. The feeling he got from them was sceptical at best. He told them of reports and the danger he saw, but they just laughed. The council would go against him if he spoke up without any further proof. There were some honourable people in the council, but he could tell that a lot of these so-called lords were just worried about the expenditure.

The new Lord Commander of the People's Army, Thaddius Blaquart, and his cronies would no doubt be the loudest of the opposition. Blaquart was an oily little man and would be the most vocal of his opponents. Gabriel had never caught him doing anything, but something about him just grated on him. Blaquart had claimed no knowledge of the last Lord Commanders disappearance. Gabriel didn't like how flippant this man was about his old mentor's loss and presumed death. The weasel had already taken residence in his old friend's rooms at the palace.

Blaquart and his cronies always seemed to have some sort of hidden agenda, and there were stories. Nothing he could prove, of course. Gabriel pushed these thoughts to the back of his mind and effortlessly weaved his way through the crowds.

Kishar was the Capital of the Light, a place of learning and wonder. It was home to the priests of the six forgotten gods. They could be recognised by the six-sided star they wore emblazoned on their uniforms. Each one of the gods had a place of worship, buildings of majestic beauty. The library of Anotao overlooked the coast on the far side of the royal gardens. It was the largest repository of information ever built, a memorial to the god Knowledge.

The city of Kishar was decorated in a yellow and white, gold veined marble and built on a dark yellow stone that had an almost reflective finish to it. Home to artisans and traders, visited by pilgrims to nobility, it was indeed a wonder.

Hundreds of people visited each day. Some came to pay homage, some to sell goods. They all visited with the hope of catching a glimpse of the King. The people came from all the local states, Valor, Mycenia, Tiamat, and last but not least, Delos, Gabriel's birthplace.

Walking through the merchant's quarter, the smell of ginger and thyme filled the air. He loved the bustle of it all. Voices full of promises rang out over the clamour of the crowds.

"Over here, sir... I have a sale. The most exquisite spices."

"I have no Coppers to buy such luxury goods, though I'm sure they're the best," replied Gabriel, not wanting to stop and talk to the man.

"A man who recognizes quality like yourself must have something to trade," the man implored. Then he conspiratorially lowered his voice and continued with, "I have tabac from the northern reaches of Alesia. It'll be gone later."

"Isn't that illegal in Kishar... I don't want to get in any trouble." Gabriel whispered feigning innocence.

"Keep it down! Look, whose going to know I won't tell anyone?"

The man was persistent. Gabriel admired that. All good things came from tenacity. "I haven't had tabac from Alesia in many years." He spent a moment haggling with the vendor. Not doing so would bring suspicion, and he didn't want to draw any undue attention, and the tabac was hard to get in Kishar. He purchased the pouch before disappearing back into the crowd.

It wasn't a short walk, and he had to contend with lots more hawkers shouting their wares on his way.

"Fish... fresh fish!"

Gabriel ignored the man, as he did with several more hawkers along the way. He was in his element. Gabriel had never been comfortable in the palaces. That life was too soft for him. He yearned to be out in the field with the men. No chance of that now. He had plans to put in motion. Something big was coming, and no matter if the people believed him or not, he would be prepared.

Gabriel acted the role of scholar well. He was no longer in his imposing black and silver armour of the Lord Marshal, in which he was the epitome of the word indomitable. Normally, he would also wear the elemental sword of his station on his left hip. His hand was occasionally reaching for the reassuring touch of the hilt that wasn't there. It was inside one of the map holders he was carrying.

The weapon never left his side, even on a delicate mission like this. The sword was a gift of rank from King Leander himself. When the old Lord Marshal retired, Gabriel had been the next in line to inherit the sword. It was a tradition spanning many generations, over hundreds of years.

The sword carried the bearer's memories, from the recently retired, to the long dead. It was a wealth of knowledge beyond its elemental blade. The knowledge and the experiences were all events he could visit, including battles long gone and strategies that won wars. The sword carried the abilities learned over many men's lifetimes, and he was the benefactor of all of it. Without physical contact, the knowledge contained was like all other memories, foggy, and they came randomly. When the sword was away from his side, the memories of so many lifetimes were overwhelming. It was something all of the bearers either mastered or went insane, trying to silence the voices.

Gabriel was one of a few people to receive an elemental weapon cast by an ancient master from a time long gone. Assai was a craftsman capable of exquisite beauty and elemental crafting. His was a skill brought to High Garden during the Great Emigration around six hundred years earlier. Assai's talent disappeared with him just after the Chaos wars around three hundred years ago.

The weapon was elemental, with a blade made from air. It would never rust or dull, and in the hands of the worthy, it could cut clean through stone.

Why Gabriel was having flashbacks from so long ago this morning was a mystery to him. He continued to the library as he relived another memory. This time an attack that had turned the tide nearly three hundred years ago.

*

Ninti Enlil had fought amongst ranks of the Dread lord's disciples that day. Fidelus and other creatures of the dark, all to get to a valley within the mountains of Gelal. Here the five remaining Dread from the great emigration had pierced the veil. They had become powerful beyond measure. Their names had been erased from history, yet he knew them all. They were lost souls devoid of humanity, trained from childhood to kill and inflict pain.

Gabriel couldn't really explain what he saw in the memory, just that Assai an elemental armourer somehow made them all disappear. One minute there were five giant chained dragons, their legs had been removed and yet they still slept. Creatures of darkest night sang in guttural voices and the rhythmic beating of drums. There was a commotion he couldn't make out, then there he was walking amongst them, a beacon of light. Gabriel looked away, and when he looked back, there was only Assai. Whatever these Dread had planned had been stopped. The Light had won.

The memory clung to him; it was too easy. Something about the recent reports of attacks had a familiarity to that dark time. He was still lost in thought when he reached the end of the merchant's quarter. Gabriel needed proof. Maybe he would find it in the library. There he would see the King's head librarian Emmel and hopefully find answers.

At the entrance to the royal gardens, four guards of the people's army stood at watch. The one nearest to him was chatting with one of the female gardeners. "It's a beautiful night. Come for a walk with me." He flirted.

The girl was giggling at the man's advances. Usually, he would reprimand the guard, but today he wasn't the Lord Marshal and Hand of the King.

The archways that led to the gardens towered over him. There was a cooling breeze as he walked into the shadow of the barbican. The entrance sculpted from a rare white marble into trees that spanned the width of the road, easily thirty feet tall. They towered over him, cradling a walkway that adjoined the outer and inner walls. At the entrance to the gardens, a pair of white oak doors stood open in the two archways. In the garden any magic ability was absorbed, strengthening the wall and gates. Gabriel was reasonably sure if the world fell, this place would still stand.

If Gabriel was the King's right hand, the man he was meeting was his left. It hadn't taken long to get to a private grove.

"That's close enough, laddie." It was Bishop, but he sounded ill. "Yer a sight fer sore eyes, but we cannee be seen together."

"Why, the secret meeting old man?"

"Still young enough to teach ye a couple of things laddie. Now make yerself comfortable."

Gabriel found a rock to sit on and got out his pipe.

"Is that Alesian tabac I smell," Bishop asked.

"Yes, shame you can't be seen with me." Gabriel chuckled as he blew out a large cloud of smoke. He was also fully aware of Bishops dual physicality and that he was probably naked behind the bush.

"Well, I'm glad ye can still smile, though what I'm about to tell ye may change that. The stories of Sokar and Dren are true. A powerful warlock has created a vast army. Dark magic the world has'ne seen in generations and someone, or something, is coming. They have built an unholy army that is pushing north."

Gabriel was glad to know he wasn't going mad. "I thought as much old friend. Do we have any proof I can show the King?"

The man in the shadows laughed. "We do not need proof laddie. Do ye need proof to know you have an arse, or do ye trust that yer hands dinnee lie to ye?"

Gabriel laughed at the example. "I wish it was that simple. Using your example, the King's behind is currently surrounded by the armour of the people's representatives and his hands are struggling to get a grip. Maybe if the other hand stopped wandering and helped with the clasps?"

"There is more te this than ye know. Prophecy is coming to pass. The one who was lost has been found, and he wears a great serpent at his wrist."

"All the more reason for you to stay and help."

"Do ye know the rest of that prophecy?"

"No."

"That is no surprise laddie. It's from before even the bearer's beginnings. When memories of the past walk the land once more, unless the one who was lost is found with lightening at his wrist, a dark soul shall take his place bringing death and destruction in his wake."

"And you believe you have found him?"

"I cannee say for sure, though I have found a man with a serpent at his wrist and he was lost and now found. Aleator Darkwing is among us once more. The lost hero has returned."

"Tor is alive? Where is he now."

"I do not know fer certain laddie, and that is why I must leave. You must warn the king."

"I understand the importance of the news. I also know Aleator Darkwing, and he is no destroyer. It seems to me that if the prophecy is to be believed, for good or bad, he is central in our cause. I will send a squad of my best to escort him here."

"Ye cannee go interfering."

"Okay, they will observe only and protect only if necessary. It seems to me if the man is good, he may need help, and if he has become the unspeakable, we need to know where he is." Gabriel didn't believe the Spymaster had no idea of Tor's whereabouts. "Where is he, Bishop?"

"Yer men they cannee be seen, and from what I've learned, we have likely been infiltrated by the Fidelus so we must be cautious."

"My best old man, without them you risk his life and with it possibly of the prophesized hero able to save us all.

I ask again as the Kings right hand, where is Aleator

Darkwing?"

"Somewhere near Idrienne. I cannee be more accurate than that laddie. It's why I cannee stay to argue politics. You guard against the known. It is your task to prepare and defend. Warn King Leander. My role has always been to seek out any threat, more than that to eliminate if necessary."

"Dinnee fret, I have'ne plan to jump in feet first. We have one advantage. There is still time."

"What will you do?"

"We must figure out the extent of the infiltration and the attacks against us. I must travel te Manthripur and meet with the Oracle. I need ye te secretly get us information from the historians, anything you can find on an elemental arm brace inscribed with the words Ib'ren Cohar and crafted around the same time as yer sword. Ask Emmel aboot a serpentine brace made of gold. The runes on it are ancient and powerful crafted by someone as skilled as Assai."

"So, you will be back?"

"Yes, be ready laddie, and do what ye must. It's time for the Athanatos to join the fray."

The Rise of Thaddius Blaquart

Chapter fourteen

Lord Commander Thaddius Blaquart of the People's Army sat in his office and smiled contentedly to himself. He inhaled deeply and sighed out the pleasant scents of the room. Of all of his possessions and properties, this one room was his favourite. It was his reward for all of his hard work, toil, sweat, and misery that this godforsaken army had put him through. Blaquart was now reaching his fortieth year and had progressed from a grunt to an advisor in the king's court, a minor miracle for a soldier in the People's Freedom Army.

He had joined when he was a young man, trying to escape from a drunken and abusive father, only to find the army full of drunk and abusive men just like him.

Blaquart spent his early years in the army as a grunt, digging latrines and cleaning the soiled clothes of his betters. It was during those first years he had learned to hate and despise people even more. He had been looked over, ignored and poked fun at by the people who were supposed to respect him. No, Blaquart thought to himself. He would teach them all respect, and at the end of his sword if necessary.

Things did change dramatically for Blaquart; it all started around three years ago.

Finishing his duties for the day he stunk of exhaustion and worse, it had been a full day of filling in old latrines and digging new ones. Blaquart lay down on his filthridden bed, in his tiny little tent, and dreamed of having a beautiful room where he despatched orders. It would be further decorated with some pretty young woman bringing him tea. He had always longed for power. Now the dream was the reality. Over the years, the digging had given him a formidable if unassuming frame.

At the time the army was to offer protection from the nomadic tribes of Thalls that roamed the plains. For the most part, the Thalls were tribal and stayed in their lands. A fractured society that offered very little in the way of danger to Kishar. They had been having border wars for as long as Blaquart was alive. The main threat was a large bird they had domesticated and farmed. The army called them Terror Birds. They were ferocious in battle and as fast as horses over short distances.

The Thalls would regularly raid the settlements, taking livestock and woman to satisfy their needs, but the people paid taxes to be protected. It was tedious work, and Blaquart cared little for the settlers and certainly not enough to get in a fight with one of those oversized chickens the Thall rode.

Blaquart remembered contemplating deserting from the army. That night when he had fallen asleep and dreamed. It was unlike any dream he had ever had before. He could feel and smell every aspect of the vision. First, he found himself floating high above his campsite. He could see the soldiers drinking and laughing below. Then, in a blink of an eye, he was flying through the air so quickly and fiercely that cold night air battered at his face.

Chilled to the bone, he began to shiver in his dream. The world had become a confusing blur. He remembered screaming out in frustration when suddenly, he came to a standstill. It was pitch black and had a smell like sulphur and death. From the darkness, a voice had spoken to him so quietly at first, but yet it spoke with power. Blaquart didn't realise it then, but it would be a meeting that began his epic rise to power.

"Thaddius Blaquart," A sibilant voice whispered across his senses, reverberating in a deep and menacing tone. "You have been trodden upon for far too long. Left to rot at the bottom of the pile when you should be ruling over these malcontents."

The words were like a winter's wind, cold and shocking to his mind.

The voice spoke again in a low hiss. "I have been watching you, Thaddius. I watched your father beat you and your mother daily. I also watched your mother abandon you to that abusive pig."

The words formed images he did not want to see but appeared before him anyway. His father and mother's faces stern with disapproval for him. His father's fists clenched ready to lay out the day's punishments.

Blaquart watched on helplessly as the scene played out before him. Images of his father's angry face and swinging fists pommelling him, while his mother just stood there smiling. He was sure she had never smiled before, but his thoughts were hazy. Eventually, the sequence faded away.

Then the voice spoke again. "How many years did that man take out his frustrations on you? Why was it that your mother did not care enough to help her son?"

It was a fair question, but somehow also an accusation. Not that far removed from own questions that he had spent his life trying to answer.

The images blurred again.

"I know you would take your vengeance eventually."

Blaquart could almost hear the voice smile as it spoke.

Then the images formed another shape in front of Blaquart. His father was sitting in his old smelly chair, stinking of beer and sweat. It took a moment before he realised where, or more importantly, when, he was. His heart began to beat faster, feeling himself advance on his father without having any control over his movements, looking down to his hand, already knowing what he would find there, a knife sat firmly in his hand as he began to raise his arm. The blade shone in the dim light moving ever closer to his slumbering father.

It was so vivid he had forgotten it was a dream. He was a boy again and what he needed to do next was clear. Fear grasped Blaquart as he stood above his father. His breath caught as he put the knife to his father's neck. He would kill his father this night, and there was no turning back now.

The fear and anxiety he felt nearly shattered his nerve. As the point of his knife touched his father's neck, his father's eyes snapped open. Meeting those eyes with his own cold relenting stare, he saw his fathers were filled with rage, but there was also fear there. It triggered something primal in Blaquart, his brutish father was afraid.

Suddenly his father went for the knife, but it was useless. Blaquart already had the blade at his neck, and he pushed. Sliding the blade into his jugular as his father gurgled some last obscenity. Blaquart wrenched the knife from his father's throat and slammed it into his chest again and again. Blood dripped from his hand and flowed down to pool on the ground.

The image dissipated and Blaquart was left breathless and confused, yet somehow satisfied. His heart was racing, and tears rolled down in cheeks. He had no idea how this dream had made him feel so cold and fearful. Every nerve in his body was on edge. There was something else that he hadn't felt before, a sense of pride, and a need for more power and control. The image of his father's fearful eyes floated in front of him, and he smiled.

"Yesss..." the voice hissed as if responding to his thoughts. "That's it, Thaddius. Let that feeling grow. Fill your soul with hate and demand what is yours!"

"What are you?" tremored Blaquart's voice in the darkness.

"That is not important. If you want the power I can bestow, you must have resolve. Do you want to stop being afraid?" The question echoed eerily.

"Yes, more than anything!"

"Anything?" The voice asked a second time.

"Anything!" Blaquart responded with more confidence than he felt.

"Good, you will need that resolve you had as a child. It will be needed for the challenges ahead. If you do as I say, and have faith in my word, you will rule a whole new empire. You will be the most powerful human on the planet. Your words will carry power as never before, and enemies will shake at your very name. Can you see it,

Thaddius Blaquart?"

The dream had changed again, and now he was in Kishar sitting on the throne. The hall was filled with men on their knees. He watched them rise and chant his name; his heart was beating fast now. The admiration in their faces was intoxicating. As he rose from the throne, the hall erupted with applause.

"Is this what you want?" Asked the sibilant voice in his mind.

"Yes!" Blaquart had never had such dreams, but now he could think of nothing he wanted more. "What must I do?"

"All you need do is give me a sacrifice and whisper my name into a flame when you have done the deed."

"You want me to kill someone?"

"Yes. If you want power, I must take it from somewhere. There must be someone you hate, someone that mistreats you, someone…" The voice trailed off. It was so seductive that he felt it energise his soul and light his desires. A name popped into his head, Darwyn Lalola.

"Yessss... that's it. You can have all thissss."

Lalola was Blaquart's commanding officer, a real ballbreaking bastard, and the main reason why Blaquart had not moved any further in his army career. He regularly reported his misdeeds and took credit for Blaquart's achievements. If his sacrifice was the price, it was a cost he was happy to pay. He needed to see his father's fear again in those eyes.

Blaquart's pulse was throbbing to the rhythm of his heart, like jolts of electric pumping through his veins. He had never felt so alive.

The royal hall faded to darkness, and he was floating in the dark again. He drifted towards a large ornate mirror. In the reflection, he was wearing some kind of brace; the eyes that looked back at him were electric blue. He looked a force of nature. His reflection spoke. "Look at you. You're nothing but a worthless ditch digger, aren't you?" "No!" Blaquart replied angrily.

"No!" The reflection replied incredulously "But you smell like a peasant you poor deluded fool. Well, never mind that, let's focus on us or should I say me. I am what you that you always wanted to be, and you could be. You just have to say yes and free me, and no longer will we be tormented by bullies. Take my sword, and all of this will one day be yours." The mirror image had gone back to just mimicking him except for a rather plane looking bonehandled sword his reflection wore at his hip.

"But how do I take it?"

Eerily the reflection stopped copying him and beckoned him closer. He floated forward at the image's command. His mirror image reached forward, its hand reaching through the glass, but what came through was not human. The arm protruding from the centre of the mirror was made from molten stone, fire and smoke holding the sword out for him.

Blaquart suddenly had doubts. His mind filled with fear. The reflection took the sword back.

"What I am offering mustn't seem of value compared to your life of being a shit digger?"

Blaquart tasted dirt in his mouth, and his head spun. His body felt as if it had been abused and tortured, every muscle and fibre ached like he had toiled all day digging those forsaken latrines. Blaquart's fear was suddenly a cold reality as his reflection stared at him malevolently.

Disdain was clear in his reflected features. "Choose!"

"Yes, I will do all you ask. I will take the sword and give you your sacrifice. Show yourself! Let me know this is more than a dream."

His reflection stepped forward once more, the arm just as horrifying. "Take the sword and answer me thissss...

What will you do once you have killed your captain?"

"What would you have me do?"

"Take the sword, and I will remind you and give you proof this is real!"

Blaquart snatched away the proffered sword. He could see runes on the blade, but as he brought his arm back another hand shot out of the mirror and grabbed his wrist, making him drop the newly acquired sword. His reflection dragged him nearer.

"So, you remember my name." The thing in the mirror declared. It turned his wrist and with a burning finger seared a single word into his skin. He screamed in pain and beat against the mirror with his free hand, but it had no effect. Finally, when the reflection had completed its gruesome task, it suddenly let him go.

"Give me a sacrifice! You must call me when it is done by saying my name into a fire. I wrote it on your arm, so you don't forget. I am Achill!"

The voice hissed out into the darkness, and he was falling again. Spinning and spinning until he eventually hit something substantial. Blaquart opened his eyes, he was shocked to find that he was no longer in his tent but in the middle of an empty field. He could smell cooking meat. He looked at his arm, and once more, he felt the agony of each letter.

As his eyes focused in the darkness of the night, they fell upon the terrified face of Captain Darwyn Lalola. He was lying tied up and gagged. He appeared stunned and confused. Blaquart looked around to see if anyone else was about, but he was alone. That's when he saw the scimitar stuck in the ground. It glittered in the moonlight. It was like it called to him. It was a notched bone handle with an ever so slightly curved and wickedly sharp blade.

A noise broke him from his admiration of the weapon, and then he noticed Darwyn's eyes were open. They were dilated with fear, and they were staring at Blaquart and his newly acquired sword. That was the same look his father had! A desire lit up within him. Whether this was still a dream or not, Blaquart wanted to see his father's death stare once more. He launched himself at the immobile Darwyn Lalola thrusting the blade through his hated captain's chest. Lalola could only let out a muffled scream as the scimitar pierced his chest.

Blaquart was face to face with his dying oppressor now, taking in the fear and pain. He twisted the sword in Darwyn's chest and relished as the light in his eyes extinguished. Suddenly the blade began to heat up. Blaquart released it and leapt away from Darwyn's' body. Lights and symbols floated from the body. The ground started to rumble, and a high-pitched noise came from the blade. Darwyn's body ignited.

"ACHILL!" Blaquart screamed into the fire.

No sooner had the name left his lips a wind kicked up from nowhere. Lightening crashed into a nearby tree. A high-pitched noise got louder and louder. The area became so bright it was unbearable. The last thing Blaquart saw was a mass of flaming symbols swirling around Darwyn's infernal body.

He could take no more and huddled himself into a fetal position and shielded his eyes and ears. The crescendo built and built until a loud crack of thunder sounded. Then silence descended over the field. When Blaquart finally looked up, the wind had died down, and the storm passed. All that remained was Darwyn Lalola's crisp, burnt body. A foul odour hung in the air as Blaquart surveyed the scene in front of him. The sword with the bone handle was still stuck in Darwyn's chest.

A strange noise started to come from the direction of the burned body. Hesitant at first, Blaquart cautiously crept toward Darwyn's corpse to retrieve his sword, and unceremoniously put his foot on the dead man's shoulder and wrenched the sword free. It was surprisingly cold to the touch. Darwyn's burnt chest it expelled viscera and noxious gases toward him. Blaquart jumped backwards taking the blade with him.

He had wiped away the viscera and gunk from his eyes to find the mutilated body sat upright with its rib cage cracked open wide, the smell was obscene. He had dug shit ditches for longer than he'd care to remember, but this smell was different, the kind that made you want to gag.

He noticed something moving within the open torso that shouldn't be there. It was a black oily substance that seemed to be undulating and bubbling. Then it started to climb out of the body stretching and clawing its way until it stopped just a foot away from him. It began to boil and bubble. Moments later, it stopped and drained into the soil.

Blaquart hadn't realized he'd been holding his breath and gasped for air. Puzzled and confused, he wondered what had just happened and where in the world he was? Sheathing his new sword and gather his wits. He could almost see the stars. The ground started to steam, and a warm mist settled over the deserted field. Something flashed past his face. It was as black as night and seemed to eat at the light of the moon. He lost sight of whatever it was as quickly as it came. Scanning the area had become near impossible, but the land was empty all around, just eerie silence. Even the creatures of the night had disappeared.

A chill ran up Blaquart's back as an unearthly cold settled over the land in contrast to the warmth of the mist. His breathing was heavy and laboured, panic rushed through his body, setting his nerves on fire. The wind picked up, clearing the fog that previously obscured his view, revealing a creature he could only describe as evil incarnate.

His breath caught in his throat as he examined the dark figure in front of him. Blaquart's eyes could not entirely focus on the face, it was as if he was forced to look away, but the thing in front of him was so close that his eyes had nowhere else to look. The face was jet black, and the skin seemed to undulate around a space where a nose should be. The creature's mouth was filled with dangerous-looking teeth. The thing that disturbed Blaquart the most were the eyes. Just two hollow pits of darkness with irises of fire that threatened to open up and swallow him.

Tilting its head to the side as it spoke, "Now you know me, mortal... I am Achill, look upon the face of your saviour. That is the scimitar of Alal you now carry. Let it guide you and give you the strength you need to crush your enemies. The more you kill, the better your fortune. Over that rise is your camp. It is time to take what is yours."

Achill waved his hand, and a portal of fire opened behind him. Just before it disappeared into the void, it spoke once more "I will be watching you, little man. You know how to call me if you survive. Go back to your camp. Our master has initiated his plans for you. Go now." The words were said with menace and dark promise.

Blaquart took one last look at the mutilated body of

Darwyn Lalola. Seeing the fear in his eyes had been so sweet, but now he had a desire to run, to get as far away from Lalola's body as possible. Running back to camp for all he was worth.

As he reached the top of the rise exhausted and near collapse, he saw that the camp was in disarray. Thalls had attacked. He could see skirmishes all across the camp.

Thall Ambush
Chapter fifteen

The moon bathed the campsite in an otherworldly light. Shadows moved just beyond the camp perimeter. What he saw shook him with dread and fear. In the history of these lands, the tribes were more likely to attack each other than join forces. He didn't know why but the Nomadic clans of the Thalls had formed one massive raiding party.

Blaquart wanted to run at the sight of the marauders.

They were swarming over the camp on their giant Terror Birds and killing indiscriminately. His hand went to the hilt of his new sword, and it fired feelings in him like nothing he had ever felt before, fanning the flames of hate he had thought long buried within him, now only a bloodlust remained. Running into the midst of the battle with a strange smile on his face, scimitar drawn.

He would typically hide, but he had lost control of himself. Some strange craving was driving him to attack, wielding his new weapon like a man possessed. Which for all intents and purposes, he was. It felt as if he was sitting within himself, watching as his body hacked and slashed, contorted and weaved. Enemies fell before him. One of the Terror Birds had found him and attacked, all talons and beak. Sidestepping and bringing down his new blade Blaquart took the bird's head clean off.

Blaquart felt exhilaration like he had never felt before. He could barely hold a sword before today. Now, he was some golden warrior from the legends of old. The crowd of men fighting in front of him dissipated as if he had reached the eye of the storm. Madness swirled around as he stood there in a relative peace, surveying the battle.

He looked around and saw countless men dying, screaming and wailing. He saw his father's dead eyes in their faces begging for release. Blaquart smiled to himself as he launched himself once more into the fray.

Just ahead of him, his commanding officer was being set upon by four of the raiders. Lord Commander Laforte was holding his own for now, but there were just too many for him to fight off. Blaquart had no love for the man, but his scimitar had fired his blood like nothing he had ever imagined possible. It was almost too easy as he marched towards the Lord Commander, leaving death and destruction in his wake.

When he reached Laforte, Blaquart dispatched the first enemy by driving his sword through the Thall's back and out of its chest. The second raider was stunned at the sight of the scimitar protruding from the fellow Thall. It was enough of a distraction for Laforte to finish the job. With a quick thrust to the heart, one more fell. Pivoting like a dancer his sword created a bloody arc as it sliced across the third marauder's unguarded neck. Laforte ended it with a graceful pirouette using his momentum to behead the final Thall. The head hit the ground with a thud and rolled to Blaquart's feet. It still had a look of surprise on its face. Blaquart had to admit Laforte was a skilled fighter.

Laforte turned to Blaquart and looked him up and down as if weighing him up. With a bemused expression, Laforte asked, "what's your name, lad?" Laforte shouted the question over the clashing of steel and cries of war.

"Thaddius Blaquart, Sir."

"Good work soldier, but it's no time for talk. We need to regroup with our army and push these bastards back!"

For the rest of the night, Blaquart fought alongside Laforte until they were both covered in blood, and they had pushed back the marauding Thalls. By the next morning, they were covered in dirt, blood, and God only knows what else. They had forced the clans back, but at a high cost to both sides. The stench of death covered everything. Scavenger birds cawed at the morning sky as they feasted on man and Thall alike.

After the battle had finally passed and the wounded and dead were being seen to, Blaquart found himself within the Lord Commander Laforte's tent. Exhausted and in pain from the battle, and using muscles he didn't know that he had, Blaquart found himself worn, his hands trembling uncontrollably from the thrill of the fighting. He was not a warrior and had never been that close to battle before. Blaquart had never been in a fight that he hadn't run away from or lost. So, to have fought with such skill and intensity shocked him. He could only put it down to the bone-handled scimitar Achill had given him. Blaquart shook his head and moved on to less fearful thoughts.

Blaquart watched Laforte receive several stitches without complaint. He was a bulky man, even without his armour. Nothing seemed to stop Laforte. He had received wounds that would have killed lesser men.

Laforte looked up from a wicked-looking wound he was having stitched on his left leg, meeting Blaquart's gaze. "Thank you for helping me back there. Those four assholes were wearing me down. Without you, they may

have succeeded. What's your rank, soldier?"

Blaquart, felt himself start to squirm under the direct question. "Sir, I have no rank in your army. I'm one of the latrine workers."

Laforte stared at Blaquart incredulously, before breaking out into a fit of laughter. It took him a moment, but he managed to compose himself before breaking into laughter once more. In between his laughs, Laforte would exclaim, "A fucking shit digger... hahaha. Saved by a fucking shit digger!" Finally, Laforte calmed down. "Oh, I'm sorry son. I don't mean to be rude, but why the hell are you digging latrines? I saw you with your blade out there. You're like a seasoned veteran!" Laforte was still chuckling as he was talking.

"Tell you what, kid, stick with me. You ain't going to be digging shit no more." Laforte promised with a big smile upon his face. "Go home, kid. Get some rest and then tomorrow, we can talk about your new position."

Blaquart nodded to Laforte and left the tent to the sounds of Laforte's chuckling to himself and exclaiming, "A shit digger. A fucking shit digger... hahaha."

*

Achill watched as Blaquart left, floating in the shadows, unseen, smiling a satisfied smirk at fulfilling his part in the plan and it worked perfectly. He had controlled Blaquart like a puppet. He had whipped up the tribes to attack the camp. Achill had only been back in this realm a few hours, and already he had created so much carnage and death that he could taste the blood in the air. With that, the shade faded out from the tent and into the night.

*

In the few years that passed, Laforte became Blaquart's mentor and father figure. He taught him everything from army etiquette to fighting and strategy. He helped Blaquart gain promotions over his peers, championed him when it was needed. Now and then,

Achill would appear in Blaquart's dreams. It was here that Achill would tell Blaquart what was expected of him from his new God, Alal. The Djinn was continually reminding him of his obligations.

Achill taught Blaquart how to channel his new blade. As long as he had the Scimitar close by he would benefit from the skills and the knowledge of all those that had been slain by it. The idea that he could become more powerful than the king himself was intoxicating. He barely believed at first, but as time passed, he became more and more adept with the scimitar. Laforte, his mentor, was teaching him politics and strategy. It hadn't taken him a long time to learn how to make people do his bidding and follow commands.

Blaquart did not stop there. His greatest thrill was torturing people. To see the fear in their eyes was like wine to a drunk man. The control was both alluring and arousing to him. He had potions that would make people gnaw off their own fingers if you asked them, and ask he had!

After two years of tutelage, Achill had told him it was time to remove Laforte and take his place. Blaquart had gained enough knowledge, connections and rank. It was time to move up, and his mentor was in the way.

Over the next few months, Blaquart had been slowly poisoning Laforte's nightly tea. It would appear to anyone else that it was just his sickness getting worse. Feining support he had drawn up recommendations for Laforte to sign in preperation of his death. Most important to Blaquart was making sure his name was at the top the list for the position of the Lord Commander.

Blaquart had been Laforte's right hand which irked the other generals. So, when his mentor seemingly disappeared, which both confused and annoyed Blaquart. The council would not award anyone the rank of Lord Commander before a body was produced. Blaquart knew different. No one survived the toxin; the disappearance of the body was even a mystery to him. It was hardly like he could say he knew the Lord Commander was dead because he'd poisoned him, which left him in an awkward position politically.

He could levy for the newly opened position of Lord Commander. Eventually, the council caved to Blaquart's campaigning, in just a few months he had managed to assume his mentor's position. Sat in Laforte's office, the office of the Lord Commander; his office. He smiled contently and took in a deep breath. It smelled so much nicer than digging latrines.

It was then that a chill ran up his back, and he knew that Achill had paid him a visit.

"What are you doing?" Achill's spite filled whisper of a voice asked.

Blaquart felt his temper rising. At first, he had feared the Djinn, but time had cured him of that affliction. He now had just as much contempt for it as it had for him.

"What do you want, Achill?" he replied with just as much spite. "Have I not succeeded in what you wanted of me? Am I not the leader of this army? Why, if I wanted, I could invade any land and blame it on the Thalls, or soon even take the throne! Can I not just enjoy one minute of my success without seeing your horrific face?" Blaquart felt a vein throbbing on the side of his head as his temper flared.

Achill stared back at him with those merciless black, soulless pits of fire he called eyes. Blaquart was starting to regret his outburst as it floated towards him. The stench of decay filled his senses, and a cold sweat broke out all over his body.

Achill stopped just a mere inch away from Blaquart's face and took in a deep breath through his slit nostrils. "You reek of weakness, you pathetic lump of flesh. You sit here thinking you have achieved the goals that were set for you! Do you believe that these chambers represent victory or true power?"

Blaquart had never even heard the Djinn speak more than a whisper. Now here he was shouting and raging at him. He shrank back into his chair under the tirade.

"Look at me, little man!" Commanded Achill. "You know the plan. You are to gain access to the king's council. If you do not see it through soon, I will personally destroy you!" Achill's taloned fingers were gouging out grooves in Blaquart's ornate desk.

"Yes-yes I'm sorry... I'm sorry! Please!" Blaquart blubbered, as he hid behind his hands.

With that, the shade backed away. "You will only have a short window of opportunity once I have distracted the city. If you have not executed the plan by then, I will return for you, and you better hope you're King Blaquart." With that, the elemental shade vanished back into the shadows.

Blaquart's heart was still pumping, sweat glistening on his brow. He looked around at his stately office, at all his treasures and realized that it wasn't enough for him. He wanted more than what he had now. Blaquart knew what he must do, and he had bribed just the right people to achieve it.

Life Lessons
Chapter sixteen

Kiva had spent a couple of weeks floating down the river Idrienne with her new companions. The current propelling them along at a lazy pace. Kiva had been amazed at the duo's stories during the journey. If it hadn't been for her misadventures, and what she had seen, she would have found some of the tales hard to believe.

They had come ashore a few day's ride from a city called Dar'vien. They had run out of supplies a couple of days after escaping and had been living off fish for what seemed like forever to Kiva. Tor, a man who had only just recently started eating so well appeared to have a newfound appreciation of regular fresh food.

The cliffs blocking them from the west slowly came to an end, and with it, the safety they had offered. Tor had left not long after they had come ashore. Tor had told Kiva he was going to see if he could find someone that he and Rek had served with, and get them some supplies.

Kiva wasn't happy about Tor going, even for supplies. She had heard them talking in the night, something about someone Rek referred to as Old Iron Balls. Rek had later told her it was Tor's father.

Before Tor left, she had the strangest conversation with him. She had been singing a song from some childhood memory when she caught Tor watching. Those azure eyes lit up as she faced him.

"You should sing more, little one. It feeds the soul." For a moment, Tor had seemed unsure of what he was saying. Kiva continued to sing, and Tor listened for a few minutes before walking away.

Kiva could see Rek was unhappy about the group separating. He and Tor had had a heated conversation, ending with Rek turning his back and stalking away from the camp. On the upside, before Aleator left, he had promised to bring her a change of clothes; jesting that he couldn't be seen travelling with a crow, even if he was a Darkwing.

She was becoming accustomed to her new normality. Kiva thought back to her first week on the boat as she watched Rek make a fire. There was a gentleness to Rek you would never see just by looking at him. At first, his mountain-like exterior had scared her. She had been unsure of him, but during their journey, he had become great a source of comfort. After a couple of days of uncertainty and Rek catching all their food, Kiva had asked him if she could help.

"Rek?"

"Yes."

Now he was looking at her; she was unsure if it was a good idea. What could a man of his size teach her, a master thief, about sneaking? Then again, she was bored and with no family left she would need to be able to forage and hunt. "Rek can I... I mean, would you show me how to hunt food?"

"Have you ever been hunting, Kiva?"

"Only in towns."

"What can you hunt in a town other than rats?" "Coin," Kiva responded uncertainly.

"Well, coin doesn't move about much." He managed to respond over a stifled laugh.

"It does if they're still carrying it," Kiva replied under her breath.

Rek laughed. "I suppose it does at that."

She spent the afternoon with Rek teaching her which plants were edible, and which weren't. When they came across some rabbits, he showed her how to make snares, and they each set a couple.

Kiva was unimpressed with having to wait. "If I had my knives, I'd show you a thing or two. I had some of the best growing up in Sha'mack," boasted kiva.

"Well, I don't have the best. Just a couple I carry because I like the look of them; more than my ability to use them. Why not show me what you can do," teased Rek, unbuckling one of his many belts and passing it over to her.

The knives were much better than the ones she had owned. Feeling the balance she spun the blade over the top of her hand, rolling it through her fingers. Kiva could see Rek was surprised at her ability. She knew he would've assumed she was just a little girl bragging.

"So, do you think you can catch a rabbit with those? If you do, I'll let you have them." Rek offered. The smile Kiva gave him was radiant and eager. Rek laughed again.

"Are you sure?" Kiva asked, unable to comprehend such a gift.

"Don't get too excited. You have to catch dinner to win them." Rek challenged over his shoulder as he set off back to the camp.

Kiva had tried numerous times to take down a rabbit and missed by only a hairsbreadth. Every time she stood to throw, the rabbits would bolt. She had even inadvertently chased a couple of the rabbits into a snare Rek had laid, which would no doubt have the giant in fits of laughter when he found out. After a couple of hours, she still hadn't even clipped a single rabbit. Dejectedly, she got the rabbits from the snares and set off walking back to camp.

The sun was setting on the horizon when she got back to Rek. He was stirring a pot, an expectant look on his face. "So, Princess, did you catch one?"

"I'm not a princess." Kiva snapped, annoyed more at her own inability than his comment. "Here are your rabbits and your knives." She dropped them on the ground in front of him. Tears of frustration welled up in her eyes. Not knowing what to say or why she was so upset, Kiva withdrew and sat in the boat, dangling her feet in the river.

*

Rek's heart went out to her. He wished she had made a kill with his knives. There had been a moment when he had seen the young girl she really was. He had to give her credit, though; she had ability. Rek decided to give her a little room. Besides, he had no idea what to say to a young girl to cheer her up.

Once the food was ready, Rek went to her. After all, she needed to eat. Kiva was crying when he found her.

"Kiva." Before she turned to face him, Rek saw her take a breath and rub her eyes. "I've brought you some food."

Kiva didn't need telling twice. After all the running around that morning, she must have worked up a wicked appetite. She took half of the roasted rabbit and devoured it.

"Tell me something, Kiva. When you had the rabbits from the snares, why didn't you just kill one with a knife and say you hit it?"

"The deal was hit a rabbit. The closest I got was chasing those two into your snare. If you give me another chance, I will prove I'm worthy of them."

"Wait a minute, did you just say you chased them into the snare?" Rek couldn't hold his laughter, which in turn made Kiva laugh and for just a moment, and the young girl she hid so well shone through once more.

"Will you tell me a story, Rek."

"If yer promise to think about where you want to go."

"But I want to stay with you."

Rek didn't know what to say, but he would not lie. "Tor should be back tonight or tomorrow, and you'll have a decision to make. Our journey is a dangerous one, and staying with us would likely be a death sentence. Just promise you'll think about it."

Reluctantly, she agreed. The smile was gone now, so Rek tried to give her some peace of mind. "Tor will get supplies, and as promised give you money to start a good life, a safe life with a normal family." He didn't seem to get the desired result and thought it best if he left her alone for now.

*

When Kiva went to her makeshift bed, she found

Rek's throwing knives under her blanket. That night she slept without the nightmares that had plagued her for so long.

Kiva woke up early the next morning and found Rek at the campfire. Sitting down and leaning against Rek, he put his arm around her.

"Don't worry about Tor, Kiva. He and his father don't have what you'd call a conventional relationship, but he will be fine."

"He's was moody for the last couple of days before he went. At least he has a family. He should be happy."

Rek momentarily noticed a look he'd seen before, but just as quickly as it had come, it had passed. There was a pain behind her eyes at the talk of family. After what happened at Idrienne, he didn't want to force the conversation. Once they were in a better position, he would ask her what was still upsetting her.

Rek wondered how Tor was getting on. He had left them on the riverbank the day before to see his father, the Infamous Captain Brea Darkwing. His father had retired from the Athanatos and opened a brothel and Inn nearby. The thought of a drink and a soft bed was appealing to Rek, but they hadn't felt right about taking Kiva into a whore house.

Rek had always respected Tor's father. The man may have a reputation, but Rek admired the fact that Brea always followed through on his word.

The Darkwing family had estates in Kishar. Rek was not surprised by Brae's lifestyle, even admired it. He would love to be a fly on the wall when Brea saw his son was not dead.

The next morning, Kiva had built an improvised spit over the campfire. Rek managed to bring down a bird as it was flying by, with his sling.

After the bird was plucked and roasting on the spit, Kiva sat down, stomach growling at the delectable smell. "Reeek... Will you tell me a story?"

"What kind of story. Do you want to hear the story of how I saved the king from a bear?" Which got a smile from her.

"No, not a silly one."

"Then what would you like?"

"How did you and Tor meet?"

"Oh, that was another time, Princess, back in the days I was smaller than you; you don't want to hear that! How about the time we protected several families from a Thall raid?"

"No... Tell me how you met!"

Rek could see he wasn't going to be able to tell a more flattering story, but he could not deny Kiva as she looked at him with eyes full of expectation. He took a resigned breath. The fire sparked and crackled as the fat in the meat dripped into the fire.

"Do you know I'm what they call a bastard child?"

"No... Why do they call you that?"

"Because I don't know for a fact who my father is."

"So, I'm a bastard child???"

"No, no, no, don't ever think like that. Our character is not defined by our connections to a family, but by our actions." Not liking where the conversation was going, he pushed on with his story. "The reason I ended up in the Athanatos is that they confirmed I had an innate connection to the element of earth, and that my father had likely been Jaden."

Kiva laughed long and loud. It was a rich and beautiful sound to Rek's ears. The Jaden had a small stature and fair looks offset by stocky frames.

"You're half Jaden." Kiva was in hysterics now.

Rek understood why it might be funny to her since he was six foot three inches, and as broad as two men. He was enjoying seeing her laugh and decided to portion out some of the cooked bird. Kiva was catching her breath, but failing at drying tears from her face as she spoke again. "Haaaahahahaaa... Who was your mother, a giant?"

Rek chuckled but answered this time as Kiva fell over in laughter once more. "My mother was a simple farm girl." He portioned some onions and mushrooms on the leaf and sliced her some meat, which he set in front of her. She had quieted at the prospect of breakfast. He could tell she had questions, even if her hunger had momentarily gotten the better of her.

Kiva contentedly ate the food and between mouthfuls asked, "Couldn't your mother tell you who your father was?"

"They say she died giving birth to me."

"Did you grow up on the streets like me, then?"

"You lived on the streets in Idrienne?"

"No, in Sha-Mack."

Rek decided now was as good a time as any to probe whatever thought filled her with pain, but he also understood that secrets had a cost, and that cost was usually a deep truth of your own. He had once badly beaten a man for mocking his Aunt and was surprised at how ready he was to share with Kiva.

"I was raised by my mother's family in Valor, at least for a while. They were kind in their way. My Uncle was a blacksmith, a large man. They fed, clothed and raised me until I was around ten summers. My uncle would only beat us when he was drunk, and Aunt Amyra would always get in the way if she could." He smiled at the memory of her trying to protect him. "She followed the old gods. I wasn't there in the end. I heard my uncle had come home in a drunken rage and beaten her to death. Then later hung himself."

"Where were you?" Kiva asked. It was an innocent question, but it knocked the wind out of him. Another time he had not been there for a loved one.

"I had been conscripted into the Athanatos. That's when I first met Aleator Darkwing. I was being tormented by a much larger Cadet called Ripstone.

Kiva understood how hard kids could be on outsiders. She had also been a victim to her share of bullies on the streets. "I hope you taught them a lesson!"

Rek laughed. "Well, they don't call me names now! But back then, I was even smaller than you. I did not grow until a few months after I met Tor, but those first months in the Athanatos were hard. The rumour was my father had been a Jaden emissary from Lagash, my mother a whore from a farm in Valor, and they taunted me endlessly

with that information. All except Tor."

"Tor wasn't like me back then. Where I would run, he would fight! He had similar racially driven run-ins due to being half Ashiri. He took a dull view of bullies. His family, the Darkwings, carry a well earned and fearsome reputation.

This particular day Ripstone had chased me up a rise that ended in a two hundred foot drop into the swimming area. Sometimes some of the older cadets would dive from there to cheers from those below. Swimming was part of the training, you see. Learning to fight in water was a skill you had to master. Anyway, at the top of the bluff, I had been cornered. I remember Ripsone taunting me 'Where you gonna run now, Dwarf Boy?'

I looked over the bluff and instantly regretted it. That way was death. Ripstone and three other boys had me cornered, and I had nowhere to run, no one to protect me or so I thought, as Ripstone grabbed me and dangled me over the edge." Rek poked at the fire with a stick. "I remember screaming and begging. My heart was beating so fast I thought it was going to jump out of my chest."

Kiva was on the edge of her seat when Rek took off a water skin he had filled earlier that morning and took a swig before offering it to Kiva.

Rek could see she wanted to know what happened next and couldn't help but tease. "So, that's how me and

Tor met."

"What do you mean that's how you and Tor met?

What happened next?"

Rek laughed. "Tor is what happened next. He punched one of the onlookers in the throat that had blocked his way, then shouted Ripstone's name and told him to bring me in. The other boys didn't want trouble with Tor and stepped out of his way."

"This is none of your business, Darkwing! I'm teaching the kid a lesson." Ripstone yelled back.

"Well, bring him in so I can also enjoy this fine lesson," Tor yelled back.

"And bring me in he did. The rage in his eyes was a fearsome thing. No sooner had he dropped me on the ground; Tor charged him taking him over the edge."

"Then let's learn togetheeeeeerrr," he yelled as they sailed over the cliff.

"I couldn't believe it. Tor had jumped from the bluff taking Ripstone with him. Later we had all been dragged in front of the elders. Ripstone had fallen badly, and the boy that Tor punched in the throat had a large bruise. They had wanted me to say Tor was the bully. I was a witness to the charges. Instead, they heard the truth, and as a result, Ripstone was discharged from service, and I had found a new friend in Tor."

"I like that story," Kiva confessed then hugged him.

"And thank you for the knives."

*

It had been a good day. Breakfast had been tasty, and she had enjoyed Rek's story immensely. The rest of the morning, she had been thudding her new throwing knives into the surrounding trees. She couldn't remember the last time she had felt so safe and happy. She was collecting the knives and putting them back in her belt when she heard Rek call her. She set off back at a run with a blade in each hand.

"These knives are the best. Thank you, Rek!" she exclaimed as she arrived back at camp.

"Kiva, go to my pack. There's an ornate box inside.

Fetch it, please."

Kiva looked up from her knives and gave Rek a big smile before she retrieved it. Placing the box on a log in front of Rek, he told her to open it. Inside the box, there was a beautifully crafted crossbow. " Today we'll see if we can find that deer from the tracks we found yesterday, but first let's see if you can shoot as well as you use those knives."

"You mean you're going to let me shoot it?"

"I'm going to let you try. If you can show me that you can be patient."

"When, now?" Kiva squealed in delight.

Rek couldn't help himself; he burst out laughing.

Nothing seemed to stop this girl. After what he had seen in Idrienne, he was surprised she was functioning at all. Kiva was as sharp as the knives he'd given her. Her joy was not unlike the sun shining through the clouds on a grey day. It made him believe anything was possible. If this girl could still smile and laugh, what excuse did he have not to?"

"Yes, Kiva, now. I don't know about you, but I'm fed up with fish and rabbits. Bring the crossbow here."

It looked tiny in Rek's hands, and he attached an arm strap that allowed it to be worn over the shoulder with quick access to a quiver of bolts, fletched with white feathers.

"Can I shoot it, Rek?"

"Well, that's the question, isn't it? Can you see that log over there? Why not try and hit it?"

Kiva aimed with the bow. Resting the stock on her shoulder, she took a breath and squeezed the trigger. The bolt shot from the crossbow like lightning slamming into a two-inch bole in the log.

Rek was speechless for a moment before asking, "You sure you've never shot a crossbow?"

"No, Rek. Why? Did I do something wrong?"

"Well, do you think you could do it again?"

Rather than answer, she used the crank and reloaded the crossbow, which surprised Rek as he hadn't shown her how to do it. Kiva readied a bolt and fired again. The second arrow stood quivering, not a fingers breadth from the first shot.

"I'm impressed, Kiva. Do you remember the lessons from hunting the rabbits yesterday?"

"Yes."

"So, what are the three rules of hunting?"

"Be patient, keep downwind, and don't be seen."

"Well said. If you think you can handle a hunt, I'll see if I can find some more vegetables. Come and get me if you bring down something too large for you to handle. If you're not back in a couple of hours, I'll come and find you."

Kiva ran over and hugged him. As he looked down, she smiled and gave him one more squeeze, then disappeared into the trees.

The Drunken Duck
Chapter seventeen

Walking into the Drunken Duck, a favourite haunt of his father for gathering information. It had been no surprise when Rek had told him his father had bought the inn. It was a smoke-filled den of iniquities. People astutely ignored Tor as he walked towards the bar, his face hidden in the shadow of his large hooded coat. He had been here before. It was one of the more private brothels you could frequent. Full of rogues and merchants, but they would keep the peace. Not for fear of local law enforcement, but primarily because the landlord would make examples of anyone who broke his rules.

It was simple here. Your dreams could be fulfilled with real women, drinking, smoking and most anything you could think of, but damage or take anything that wasn't yours, and you would get your teeth smashed in, or worse.

Today he hadn't come for pleasure. It was something much more valuable he required. Information, and if possible, supplies. He propped himself up at the bar and took in his surroundings.

A group of three men over to his right seemed to be enjoying the company of the half-dressed ladies. It was nice to see lives not so serious as his own. In the corners of the large room, bare-breasted women danced provocatively on the tables. Silk scarves circled their waists, glass beads and sequins glittered catching the light as they danced, emphasizing the sway of their hips. These women weren't just there to entertain, though. Judging by the tattoos, they were Ashiri. Trained from birth to know how to make men do what they wanted or kill them, dancing was not their only talent. They were ferocious fighters, and for any man foolish enough to raise his hand to these women, he would soon lose it as a result.

The Ashiri were a seafaring society of warrior women. They only came ashore to get pregnant, before returning to their ships and the sea. They were an energetic people, enjoying sex and making money from it, seemed a natural extension of that trait. That's where his father came in. He offered them a place to sell their wares, so to speak. Brea gained entertainment and security from the deal.

The Ashiri were from the east coast, a city called Cadia between the planes of the Thalls and the forests of the Fenn. They rarely left the coast except on rare occasion if they had a blood debt or feud.

Tor knew the Ashiri were watching him, and he could tell they hadn't decided if he was friend or foe yet. A man who had one drink too many disturbed his thoughts bumping into him, spilling ale onto his boots.

"Mind where yer standing," complained the ferret faced drunk.

For a moment it seemed a blueish light lit the dark cowls of Tor's hood. "Walk away now, life's too short."

"Who you calling short?" Replied the drunk, looking at him with rage in his eyes. His hand was disappearing into his coat.

"If your hand comes out of there with anything but coin to buy a drink, I promise the next thing you'll need to buy will be teeth."

The man snarled and went to pull his knife from his coat. Tor smiled.

"What are you smiling at you son of a goat, I'm gonna make ye bleed."

A shame the man hadn't taken in his surroundings before his blade cleared his sheath. Two of the Ashiri had taken a position right behind him, their beauty just a distraction from their brutality. No sooner had the weapon been pulled it was taken from his hand, his arm was twisted at an unnatural angle, forcing him to the floor. The second Ashiri responded by kicking the drunk barefooted in the face on his way to the ground and knocking the drunk unconscious.

At first, the Ashiri appeared to be looking at Tor, but he realized they were looking behind him. Turning around, he came face to chest with the landlord.

"My apologies, Sir, for the fool on the floor. The first drink's on the house. I will need you to take down your hood, though." The landlord motioned to the Ashiri who gave no outward sign that they had just taken down an armed man. One had her foot firmly placed on the man's face. She seemed to be absently pinching the drunks cheek between her toes. They looked at each other. The one on the left was the leader. She gave a gesture with her right hand.

It was clear the second woman was unhappy about leaving Tor and the landlord alone, but she would do as she was told. It was the Ashiri way. They took the man out to dump him on the street. They would no doubt rob him and leave him with a collection of bruises if he was lucky, scars if they found nothing of worth.

"I wouldn't turn down a free drink for saving me the bother of getting blood on myself, old man." Tor laughed, taking down his hood, and looking the landlord in the eye.

"Tor! Is that you?"

Aleator prepared himself for questions he knew he couldn't answer from the proprietor, his father.

"So, you're alive then."

"More or less, old man."

"We thought you were dead, where have you been all these years? I should probably box your ears. Poor Rek lost his mind with guilt."

His father wrapped him in a bear-like hug for a moment before looking at his son expectantly. His father was not prone to outward displays of emotion and had fallen back into his role as his old commander.

Brae hadn't lost any of his intensity or his size. Tor trusted and feared this man more than most, but he wanted to keep his cards close to his chest and keep his father out of whatever trouble he was in.

"Rek? I haven't seen him in years, or anyone else for that matter. I'd rather not talk about that. I hoped you could fill me in on what's been happening in the kingdom.

Maybe over that free drink, you offered."

His father was always off on some business for the throne when Tor was growing up. He couldn't complain. He had been fed and trained by the best in the land. He had gained many accomplishments, and yet he never felt he had earned his father's respect.

"As sharp as ever young, Tor. Still giving nothing away," laughed Brae. "It will cost you a story."

"What story would you like to hear, old man?"

"How about why your eyes are now blue. Those aren't Darkwing eyes, and why are your pupils slitted? Have you been sleeping with reptiles?" Teased Brae but he had a worried look on his face. He stepped behind the bar, fetched them two tankards and a flagon of something no doubt strong enough to strip paint.

Once they settled in a corner booth, that offered a good view of the bar, Brea poured them both a large drink. "There are no listening ears here, Tor. I called in a favour and had it spell protected. With that said, where the fuck've you been all these years and tell me straight, or I might forget you're my son."

"I was betrayed by one of our brothers. I have gone over it again and again in my mind, and I keep coming back to the same conclusion. I was betrayed by one of our own."

"Not one of the Athanatos?"

"No, I think it was someone in The People's Army. Someone with connections. There is no one else that could've given me away. No one else close enough to know where I would be, which is why I have come to you.

Are you still connected in the kingdom, old man?"

"Less of the old man. I'm still young enough to teach you a thing or three. In answer to your question, yes, I still know a few people. Why?"

"I have spent the last three years being tortured in some perverse attempt to break my spirit for some vile ritual. They should have killed me! A mistake they, whoever they are, will soon live to regret. I want to know who profited from my disappearance. I need to find out who my enemies are."

Brea seemed shocked, anger plain on his face that his son had been held captive. "That much I can understand, Aleator. I will approach my contacts for you. Any idea where they kept you? It may help to figure out who was responsible."

"Your guess is as good as mine. Some church between Lagash and Idrienne. I still have giant holes in my memory."

"What happened to your eyes?"

"That's one of the things I'm trying to figure out. Will you help me find out who betrayed me? So I can get them, just like you taught me."

Brea laughed "You remember my training, but not years of torture."

"Well, you hit harder than they do, old man!"

They laughed together for a moment in the smokey back room and forgot the past, just drinking and enjoying each other's company. Tor couldn't think of a time he had drinks with his father. They had talked into the early hours before he retired to bed.

Tor was settling into a room upstairs in the inn. He had a lot on his mind, and the drink had made him a bit foggy. It probably didn't help that he hadn't eaten much before drinking. Though Brae did share what tasted like the best beef stew he had ever had and a large crust of bread. There was a bed and a side table, but little else in the room. For Tor, it seemed a luxury he hadn't had in a long time. Taking off his shirt and boots, he was about to make himself comfortable when Argento asserted himself. "So that's your father. He seems strong, and he is clearly proud of you."

"What makes you say that?"

"We dragons are quite perceptive. I thought you knew." Tor could sense the dragon was amused. "What is next, Aleator?"

"We need more information about our enemy. I can think of no safer land than that of the Anunnaki home in Manthripur to get our bearings. We can see the Oracle on the mountain. She is rumoured to have a grotto where she grants three visions, past, present and future. Hopefully, she can help us get a clearer picture of what is going on."

"Why didn't you tell your father that you are with Rek?"

"The world of man is changing, and I fear not for the better. It seems we have death on our trail, and the less my father knows, the safer he will be. I only told him as much as I had to."

Argento sensed there was more than he was saying.

"You care for this man then despite your anger at him?"

"It's a long story."

"The good stories always are." The dragon purred in his ear. A strange rumble like boulders rattling down the side of a dry well.

Argento sensed Tor's reluctance to talk about his father. "As you wish. Another time." He relented.

Tor caught a glimpse of himself in the small window in the room. Argento's light reflected in his eyes. He also noticed he had put on some weight and muscle since his escape from confinement. His arms and chest had filled out beneath the layers of healed scars. Argento told him he could probably heal the scars completely when he was a little stronger, but Tor had declined the offer.

"They are a reminder of all we need to pay back, though I thank you for the offer and may take you up on that when our enemies are dead."

He could sense the dragon's indecision. It didn't seem to understand his reluctance to talk about his father and their past. Argento seemed to let it go, instead reminding him of his promise to Kiva.

Tor was unsure of the relationship between Argento and Kiva. The dragon sensed something curious in her, that much he knew. There was a strength of survival about her which was something he could relate to.

Sitting on the bed, he thought about the last couple of weeks and of what Kiva and Rek must be doing.

Whenever she sang, there was a musical quality that would draw the Dragon forth. There was something important about this girl. What it was he didn't know, but he would figure it out.

The dragon receded once more to the corner of his mind. It was comforting for Tor. It was like he could feel Argento's strength radiating like the fire from a cooking hearth. If he needed the Dragon, he knew it would be there in seconds. It almost had an addictive quality. His blood pounding in his veins. Fuck, he had beheaded a troll... Alone!

Walking over to the bed, he had an appointment with a good night's sleep; which was interrupted by a knock at the door.

"Aleator?" His name was pronounced with an eastern droll in a husky voice filled with promise.

He opened the door and came face to face with one of the Ashiri. It was the one that dragged the drunk out downstairs. There was no doubt that she was beautiful; she possessed the most bottomless green eyes. She brushed a hand through her long auburn hair, pushing it behind her shoulder and ear, revealing the arch of her neck. Tor's eyes followed her hand as it slowly traced the curve of her full left breast down to her thigh.

"I have no money," Tor mumbled, eyes following the lazy movement of her hand.

"There is no charge for Athanatos." Her hand reached over to his bare chest, feeling the warmth of his body. "Don't be nervous," she whispered seductively, stepping up to him and gently pushing him back towards the bed.

He didn't stop her. She was close now, and his blood stirred in a way it hadn't years. Climbing atop him, the material around her hips rode up, and her lips brushed against his. She took his hand as she kissed him and placed it between her legs. Argento woke for a moment in his mind, but Tor ignored the dragon flipping the Ashiri onto her back. He kicked off his pants and lost himself in the pleasure of her body.

An hour had passed, and the candles had started to dim in the room, unlike his ardour. The Ashiri had moaned with pleasure and was now riding him with a determination in her eyes.

Tor was close to release when Argento's voice echoed through his mind. "Something is wrong… Beware, there is darkness here."

It took all his effort to take in the room, and he wasn't a moment too late. The Ashiri looked like she was arching her back in the throes of passion, but the shadow she cast seemed to be changing shape, and it was somehow darker, almost bottomless. As her head came forward, the eyes that looked at him were no longer green. They were black as the night itself. Her hands became visible once more, as a blade of darkest obsidian appeared clenched tightly in her hand. Where the blade had come from, he did not know.

Seeing an imminent threat, Argento took control. Raising the Ib'ren Cohar, Tor's arm blocked the attack with such force the knife smashed, and the pieces clattered to the floor. He followed up the block with a right cross that sent the Ashiri flying from the bed, hitting the floor hard. The entity was astonishingly fast, she was already up and attacking with another knife as he leapt from the bed.

Dragons instinctively had a hatred for the dead, and this one had a stink that filled the room. Argento leapt at her, kicking the possessed Ashiri so hard in the body that she slammed against the wall with a loud thud, even splintering some of the wood panels. No sooner had she hit the wall then Argento was on her again, twisting her arm at an unnatural angle behind her back pinning her to the floor.

"How dare the servant of a forgotten god attack a DRAGON!"

People must have heard the commotion coming from the room. The woman he had just shared his bed with was shouting general obscenities while he pinned her to the floor. Tor had his knee planted, firmly pushing between her bare shoulders.

Argento wanted to kill it. The venom in his voice as he spoke, it even gave Tor chills. "Who sent you, Wraith, that you fear more than ME?" The last word seemed to echo in the room.

The entity didn't seem fazed. "I'll say nothing half breed. Do as you will. I will come back again and kill you while you sleep," hissed the creature beneath him.

Argento raged, "Answer Me!"

Tor had noticed a black pearl clasp fastening the material around the girl's waist. It was burning against the flesh of his bare leg.

"The clasp," he screamed in his mind at Argento. Reasserting himself, Tor ripped foul gem off her and threw it into the corner of the room.

At that exact moment, the door to the room seemed to explode inwards. The fight had gone out of the Ashiri beneath him. He didn't know what the new threat at the door was. He let Argento retake control. The blade in the Ib'ren Cohar extended from his brace, whipping about and forming a wall of death, Argento turned to face the next intruder ready to eliminate any possible threat.

Brae stood in the doorway, his massive frame blocking the other Ashiris entrance. They were trying to force their way past to help their fallen sister. Brea was shouting his name.

"TOR! ALEATOR! STAND DOWN!"

The blade of the Ib'ren Cohar was moving like a cobra attached to his wrist, matching any movement the big man in the doorway made.

"Hold your ground, old man. I will not hurt her. Lower your weapons," Tor advised to the rather angry looking Ashiri behind Brea.

"Okay, Okay, no reason for this to escalate, son." Brea said, trying to be reassuring to all parties.

"Son or not, if he doesn't get off her now, I'm going to cut his fucking eyes out," yelled one of the women.

Brea seemed to be trying to calm them down.

Taking in the scene, it appeared the threat was over. Argento decided he was no longer needed. He receded to the corner of Tor's mind.

It was a weird sensation like having the power of lightning, or a tornado, just within reach whenever you needed it. Argento filled Tor with strength when he had none.

The formerly possessed Ashiri below him began to stir. Tor moved to the far side of the room and put on his pants before grabbing his shirt and finding the dark crystal broach.

"You can let them in, old man, but be warned if they attack I won't be held responsible for their deaths." The way it was spoken so plainly it almost didn't sound like a threat, which made it all the more threatening.

The innkeeper let the Ashiri past, and they ran to their fallen sister who seemed to be trying to stand up. Tor noticed the Ashiri he had slept with flicked some sort of gestures with her hand in the direction of her sister's, which seemed to reassure them enough to put away weapons. Using the arm of his shirt, Tor picked up the clasp. It was no longer hot.

Turning to the Ashiri, he asked with as tempered a voice as he could manage, "Where did you get this?"

There was something about the runes on the stone he remembered from his time in the dungeon.

"I took it from a passing merchant who got a little too fresh for a man with no coin." Her eyes were the deepest green again, and Tor felt a little guilty for the bruise on her left cheek that had started swelling.

"This is a thing of evil. Do you remember the name of this trader or where he was going?"

"Said he was going south, he had a bag of them, and I didn't think he'd miss one. I'm so sorry, Tor!"

Tor excused himself and went back down to the bar. He was still shaken and in need of a drink. He spent what remained of the night in conversation with Brae. His father had agreed to get a message to Gabriel, the Hand of the King and leader of the Athanatos. The message that he was still alive and that the threat from within was genuine. Trolls and Nightkin were migrating overland. Something was going on in the south.

After some sleep, he set off back to the campsite fully resupplied and dressed with fresh clothes, new boots, and his father had even kept his swords. They had been given to Brea as proof of his son's death. The only thing Tor kept was the coat he had taken from the dungeon. Tor felt better than he had in a long time, and for once, he and his father had not fought. Instead, his father had listened. They still had their differences, but deep down, Brea was still his dad.

Knock Knock Jokes
Chapter eighteen

The Spider had been following the progress of his prey as they floated down the river Idrienne. He watched over the cliff tops, checking that they hadn't gone inland except at Idrienne. From his vantage, it appeared they had run from a group of smaller creatures, probably Nightkin from what he could see of their tracks. He was hot on the trail, maybe only a day behind.

His Night Wargs were fast. Even with the river's current carrying his foe, and as long as he stayed with the cliffs, he wouldn't be far behind. When he caught them, he would kill the large one quickly.

The Spider hated them for making him hurry past farmsteads, leaving perfectly good victims to go about their daily business. Passing one such farm, he noticed a teenager. The boy was playing with a red cape, twirling and laughing. The Spider wanted that cape. How he wished he could stop and take it. He was picturing himself dancing around the dismembered corpse wearing the boy's cape. Dismissing the thought from his mind, he urged his Wargs to a faster pace.

He hadn't gotten far before his childish nature had gotten the better of him, he'd barely been able to stop to eat as he made up for lost time, his only real satisfaction was his new red cloak. Soon he would be at the end of the cliffs. He would ford the river first, but he needed food and rest for both him and his Wargs. Otherwise, his mounts might overcome their fear and try and take a chunk out of him. That would be regrettable. They were rare, and he didn't want to kill them. They would be hard to replace.

Dismounting, he sent his Wargs backtracking to make sure he wasn't followed. He also needed them out of the way, so their scent didn't disturb his hunt. They disappeared like shadows chased by the light, one moment they were there, the next they were gone. He was not worried. They would come back when he called. He had spotted some tracks and climbed a tree to watch and wait.

*

Kiva was still surprised Rek had let her use his crossbow, especially after giving her his knives the day before. He had told her.

"You could put a bolt in the crack of a man's arse across a field with that aim of yours!"

The compliment had made her laugh. There was no lack of honesty in Rek.

The day before Rek had taught her how to read tracks and she was determined to impress him. She found the ones Rek had said were deer down near a shallow stream, 'would be food fit for royalty' he had mused. After her experience with rabbits, she understood an essential part of hunting was patience. So, she settled into a comfortable position with her crossbow and checked with a wetted finger that she was still downwind.

After what felt like forever, Kiva heard something on the other side of the clearing. A moment later, a beautiful creature came into view, sniffing the air and checking its surroundings. On another day, she may have just admired its proud stance and graceful movement as it came out of the trees, but today she was hungry. Taking a deep breath, she lined up her bow, ready for the kill shot. The animal seemed to be holding back, not wanting to enter the clearing and hugging the shadow of the tree line.

Keeping her breathing even, Kiva focused on her target. All the world faded away except for where she wanted the bolt to go. She waited breathlessly for the animal to step closer.

Step out it did. The deer slowly moved forward, but without warning, something from her worst nightmare dropped from the branches onto the deer.

She froze watching in abject horror as the poor creature tried to shake off what appeared to be some sort of giant spider. It had six of eight arms wrapped around the deer's torso and neck. Under a red hood, a black carapace glistened as the sun caught its form. What appeared to be some sort of head momentarily pulled back, revealing white gums and rows of vicious-looking teeth. The whole head seemed to be a giant mouth only visible for a second before snapping forward, repeatedly ripping into the helpless deer's neck.

Unable to move, all she could do was watch silently as the creature tortured the poor deer. The monster

surprised Kiva once more as it performed some sort of parody of walking like a human on the bottom two of its six arms. It had no legs she could see and worse still, it had begun to talk. Flourishing what appeared to be a red cape it told a joke, of all things!

"When is a deer not a deer? When it's dribbling down my chin. Hahahahaha."

The evil thing seemed to enjoy the suffering of the animal, snapping its maw in front of its face and taunting it as it died. The animal started to shake, frothing at its mouth as the light went from its eyes. The creature disappeared, dragging the deer into the undergrowth.

Kiva couldn't believe what she had just seen. Sweat beaded on her brow as the realization of what had just happened sank in. Whatever it was, it wasn't worth waiting around for, and Kiva set off at a sprint back to Rek.

She ran so hard after her ordeal that she nearly tripped over her own feet trying to get away. Arriving back to camp she saw Aleator's unmistakable figure with Rek. Even at this distance, she felt safer already. She was pale with fear and out of breath as she reached her companions. Kiva launched herself into Rek's embrace finding safety in his shadow. She tried to talk, but she was still in shock and clung to Rek for dear life. "What's wrong little one? If you keep squeezing me so hard, I may end up with broken bones."

"Sorry, but there's a th-th-thing killed the d-d-d-deer." Kiva stuttered, catching her breath and reluctantly releasing Rek.

"Your safe now. Calm down. What do you mean a thing? I thought you were hunting deer, not a thing. Not that you couldn't hit something in the afterlife with that aim of yours."

"The deer was dead before I got a chance to get a shot off. Some dark creature fell out of the trees and killed it."

"Don't worry, Kiva. You're safe with us. What sort of creature was it?" he coaxed.

"It was black, and it was all arms and teeth wearing a red cape."

Rek had a flashback of the creature that had chased them off the ridge before they had set off for Idrienne. That thing was dangerous. "Did it have a giant eye for a head?"

"Yes."

"Did it see you?"

"I don't think so."

Rek didn't want to scare her more than she already was; he needed to keep her occupied while he spoke to Tor. Tor seemed to have the same idea. "There's a present in the saddle for you Kiva."

"Thankyou Tor."

"It's a new dress. We can't have you in rags."

Kiva's face dropped; she didn't want a dress."

Tor laughed as he spoke. "Or I did also find one of my old Athanatos cadet uniforms you can have."

Kiva spun around and hugged Tor "Thankyou."

"Start getting our stuff in the boat."

Kiva was a practical girl, and if they weren't panicked, she wasn't either. Being back on the river had never sounded so good. Not wanting to waste time, she unsaddled the horse and loaded the boat while Rek and Tor spoke in hushed voices.

*

Half an hour later, the Spider was satiated, and he sat cleaning his teeth with one of the deer's broken ribs. His Night Wargs pushed through some brush into the clearing. They had blood on their fur, which meant they had killed something as well.

"SIT!" The Spider commanded.

They came to heel on the opposite side of what remained of the deer.

The Spider moved slowly toward the larger of the two beasts. "I see you were as lucky in your hunt as I was." He ran his hand around the Wargs bloody muzzle, then licked as his fingers.

The smaller of the two Wargs whined and snapped at the larger one, frustrated at having to wait. The smell of the kill filled the air.

"Well, Fang. I take it Claw made it to your last victim

first?"

The Warg responded with a growling bark and showing its teeth. Claw just looked at the remains of the deer and waited.

"Knock knock," The Spider asked his Night Wargs jumping over and covering the deer. "You're supposed to say, whoooo's THERE?"

Fang whined. Looking at the Wargs, The Spider continued anyway doing both sides of the conversation.

"Who's there?"

"My?"

"My who?"

"Myyy DeeeEEEER.... Hahahahahahahahaha"

He jumped from behind the dead deer in between the Wargs, something very few creatures could attempt without being ripped to pieces. Closing his mouth, he looked at his unimpressed audience, before belching in Claw's face and going for joke two. It was after all, all about timing.

"Knock Knock."

"Who's there?"

"Who's asking?"

"Who's asking who?"

"Well if you don't know who's asking, how do you expect me to hahaHAHAhahahHAHA. Dig in boys."

"Hahaaahahaahahahaha." Cackled The Spider as his Wargs tore into the remains of the deer.

Now that they were all fed, he needed to take in his bearings. Taking note of the trees around him, he climbed the tallest he could find. From here, he could hear his Wargs ripping and tearing at the meat below him. The opening for the mouth in the giant eye was closed, and it scanned area.

Looking down on the land, one of his many gifts allowed him to see the passage of time. Tracks began to stand out across the clearing, each broken blade of grass a story in the Spider's mind. Looking downhill towards the river in the distance, he could see a child's footprints. He followed them up the hill, close to where he had killed the deer. The child had been practically in his grasp and would've been a much tastier prey.

He was furious. He could see the tracks running from the clearing. He hadn't seen the small human, but it had seen him. From its place of hiding, it must have run. He could see snapped branches, leading away from the clearing. Looking northeast, he could see the river and what looked like his quarries boat pulling away from the quay and the child was with them!

The Spider's anger exploded. He had been so close. If he'd caught the girl instead of the deer, he'd have them now. "No-No-No-No-NoooooOOOOOOO!" he raged to

himself, sliding back down the trunk of the tree. As he hit the ground, he whistled his Wargs. They had just eaten so they would be slow, but he was too close to lose his prey again.

Bad News, Worse News
Chapter nineteen

Gabriel remained seated where he was in the royal gardens for a while after Bishop had left. Puffing on his pipe and enjoying the bittersweet taste of his tabac, he mulled over what the Spymaster had warned. The Sokar and Dren were back in the realms of man once more, and war was fast on their heels. Gabriel shuddered at the thought. Only the gods knew what else was waiting to unveil itself from the past.

It had been around three hundred years since the Chaos Wars. It was a time of great darkness and evil. So long ago now, most people believed the stories of that war were just legend and myth. Even the memories passed down through his sword, Ninti could barely describe those events. They were just flashes and glimpses of great battles and twisted monsters. Gabriel had been tempted to take out Ninti right there and then. If he focused long and hard enough, he was sure he could unlock those shrouded memories.

Gabriel huffed and tapped out his pipe. It was neither the time nor place to be meditating with Ninti. He wanted to keep his disguise intact for now, and Bishop's requests were important. He let out a great sigh and made his way to the library.

Still, in his scholarly gear, he faded away into the crowd. This was helped by the fact that Gabriel was born with average looks, height, and weight. He was also an exceptional fighter and leader. Character traits that had helped him to become the lord commander of the Athanatos.

He had always been underestimated and could easily catch his opponents off guard. Gabriel, and his boyhood friend Brea Darkwing, had gotten into their fair share of trouble. Of course, nothing they couldn't fight their way out of, back-to-back. His foes would always attack as if there was no danger for them. The thing was he didn't look threatening until he moved. By then, it was already too late for his attackers to acknowledge.

His commanders were always impressed whenever he would complete a task quickly and easily. His progression through the ranks had been fast, and he even gained acclaim being one of the youngest swordmasters in the Athanatos.

Receiving an elemental weapon was no small thing, ceremonially or physically. In front of the lords and ladies, he held the sword by the blade and knelt before the King who accepted the handle and pulled the sword free, cutting Gabriel's hands and smearing his blood along the edge as it went.

King Leander had pulled the sword free and raised it high so all could see as the blood disappeared into the blade. When the sword was passed back to him, it began to shimmer. It had been the proudest day of his life, Gabriel remembered the cheers from those present. He had raised the weapon for all to see.

That was over twenty years ago, how times had changed. Gone was the old guard, so familiar and reliable.

The lads that had replaced them were a different breed. They were young and enthusiastic, but not as bright. Gabriel wondered if his commanders had thought the same of him.

He controlled all the guards within the Royal Palace. This had always caused some jealousy and friction between the People's Freedom Army and the Athanatos. The leaders of the army would still insist that it was their duty to protect the king and that the Athanatos should be merged into the Peoples Army. Luckily, the Royal family would insist on the autonomy of the Athanatos. Safe in the knowledge that they would not be infiltrated so easily and therefore protect the family more effectively.

The King had absolute trust in Gabriel and would always take his counsel, even his opinions on state matters. Leander had come to depend on him for more than his protection against unseen enemies and foes. In truth, his task of protecting the king was easy. The kingdom had experienced unprecedented peace for as long as he could remember.

The giant Anunakki in the North were content with keeping to themselves in Manthripur, and no army would ever attack the ancient civilization, as it would be suicide to do so while climbing their mountains. Not to mention the wondrous inventions they possessed.

As for the south, they had been shrouded in mystery since the war. Up until now, they had stayed out of the affairs of the other nations. His only peace of mind this afternoon was that the great river Ouroborus was near impossible to cross, without using one of two land bridges.

The first was at Uxmal, the land of the Jaden. The second connected near Tasad, the home of the Fenn.

Gabriel put all this to the back of his mind; he had things to do. With his scouts and Bishop's spies both reporting back of monsters and beasts raiding small towns alongside the southern border, at least one, if not all, the bridges must be under enemy control. Even if there was no proof of this, he knew it to be so. Empty towns and tales of the Va'nahual could not be a coincidence. Even if the only signs of violence and carnage had gone, people and farmsteads did not just disappear.

Bishop had found Aleator Darkwing after so many years. Gabriel had to let Tor's father know. His boyhood friend had left the Athanatos when the search had been given up for his son. Gabriel had tried to persuade his friend not to quit his commission, but once a Darkwing had decided a thing was to be done, you could either be mowed down or go along.

Brea had decided to set up his own spy network. He'd called them his Crows and continued to search for his son. He agreed to let Gabriel know of any threats he uncovered. At least he had some positive news for his old friend and just maybe some information for him. Somehow Aleator was involved. The timing of it all was just too close.

Gabriel had learned to trust Bishop's judgement in these matters, and he also knew the kind of man Aleator was. But where had he been for the last three years? The Gods only knew what Tor was doing during that lost time. There was nothing that he could do except warn the king, wait and trust in Bishop.

After a short walk, Gabriel arrived at the library entrance. The building itself was as grand and ornate as the rest of the library. The entrance exaggerated this to another level. Six immense marble columns greeted him. Upon the columns lay a great pediment of a scene between the dark armies of the Dread, charged by the heroic forces of light. In the centre of the scene was the long dead King, Anotao himself. He was the first king of the West and was responsible for bringing law and culture to the lands of man. He was also remembered for commissioning the rebuilding of all the great fortified cities dotted around High Garden.

The library itself was built in his honour when he passed away. Gabriel knew something of the man himself, through the shared memories of Ninti.

Entering the library through giant ornate double doors. The inside was as grand as the outside. Shelves of books lined the walls up to the domed ceiling. Statues stood in between each bookcase depicting the great kings, queens and warriors of legend. Scattered around the library were large ornate tables and chairs. In the corners, luxurious couches that looked more comfortable than most beds Gabriel had seen. Underfoot lay a lush, red carpet that dampened any footsteps. It was so effective that the library felt tranquil. It was as if someone had just painted the scene on a canvas.

Gabriel took a moment to take in the beauty of the place. Nowhere else was quite as peaceful as here. He loved the smell of the old books. He would come more often if he weren't so busy with the affairs of the realm.

The place appeared empty, but Gabriel knew that there would be attendant librarians between the isles or in any of the other eight libraries. Four either side of a large corridor that ended in a Giant statue. He was unsure how the library was organised although he believed the books up in this grand hall were for general consumption, but the other libraries were harder to access, the books they held were priceless.

Gabriel looked around for the Librarian, Emmel. As usual, he was nowhere to be seen. Probably off somewhere tending to his books or engrossed in one of them. Sometimes he envied Emmel. He must have read at least two-thirds of the books in here, which was one hell of an achievement considering that some of the larger books would take Gabriel half a lifetime to read.

Pushed for time, Gabriel needed to get Emmel's attention, and he knew exactly how to do it. He walked over to one of the ornate tables and made himself comfortable. Filling his pipe and lighting it, he inhaled the sweetly scented smoke, and then exhaled, watching as the blue-grey smoke floated off into the library.

A few short moments passed, Gabriel heard a low and anxious murmuring, which seemed to be getting more and more panicked as it got closer. He smiled as Emmel came whirring into the main hall and straight to where he sat.

Sweat gleaned his face as he charged towards Gabriel with a bucket of sand in his hands. "Put it out! Put it in the bucket now, you great oaf!" Emmel exclaimed.

Gabriel tapped the contents of his pipe into the bucket, and it died out. He grinned sheepishly, "Greetings,

Emmel. How are you, my old friend?"

"I would be much better if you would stop smoking that awful stuff in here. Do you even know what that foul smoke does to my books and I won't mention the damage the fire would cause!"

Emmel was a short, overweight man with a slight stoop from his constant reading. He also had a rattish look to him that made him look quite repugnant. Even when he smiled, it would appear as if he was sneering. It was unfortunate, as Gabriel found the man to be one of the warmest and most pleasant of people that he knew. "Sorry, Emmel. I mean no harm, but we need to talk."

"I'm sorry, Gabriel. I am far too busy with my other duties to deal with you right now."

Gabriel looked around at the empty hall and raised an eyebrow. "That's okay. I'll just wait here until you're not so busy." Gabriel sat back in his chair once more and took his pipe out, tapping out the remains of his last smoke on the table. From the corner of his eye, he saw Emmel turn a beetroot red as his temper rose.

Then with a sigh, Emmel relented. "Okay, I can spare a few minutes for you. What is it that you want?" Emmel slid into the chair next to him.

Gabriel put his pipe back into his pocket and saw Emmel sigh once more, but this time with relief. "Well, it's not what I want. It's Bishop..." Gabriel explained to Emmel what Bishop had asked.

The librarian looked bemused as he sat back, scratching his chubby chin. "Hmmm, I do not know what I could tell Bishop about the families that he would not know already, but I shall look none the less. As for the weapon, well, a name would be helpful. As you can imagine, there's been a fair amount of weapons made over the years," Emmel mused.

"He did mention something about it being in the shape of a serpent and gold."

Emmel held back a snort of laughter. "Was that all he requested? Many weapons were made as such in that age.

"He also proposed Assai may have crafted it, and the inscription on it read the Ib'ren Cohar, but that is all I can tell you," replied Gabriel.

Emmel's jaw dropped almost to the floor. "You are joking, right?" He looked extremely nervous all of a sudden as he rose from the chair and began pacing back and forth, rubbing his chins almost frantically. Gabriel furrowed his brow and watched as the librarian manically walked toand-fro.

"Emmel, is everything okay?" He asked with some concern.

"No, no, no. We are not okay, Gabriel. Not in the slightest." The tension in Emmel's voice was clear. "If you're correct in what you ask, then we may be on the precipice of an evil not seen for centuries."

Emmel was not one for dramatics, so his words and his animated gestures had Gabriel worried.

"Come with me, Gabriel. I must show you something."

Gabriel followed him out of the main hall, down the large corridor that went past several more rooms, each containing thousands of books. At the end of the hall was a statue of the god of Knowledge which they went behind.

Emmel stopped and turned to face Gabriel. "What I am about to show you only a handful of people have seen.

Whatever you do, do not touch anything,"

Turning to the wall, Emmel began tapping individual bricks with a rather plain-looking ring he was wearing. Gabriel's eyes widened in astonishment as a section of the wall rippled, as a pond would if hit by a pebble. Then the stone disappeared and in its place a gateway to another place.

Gabriel was amazed. He had heard of portal stones, but he had never seen one. A way to instantaneously travel from one place to another; it was a skill thought lost since the last great war. He gave Emmel a questioning look. "I never knew you had any elemental ability?"

"All head librarians know a little magic. It's a perk of having so much knowledge at hand. Now come this way." Gabriel looked around in wonder. He was standing inside a vast cavern, lit with what seemed to be thousands of tiny stars that filled the ceiling of the cave. "Where are we?" He asked in wonder.

"This is the King's vault, deep inside the mountains of Manthripur. There were several gateways carved from the same stone and spread across High Garden as a means of escape at the end of the Age of Wonders." Replied Emmel, with a hint of pride and love.

"I have served the king my whole life. How is it I know not of this place, Emmel? In all my service, not once have I even heard a whisper of such a place?" Gabriel was a hard man to surprise, but as he looked around in sheer awe, he was near speechless. He looked upon his friend with new eyes as he followed the little librarian.

"I never said which king and much like you, Gabriel, I was charged with a great gift and burden as head librarian. This is where we keep the most dangerous books and relics of evil we have ever found. Some even date back as far as the Chaos Wars, some even older. We keep them here because if they fell into the wrong hands. Well, let's just say my little trick with the wall would pale into insignificance. These books contain knowledge that could upset the balance of the whole world."

Gabriel continued to take in his surroundings. Whole sections of cavern walls had been sculpted into recesses for bookshelves, that went as high as the ceiling without a single space left to be filled. At the back of the cavern, Gabriel noticed a large table that had a cluster of what looked like stars high above it, illuminating the area with a soft glow. The faint light was reflecting off crystals all around the cavern. A pair of enormous glass panels stood behind the table. As they walked towards them, Gabriel realised that etched upon the panels were line upon line of scripture and markings.

"What are they?" Gabriel asked as he slid his fingers along the smooth outlines of the etchings, amazed at how they caught the light.

"They are wards, placed there to protect the tomes inside." Emmel beckoned Gabriel to sit at the desk. "Please, sit. What we need is in here."

Gabriel sat in the old chair, next to the huge table. He realised as he sat down, it was not made for comfort. In fact, the chair was downright hard to sit in, but he guessed it was designed to keep its user upright and awake.

Emmel began to hum, and underneath the low hum, Gabriel could just make out the librarian forming strangesounding words. Suddenly, the cavern rumbled. Emmel remained transfixed at the glass panels. Gabriel defied his urge to run and take cover. The etchings on the panels began to glow one by one as they lit up a brilliant blue, shining brighter and brighter until Gabriel could look no more. He shielded his eyes until the rumbling had stopped.

When he finally opened his eyes, Emmel was running his finger along some rolled parchments. Zeroing in on what he was looking for, he exclaimed, "Aha! Found you." He brought a handful of papers to the table. "These are what you're looking for." He laid them flat on the table, using a couple of old paperweights to keep them from rolling up. The heading on the first paper read The Damnation of Dragons and the Dread. Emmel's' hand was shaking, and a sheen had appeared at his forehead despite the cool surroundings. Nervously, he spoke, "I think what you described is a weapon of Khnumm, not Assai."

"Khnumm? I feel I should know that name?" Gabriel replied.

"There has been a lot of effort to try and wipe him and others from our history. But I am afraid that we have failed in our efforts." Emmel took a moment to compose himself. His hands were shaking as he clasped them together in an effort to soothe himself. "Do you know of the weaponsmith by the name of Assai?"

"I know of Assai. He made Ninti," recalled Gabriel.

"Yes, indeed, he did. He created hundreds of weapons and each elementally unique. Assai also found an apprentice with a similar gift to his own, yet nothing compared to his mastery. The apprentice grew jealous of his mentor's fame. It corrupted the young man and made him vulnerable to temptation.

Khnumm sought to seek his own fame and fortune and designed a weapon of limitless power; The Ib'ren Cohar. He had only mastered the transference of memories previously. This new weapon enslaved what it killed and became one with the killer. A bearer would absorb the power from the soul imprisoned within its structure. The more powerful the soul of the creature, the more powerful its bearer would become.

When Assai discovered what his apprentice had devised, he tried to stop him, but Khnumm had other plans, all he needed was some blood on his new blade, and he would know all Assai's methods. Assai misjudged his student's ambitions, playing into his apprentice's hands. Khnumm attacked dismembering his mentor with one foul sweep.

Assai cried out and fell to the ground, a broken man. His left arm severed just below the elbow.

Assai should have killed Khnumm there and then, as with his knowledge, what followed would nearly end all life as we know it."

"Khnumm travelled to the five Dread Warlocks. Alal, Satet, Tao'nas, Uruku and Falan, dark warlocks that craved dominion over all humanity. At first, they laughed at the young weaponsmith, until Khnumm surprised them, lashing out and striking Falan with the blade he had used on Assai. This attack was not a wounding; it was a fatal blow stealing Falon's very essence.

The other Dread understood real power and what they had just seen could offer them that. Khnumm had gotten their attention, and now he was one of them. This joining gave the enemy a much-needed edge during the Chaos Wars.

The only thing that saved us was the Dread's greed and lust for power. Not content in conquering mankind, they set their eyes upon immortality. With great effort, the Dread trapped five dragons, and Khnumm would craft them an Ibren Cohar each. With the elemental power of dragons, the Dread would become unstoppable. Their plan backfired, and it nearly destroyed them entirely."

"Okay, Emmel, that's all very interesting but what does that have to do with the brace?"

The librarian didn't look happy at being interrupted. "To understand the threat, Gabriel, you must first realise the bigger picture. All of your questions will be answered."

From the look Emmel gave him, Gabriel knew it was a time to listen. He knew nothing annoyed the little librarian, like being interrupted when he was talking, and Gabriel had seen the look that was being levelled at him before, daring him to speak again.

"I apologise for interrupting. Please continue."

Taking a moment, Emmel poured himself and Gabriel a glass of whisky from a decanter that sat on the table. "Drink Gabriel, for there is much more to tell."

Gabriel tried, unsuccessfully, to get comfy in the old chair as he took a sip of the whisky. Emmel shimmied his way up on to the old table. Once seated on top, he downed his whisky in one gulp. With a satisfied sigh, he put his glass down and turned to Gabriel. "That whisky is over a hundred years old. I was saving it until some sort of celebration or when a momentous occasion happens. Ah well, this isn't it Gabriel, but damn if I don't need a drink to tell this tale."

"There is still a threat of return. Tales of prophesy and accounts of a weapon that has appeared throughout the centuries. It was a brace that matches your description. It has attached itself to the arms of many bearers, all of them cruel.

Any time it has appeared in the past, a great war has followed it, with its bearer always the driving force. If what you have told me is true, then dark times are not far away." Emmel finished by pouring himself another glass of whisky.

Gabriel sank his whisky with a large gulp and sighed.

"That is bad news, my friend. Was there any bearer of the brace that ended up being good, or fighting for a righteous cause?" He feared what the answer might be.

Emmel shook his head gently in reply. "None that I know of. All accounts say that the wearer would eventually lose his mind to the damned thing, and end up being killed or even killing himself."

Emmel collected both glasses and poured another drink for himself and his friend. "If you know who now bears the brace, you must bring it here away from the petty rivalries of man."

Gabriel could tell Emmel was thinking to himself. He looked as if he'd remembered something and was looking over his shelves of books. "I know it's here somewhere... Aha!" He had an excited look on his face now.

"What is it?"

"This is the journal of Assai. It documents the escape from The Age of Wonders. The change of power with the banishment of the old gods, politics of the new lands and records of its people."

"Yes, all very interesting, but what does it have to do with what's happening now?"

Emmel's look had been more hopeful now, like a parent waiting for its child to figure something out themselves. He opened the book facing Gabriel, tapping the index page. "Assai kept a record of all things he thought of note, including the forging of the Ib'ren Cohar. It also speaks of an artefact called the Sun Disc used to turn humans into beasts, but after the Chaos War, it was given to the Griffins to protect. Maybe another has been found. You will have to research the clues in this text. You cannot take the book from this place as the wards protect all within. I will leave you to your studies."

"How will I get out?"

"I will be over there. I am restoring some records from before High Garden.

With that, Emmel left Gabriel with his thoughts and a rather lovely whisky. Taking his coat off and placing it on the chair as a cushion, he looked over the index.

Journal of Assai

Chapter twenty

The book was a treasure trove. Gabriel couldn't help but read some of the earlier stuff. After all, this was the journal of a historical legend. The preface was Assai's thoughts on the new world.

Little is known for sure concerning what happened after we escaped the Great War. So much has been lost and even more forgotten as life goes on. There are always those that survive, areas that escape.

I am much stronger in this new time due to my connection to the elements a rare gift in the Age of Wonders. Without the gods, humankind has lost its connection to magic. Only in dreams can you now create with a thought. The power has been transferred to the elements and I can't help feel some responsibility. Over millennia we travelled in the Great Emigration to escape absolute annihilation.

Over the ages, the elements have brought forth new life of their own, and we have found ourselves in a bountiful land. An unexpected advantage of severing from the old gods was that all those bound by curses and dark thralls were released. There is still deep unrest in the people; for what they have lost is great, but the war is over, and we are alive. A new society builds itself from the ashes, and old creatures mingle with new spreading out across High Garden, our new home.

Very few histories are complete and for the most part, lost to memory. I decided to keep this journal as a record.

Gabriel skipped ahead a few pages.

The Thalls

From what we have gathered of the Thall, they are fearsome in combat and very territorial. They pray to elemental gods. Scouts have told us they have a society farming the local wildlife, including a giant carnivorous bird. They have communities and agriculture that they rightly feel they must defend, and with some of the things that escaped with us, it is understandable. Talks have been tried and failed.

The Thall (less evolved humans) have walked the land in peace and harmony with the elements until we arrived escaped from the Creator's rage.

From what Gabriel read, not much had changed in six hundred years. Skipping ahead, the artistry in the book was just exquisite. There were a couple of pages under the title,

Hope

We have made new allies in this time. The Maja a giant race of creatures made from stone and their children the Norns, trees that can move and speak. They have helped agree on terms and to settle peacefully on High Garden with the Thalls and other creatures.

There is hope of a golden future. A great city was built on the ruins of an ancient one, and it was named Kishar; The City of Light.

To the south in the more uninhabitable lands, elemental races like the Maja and the Norns had taken root. They had agreed that the Jaden could live their

mountains in the south-west and the Fenn the forests of Tasad. The Jadens natural affinity for the element of the earth helped to bridge the two alien societies of human and Fey until a mutual respect had formed.

The Anunnaki walk the land as teachers and builders. Physically they tower over most races. On average they stand at eleven feet tall in adulthood, thick-skinned and intelligent. They had been created by the God of Knowledge. Everything they do is measured, spending a lifetime in pursuit of a solution to some grand puzzle would be seen as a life well spent. To the Anunnaki, a mystery needing to be solved was irresistible to them and sometimes to their detriment.

Called giants by some, but never to their faces, it was offensive to Anunnaki to talk about size. Curiosity brought them to the low lands, ingratiating themselves into the races, lending a giant helping hand and learning all they could about the societies of High Garden. Without the Anunakki we would never have succeeded in the Great Emigration.

War

Three hundred years of peace have passed since the arrival, and An ancient cult called the Dread has fortified the south and are building an army.

The land has been thrown into turmoil. And my apprentice has betrayed us and gone to the other side. I fear with my knowledge he has created a Sun Disc.

There are reports of whole towns disappearing overnight and sightings of strange creatures in the south. It is rumoured the enemy is creating chimaeras. I surmise these things are connected, and the missing villagers are in fact being turned into these monstrosities we are calling the Va'nahual.

The Enemy

The Dread had brought five dragons through a rift into High Garden. They were captured using the foulest magic, and with it, the Dread would become godlike and become weapons that could dominate and rule the entire land.

While the majestic creatures were sleeping, elemental beasts of claws and fangs. The Dread had mercilessly removed the wings and legs of the sleeping dragons. Their forges rang with the sound of hammers. The bones from living dragons were melted down and forged by my former apprentice, Khnumm, using dark harmonies and chants that gave rhythm to the hammers and somehow kept the Dragons asleep while they were being mutilated.

The forging of the Ib'ren Cohar had been a success, and the Dread lords took a blade each which they quenched in the blood of the creature it was made from, and to my shame so did my apprentice who was now one of their number.

When dealing with creatures as powerful as dragons, it was important that no mistakes were made. One by one, they took the final step and plunged the blades into the dragons. All was going to plan for the Dread, and immortality was at hand.

Then the Spirit Dragon opened its eyes in immeasurable pain and desperately snapped at the Dread warlock Alal; instinctually delivering one last attack. Teeth tore through flesh and bone as the Ib'ren Cohar's blade *pierced its eye. It spat out the chewed remains of its captor as it spasmed in its final death throes. It was in that moment all theDread fell to the ground as the Ib'ren Cohars bonded to their bodies, and the dragons were forced into servitude.*

Khnumm had crafted a weapon to steal my knowledge, but he had not killed me, which was his only mistake. I was supposed to wait for the Army of Light. Instead, filled with rage at what my apprentice had done, I called on the elements I had named so long ago. I connected to all of them at once and walked into the clearing, I could feel a tear in space that they had used to bring the dragons to this realm. Reaching forward with all my senses, I had somehow manifested a hand of light. I don't know how, but I reopened the rift drawing power from the volcano itself. I used the tear created by the Dread and changed the location to a place without magic, and while the enemy was distracted with their transformation into Dragonborn, I pushed them through the rift and sealed the tear behind them.

*

Gabriel thought of Khnumm's betrayal of Assai. It was a sad story. He was betrayed by one he loved and even looked upon as a son. Assai had vowed to fight until his error in training him was resolved. He forged elemental weapons for the Athanatos to combat any kind of resurrection.

After he banished Khnumm and the Dread which ended the Chaos war, it was believed Assai had lost his mind and retreated from his life, no longer interested in the petty squabbles of humankind. There were no more entries after that.

Without their leaders, the Va'Nahual were defeated and banished once more from the realms of man, the device used to create them was hidden away. The Dread cult called the Fidelus went underground, and peace returned to High Garden.

Gabriel spent many hours in this hidden library before thanking Emmel and setting off back to the palace. He had not been looking forward to seeing the king with such ill tidings.

When he arrived back in the throne room, he was dismayed at finding Blaquart there. His ladylike heels clicked on the stone floor. The jumped-up little shit, Gabriel thought to himself and decided to ignore him.

"Leander may I speak with you." Gabriel figured from the look on the king's face that he was glad of the interjection. Looking to Blaquart then back to the king, he added, "alone."

Blaquart came to a standstill. "You can't order me around like some lackey. I'm the Lord Commander of the

People's Army if you were anyone else..."

"But I'm not anyone else. We are who we are," Gabriel interjected and could not hold a further retort. "I try not to judge you too harshly as they say you cannot truly know a man till you've walked in his shoes, but I would rather dance on hot coals than wear ladies shoes."

At this, the king intervened with a smile on his face.

Not, however, before letting out a short laugh. "Gentleman, please! you are both my trusted advisors here to protect not bicker." Leander gave them each a stern look. "Blaquart, if you would please give us a moment."

Gabriel couldn't resist smirking at Blaquart as his shoes clicked on the polished stone floor, clearly seething as he stormed off. When Leander looked at him, he stopped grinning.

"Gabriel, what am I to do with you? You know you're making a powerful enemy. He will not forget that comment easily." Leander couldn't help but laugh again as he saw Blaquart's face in his mind's eye. "What news do you bring?"

"Grave news from Bishop, my King. First, we must send our best Athanatos scouts south."

"Then this is serious?"

"If what I suspect comes to pass, we may be on the verge of the next great war." Gabriel shouted for his most trusted commander. "Raif."

"Yes, sir." The man seemed to appear from nowhere.

"Send our best scouts south and ready the men for war."

"How many should I send, Sir?"

"As many as we can spare."

The king asked. "Are you sure all this is necessary?"

"Yes, if what I believe is true, there is no time to waste!"

"Then go, Raif. We have much to talk about." The king and Gabriel talked late into that evening, discussing Gabriel's concerns.

The Mountain
Chapter twenty one

Kiva was blown away by Kalistiel. Tor had said it was a city that had grown out of trade routes, but when she saw the Anunnaki city in the heights of Manthripur, it was hard to believe. How could anything so grand come of something so simple? Travelling up the side of the mountain on some contraption of chains, metal and glass. The Anunnaki called it a Traveller, it was amazing. The conveyance could carry anything from two hundred people to a herd of cattle. There were some other people along

for the ride. Luckily, the size of the Traveller offered room for privacy.

Rek watched Kiva and once more thought how resilient she was, leaning over the rail, her face was full of hope and wonder. They had come a long way together. Rek remembered the first time he used the Traveller as a younger man, and damn near shit himself if he was being honest. He had never liked heights, but where Tor went, he would follow. He just planned on staying as far away from the edge as possible.

Kiva, however, had been immediately open to the experience. The wind picked up as they gained altitude and passed through a cloud bank. Rek couldn't deny it was beautiful. The sun washing over an ocean of clouds spreading out across the horizon. Kiva's hair danced in the breeze, catching the light from the sun. She turned to smile at him her head surrounded in a golden halo of hair. He only held her attention for a second before she turned back to leaning precariously over the railing to get a better view of clouds they had just passed through.

Taking a deep breath, Rek looked at Tor, who was sat cross-legged on the floor. He had begun meditating of all fucking things, as soon as they got on-board. Rek wanted to run over the plan, but for the first time in a long time, the sense of impending doom had dissipated, and he decided he could let it go for now. There would be time enough after Tor visited the Oracle and hopefully, they would meet up with Bishop.

*

Tor had entered the realm of the Ib'ren Cohar. He knew how to find Argento now. Everything here was an extension of the dragon. He had been visiting the dragon regularly during their journey, learning what it was to be Dragonborn. Travel here like everything else; it was a state of mind.

Picturing the dragon, and then using that image to bring himself towards Argento. Opening his eyes, he was by the side of a river. The sky was clear, and a sheer rock face ran alongside the shore. Tor realised where he was. He was back at the river Idrienne. It seemed odd to Tor that Argento would be here? Until he heard singing carried on the breeze. Tor followed the sound through some foliage and trees when he came upon a clearing with Kiva sitting on a large boulder singing to Argento. He was going to call out, but something about the song stopped him, and instead, he listened, silently entranced by the beauty of the harmonies.

When the image of Kiva finished, the world around them seemed somehow greener, brighter. She jumped down from the rock and hugged Argento's snout. "Will you teach me another one, Gento."

"No, little one, we have company."

Kiva disappeared, and the dragon raised its massive head, bringing its giant maw within inches of Tor's chest. "ALEATOR," rumbled the thought from the dragon, which in this place could shake mountains.

Tor, in response to the greeting he couldn't resist, and called his formidable companion Gento and pulling his snout down so he could see into his eyes, eyes that matched his own now.

"Why don't I remember this, Gento?"

"You were asleep when I heard her the first time.

What you witnessed was my memory of that night."

"What do you mean the first time?"

The dragon's head settled in front of him now. Deciding to ignore the question, he continued. "So, the first time I went to listen to her, she caught me, thinking I was you, or so I thought until she spoke directly to me. She asked what I was and if you were asleep?"

Tor laughed. "So, you told her the truth?"

"I am a dragon; we do not lie!"

"So, when I go to sleep, you sometimes find Kiva, and she will sing to you?"

There was a moment's contemplation before the affirmative "Yes."

Tor thought for a moment. "That language she was singing had a power. I could feel it. Should you be teaching her?"

"Not really."

"What do you mean, not really? What have you taught her?"

"Just a song, Aleator."

"The song she was just singing?"

"Yes."

"Why did you do it?"

"I haven't heard the voice of the creator since before my capture and the words you cannot quite grasp, humans can no longer hear at all."

"Then why can I hear her, Argento?" Tor could tell he had somehow amused the dragon. "Well?"

"You talk like you are still human!" replied the dragon lazily. "You stopped being human the moment you shed blood with my prison. She should not have been able to form the words, let alone see me and yet somehow; she can. She has lost so much, and when she sings, I hear the glory of the Creator. Kiva has the ability to mould thought and real emotion with sound and form."

"What does that mean?" Probed Tor, before Argento could continue.

"It means one day she will be able, with a song, to influence emotions or even bring life to the inanimate. In this way, as a keeper of the song, it will protect her. She has a natural gift, but she didn't know the words. Well, you wouldn't want her defenceless, would you?"

Tor was dumbstruck for a time. He had come to train and gained a revelation. He had wanted to tell Rek the truth for a while now and was surprised that Kiva hadn't given away that she had known. "We will talk on this again, but it's not why I came to see you. We are near the Oracle, and hopefully, she will tell us something of the enemy. I am tired of running."

"She may not tell us anything, Aleator."

Tor thought about that, but even if that was the case, Rek had said they'd meet Bishop at an inn in the merchant sector. He must know something if he was still alive. Last time they had spoken it had been brief due to an attack.

Most of that attack he had been here inside the Ib'ren Cohar, his body unconscious in the real world, carried to safety by the stalwart Rek. "Whatever happens, we will be one step closer to the one who hunts us. I only have a minute before we arrive at Kadingir. Can you bring forth a challenging opponent? I can't keep letting you fight my battles."

The Ib'ren Cohar held remnants of the many masters Argento had outlived. Argento had suggested using these remnants to improve Tor's skills. Argento summoned a Dark Fenn king named Lore. He had held the Ib'ren Cohar for nearly a hundred years.

Lore hated most races, but none as strong as that for humans. He would joke the only proper place for the other races was on a roasting spit. His ability with a sword had been unparalleled. Tor had learned a lot from Lore. He had even gained a margin of respect for Lore's skill, a natural ability for survival.

Argento understandably hated these remnants, the idea that they would dare to enslave him. He kept them tucked away in a constant state of torture.

"Argento, can you bring forth Lore?"

"Of course." Watching Tor despatch these remnants was therapeutic for the dragon. The air shimmered in front of Tor, and a moment later, Lore stepped through.

"Hello, meat bag. Miss me?"

"Only the dance."

"That is funny from a race born with two left feet." A black sword appeared in his left hand, dagger in the right.

Tor had always wondered what manner of creature had killed Lore. Even this shade of what came before was able to beat him seven times out of ten. With the Ib'ren Cohar Lore must have been near invincible. He hadn't come to puzzle out how Lore died. He had come to clear his head, and the dance helped him focus.

"I hear you, Goblin King." Tor taunted.

They began their fight in earnest. Lore charged in with viper like speed. All it took was a blink, and in that time he mounted two lethal attacks. Tor did not know how long they had been fighting before Argento banished Lore back into whatever dark corner of the cage the dragon locked them in.

"Aleator, it is time. Did you find your answers?"

"Some. I am going to bring Rek into our circle of

trust."

Tor brushed himself off and stood up, taking in the beauty of his surroundings. The view from the Traveller was something to behold. Kiva was still leaning over the rail on the other side of the platform. Rek stood as far away from the edge as possible while still in reach of her. He hadn't realised how large a part of their lives she had become.

Rek turned. "Decided to join us, then?"

"Always, Rek! I've decided to confide in you. I know you worry about what has become of me."

"Hanging off the side of a mountain is where you decided to share this horse apple."

Kiva walked over and interjected, "Come on, Rek, give him a chance."

Rek huffed but quieted.

Tor had their full attention. "When Bishop freed me, I was a shell of a man. I didn't know who I was. It was like I was adrift on a calm ocean, just barely keeping afloat, blinded by some all-encompassing fog. I was all alone, and it felt like I had been for an eternity. Until I saw lightning on the horizon, I should have been afraid, but there was nothing else other than the cold grasp of a dead ocean beneath me. The storm came to rage around me. I reached out and caught a bolt of lightning, and It pulled me from my nightmare."

"That is when I woke for the first time in a long time. I focused on my surroundings, a dank, dark cell that smelled of decay and faeces. Bishop spoke to me from the shadows. I looked up to see him as naked as the day he was born."

"I still felt in a daze, believing some dream or new tormentor had been sent to break me. A slap from nowhere brought me from my momentary reverie. I looked up. Bishop hadn't moved. He said, 'I ain't no figure of ye imagination laddie.' I was so afraid I averted my gaze lest I suffer at the hands of my new captor. I waited silently, and still, no beating came, just a whispered set of instructions, then he was gone."

"We know all th... aargh."

Kiva kicked Rek in the shin before he could finish

"Rek, please let him finish."

Rek tousled her hair. "Okay, princess. I'll hear him out."

Tor had to work hard not to laugh. Rek towered over most men. Tor knew full well how indomitable his friend was. No one told him what to do. He would occasionally get the lash in their days in the Athanatos for refusing an order or punching a senior officer rather than apologise, yet for Kiva he would listen.

Tor continued. "When I lifted myself, I was weak. It took me a few attempts before I could even stand. It was like I was drawn to the blade. A blade that I believe was going to be used on me. The blade was of craftsmanship so fine it seemed almost alive before I even held it. When I picked it up, my fears began to melt away, and for the first time, in such a long time, I had hope."

"I haven't seen this magical blade?" Questioned Rek.

"I'll get to that in a moment. On my way out of my prison, I ran into a horse handler, a disgusting man. I silenced him before he could give an alarm. That's when it happened. The serpentine dagger came to life in my hand, jumping from knuckle to wrist. The metal was like liquid. It formed into a serpent's head encircling my forearm. The last thing I remember of that place was this brace fastening itself to my arm." Tor raised his arm showing the Ib'ren Cohar to them before continuing. "This is more than it appears to be. It was forged with the darkest of magic, for one purpose, to enslave and hold the soul and power of a dragon. The people who seek that power will stop at nothing to get at it and me."

"Well, that explains why creatures from fucking nightmares are chasing us. So, the weapon held a dragon's soul... what does that mean?"

"I have begun a process of bonding with the dragon,

Argento. I'm sure you have noticed some of the changes?"

Rek didn't know what to say, which seemed to be more and more the case these days.

Before Kiva or Rek could speak, Tor spoke again. "I'm sure you've questions, so do I and in part, that's why we are here.

"I would ask a favour, Rek. Will you get us rooms in the Inn? Keep our number to yourself if asked. Say it's just you and your daughter. We should be safe here, but I don't want to take any chances. That said here's some gold. Purchase some supplies and find out what you can. See if you can locate Bishop. He said he would meet us here. Remember the people who are after us are powerful and will no doubt have spies. Be wary, however safe things seem."

"You may have been away a while, and they must have hit you pretty hard in the head brother if you mistake me for some chatty scullery maid!"

"I wouldn't share at all if I didn't trust you, Rek, but I also need you to understand, you cannot mention any of this to anyone. Kiva this is for you. Make sure Rek visits the bathhouses and find yourself some more appropriate attire." Tor flicked a gold coin in her direction which she deftly plucked from the air. A moment later he found himself tied up in Kiva's arms. The contact brought a smile to his weather-worn face. He returned the embrace.

Tor looked over her head at his friend, who was looking at him in the way that he looked at things that confused him. "Don't worry, Rek. I will meet you later, and I will answer any questions you have. Will you do this for me?"

"I will, but we will talk more on this later."

The Traveller came to a halt. They had finally arrived at Kalistiel.

"Later then," confirmed Tor.

They followed him off the Traveller. They were right behind him, but as they rounded the corner, he was already gone.

*

Rek had been unusually quiet. At first, all he could think about was how angry he was at Tor. The man was more than a friend; he was family. They had known each other for so long that he had become the brother Rek had never had. It tore him apart, knowing what had been done to Tor, but more than that, they had never had secrets from each other before. They had been inseparable. Now it felt like a massive void had opened up between them; a chasm so vast that a dragon had sneaked in and made a home; without him even being aware.

Of course, he knew Tor had changed, but he needed his forgiveness for not stopping him going on patrol alone. He should've been there. Then he gave up on the search. Over and over he played that night in his mind and the terrors that he should have either stopped or died trying.

Kiva broke him from his guilt, not by tapping him on the shoulder or saying his name. She had punched him harder than he thought possible. She knocked the wind from him with a perfectly aimed shot at his solar plexus. The look she was giving him could curdle milk.

"Rekhaert Stone," she admonished in a commanding tone. "You have not brought me to the top of the world to mope around. You can talk to Tor later. If you make my first visit here miserable, I am going to make sure you pay for it later on!" The look she gave him brooked no questions.

When she was older, she would be a force to be reckoned with, more so than she already was. He laughed, picking her up and spinning her in the air. They had spent the rest of the day exploring and shopping.

Kiva and Rek made their way through the city. She watched the residents waltz by her. Growing up in Sha'mack, she would look for easy marks to pickpocket, but here everyone seemed a prospect. Her head raced with insatiable curiosity, wondering what all these people had in their pockets. Men and women with different coloured skin, features and odd-looking clothes walked past her.

Kiva's head swivelling left and right as she tried to take in this colourful and strange city, everywhere she looked there were street food vendors, and intoxicating smells were making her mouth water.

It was a solstice celebration, and Kalistiel was alive with life. People danced in the streets. Musicians and merchants plied their wares. People sold goods outside their homes. Rek bought something for them both to eat, and when he turned around, Kiva had introduced herself to an older woman doing ear piercings and was haggling over the cost of earrings, even though the first one was clearly in place. The older woman was overwhelmed by Kiva's exuberance, and she relented to her tenacious nature.

As soon as it was done, Kiva bounced out of the chair thanking the lady. She smiled from earring to earring. Spotting Rek she skipped over. He told her the colour of her new 'pretties' bought out her eyes.

After an eventful day, they found their way to the Inn. Kiva was worn out and told Rek she was going to sleep.

Rek went down to the bar to see if anyone had heard of Bishop.

The Oracle
Chapter Twenty Two

Bishop's flight to the mountains of Manthripur had been agony and stopping to bring warning to Gabriel while necessary may have been a mistake, as the one-eyed Dren's poison slowly filtered into his bloodstream. In his human form, there was no doubt this venom would have killed him instantly.

He flew over the city of Kalistiel in the heights of Manthripur, the mountains rising in front of him. 'Not much further now' was the mantra he had been reciting as he flew over Manthripur, his body wracked with pain.

He barely made it to the old springs behind the mountains. He was near collapse. This place was a secret known only to the Anunnaki. The area behind these mountains was prohibited by Kairos the Oracle herself. Not that you could go there without a boat or by scaling the mountain. Bishop had been raised in these mountains by the Giants themselves. He made it his private playground growing up. The hot springs bubbled with healing life force from the earth herself.

It was not surprising that no one knew of this sacred place. It was hard to get to and held little reward for inexperienced explorers.

Only a few from Kesh who traded in some of the rare stones, shells and materials, found on the coastline called Eri'fik, ventured to this side of the mountains. It was the home of carnivorous creatures. Surprisingly it was not just the animals. Plants and fauna would also attempt to eat anything unfortunate enough to get within striking distance, which is why so few came inland, and those that did never left. It was not for the faint of heart.

Bishop liked it here. There was something intrinsically peaceful to his animalistic side. In this form, he wasn't something the creatures of the region would bother. After a good half, an hour soak in the spring and the pain was gone. He would have lingered in this primordial cauldron, but he had already stayed too long already.

Pulling himself from the coral pool, he gave his wing a sniff. It seemed the danger had passed. The base of his wing had some scarring. Stretching and flexing the wing, he bound into the air and headed to see the closest thing he had ever had to a mother, Kairos the Oracle!

In the furthest heights of Manthripur on the peak named Ashen'Kai, a grand opening had been carved into the stone of the mountain itself. None of the inhabitants on the mountain knew when this majestic hall was created or how the lady that had dwelt within had lived for so long.

The elder races had called this place the eye of the world. Here Kairos could follow the lines of time and power and may offer insight into the past, present or future.

Kairos had lived a very long time. Long enough that seas had risen and fallen. Alone in the mountain top, she had few visitors and longed for death, but now it was getting closer she seemed to have a lot more reasons to live.

Kairos was troubled. Whether or not the world would be broken once more by the Dragonborn would come down to the actions of so few. That morning she had been visited by her adopted son, the Griffin, Bishop. A child of a dying race, one of the few that had visited her over the ages. She had been entrusted with his upbringing and wellbeing. She watched him grow and later become the hand of the king in Kishar.

The Griffin had been created during the aftermath of the Great War, tasked with collecting and safeguarding any objects of power. Millennia had passed. The Fenn riders settled in the forests to the southeast, and the Griffin

faded from memory. Bishop understood nothing of his heritage. His future was in the making. She just hoped he would rise to meet the many challenges ahead.

He was the closest thing she ever had to a child. She had called him Bishop, which in the old tongue meant godly or blessed. In his human form, he was small. At four foot six he was rarely seen as a threat. In his feline form, he as big as a horse but broader. She loved him as much as she could anything. He would play an essential part in what was to come.

Bishop flew into the hall, and his massive wings billowed catching the air, landing gracefully, his giant feline paws padded silently across the stone floor.

"I've brought you a robe." Kairos held up the robe for inspection.

The Griffin sniffed the robe, then stepped back, his body shifting and changing. Bishop was naked once again in his mother's hall. He slipped on the gown.

"Come, child, tell me what ails you. You look hungry?"

It was said as a question, but Bishop understood it was rhetorical. Like any mother, she wanted to make sure he was fed. Unsure when he last ate, he was happy to oblige her. They sat in a large room off the back of the hall. One of the Anunnaki had brought them refreshments. His massive frame was almost comical, bringing the tea tray in on one hand.

Once they were alone, they spoke of many things. One thing she knew, without doubt, it was vital that he wait in the Keshian harbour and hire a boat that docked there named Howl.

"You must be ready to go when those who flee arrive. You must see them safely to their destination. There you will each find an answer to questions you didn't even know you had." Kairos took a drink of tea and looked over Bishop's face to see if the import of her words had registered. "Once this task is done, you may follow your heart. I will give you supplies, but you must leave here and travel straight to Kesh."

"I have told Aleator and Rek to meet me here."

"No time for that. They will come to see the great Oracle, which in case you forgot, is me. If you want to save them, then do as I ask."

"Save them?"

Kairos looked thoughtful for a moment. "Consider it a last request... My death is coming on the heels of your destiny, and it is a choice between your friend's lives and mine and I have lived a very long time. I have made my choice young cub, and I would wish it no other way. All that is left is that you find the ship and with it your destiny."

"How do you know?"

She smiled. "How does an Oracle know?"

Bishop took her hand and looking into her violet coloured eyes and saw sadness there. "I will come back."

"It will be too late!"

"But..." He shed involuntary tears for this woman who raised him.

"No buts. Dry your eyes. I am meeting my destiny. I have lived longer than any creature should. I am not what you think, but I always wanted to be. So, give me one last hug and be on your way."

Bishop reluctantly conceded. They walked to an opening in the side of the hall. He had learned to fly here as a cub under Kairos' watchful eyes.

"You will tell the Anunnaki?" Bishop would feel better knowing the giants were on watch.

"I will tell them, but it won't matter dear one."

Bishop broke down. He was crying at her feet, begging. "Don't make me go. Please don't make me go.

Don't you know…"

Kairos helped Bishop up cupping his face in her hands. "You have been the best part of my life, more than I could ever have hoped. I am prouder than you could ever know." Tears had appeared in Kairos' eyes as well, something she had not thought possible.

"I know life is unfair, but all things have their time. Yours is just beginning. Mine is at its end, and I am ready, but I need to know you will be okay. If you do as I ask, dear one, all will be as it is meant to be."

"B-b-but I love you." The words hung in the momentary silence.

She held him close. "And I love you; you must trust that what I ask is for a good reason."

The two hugged. Then Bishop dropped his robe, and his form shifted, wings unfurled, and muscle and sinew swelled and grew until he became a Griffin. Lowering his frame, which now towered over Kairos, Bishop rubbed his massive head against her one last time, and she scratched his ear. If he must leave, he must do it now or not at all. Pulling away from Kairos, he picked up a sack of supplies in his jaws. He met his mother's eyes one last time then launched himself from the room and headed to Kesh.

Over the next few days, Kairos had investigated the past and travelled along the many branches of possible futures, unable to discern anything of herself past today.

She only hoped she was prepared. Kairos understood the implications of this. Her death was coming.

*

The Anunnaki had called a meeting of the Elders. It was disturbing news that Kairos was going to die, a shock that caught them unprepared. She had resided in the mountains for as long as anyone could remember, which was a very long time. After all, they could live to be a thousand years. Some were still alive from before the Great Emigration.

Grey remembered his grandfather telling him of their beginning in this land and how he had come across Kairos' chamber. It had been one of his favourite bedtime stories.

The disembodied voice filling the chamber his grandfather had entered near one of the mountain peaks. "This chamber is not for you, Child of Knowledge. Why do you come here?"

His grandfather had told him he had near filled his pants! Looking about what appeared to have once been a pillared hall, he could not see where the voice was coming from but summed up the courage to respond. His voice quiet for one so large.

"We have travelled from the past. We seek peace." His voice had echoed throughout the cave.

"So, you haven't come to steal from me... Child of

Knowledge?"

His grandfather had said his hand had unconsciously reached for his weapon and the voice came again.

"Pull the sword, and you will die where you stand!

There is no need for violence, not if you speak the truth. Just know this, you may build on the southern slopes of these mountains, and there are also lands south-west of here open for settlement. The other side of these mountains is death to any fool enough to mine or dig into them. This mountain is mine. If you can meet those terms, you can have your peace."

His grandfather was a great warrior, but there was a depth in the voice giving the ultimatum. It resonated from the stone around him as if the mountain itself spoke to him.

"You may enter, and as a show of goodwill, I will grant you three visions, past, present and future to help guide you. Maybe, just maybe, we can stop the destruction and war ahead."

"We are not at war here."

"War, you bring in your shadow though you do not know it yet."

"What should I call you, Great One."

A small middle-aged woman stepped from a recess. "Nothing as grand as Great One. Would you believe me if I told you it has been so long since I have heard my name uttered aloud, that it has been lost to time? Anyone that does know it died a long time ago, including me. You may call me Kairos!"

After receiving his visions, Grey's grandfather left the cavernous entrance at the mountain top. Kairos had one more command.

"Whatever you do, do not make your home within this mountain, as you did in the past. That is lost to you. There are things trapped that have evolved since you once lived inside this mountain. Only death lies within now."

Grey's grandfather had agreed to the terms. It was the only time he had feared one so small, although none of the Anunnaki would dare to question her words. It was long suspected she was not the little old lady she appeared to be. She did not age, and there was iron in her. She spoke with absolute authority.

Today was no different. However, as much Grey didn't want to believe what he was being told, he had little doubt it would come to pass.

The members of the Elders looked as unhappy at the news as he was. She had been instrumental in the forging of their great new society. If not for her visions and insight, allowing them to prepare, they would not have survived.

*

Kairos was a beacon for the people travelling the length and breadth of High Garden. Sometimes there would be nothing of their future for her to see, just the past or present, but still, they came from all races and creeds to pay homage.

"I see you are thinking it's the end of the world Grey, and as I look around this room, I feel the pain. You have been like my children these last six hundred years, my salvation, but, my journey is near its end. All things pass. Do not mourn my passing. Celebrate my life. I have called you here as I require one last favour from you all."

Kairos looked to each of them in turn with genuine emotion in her eyes, memorising each face one last time.

The Anunnaki had deep-set faces with lines and wrinkles as crag like as the bluff mountains they lived in. People from the lowlands professed they were emotionless. However, it was not the case. They were the pulsing heart of the earth itself. Generally, they appeared to have a sandstone colouring with blonde or white hair and eyes of all colours buried under large brows and flat noses. Most of the Elders were around twelve feet tall and four foot wide. The general population was middle-aged, about four hundred years.

Kairos addressed the gathered Anunnaki. "Today, you will not stand guard. You will walk the mountains of your forefathers. Grey will stay with me for I have another task for him. Make no mistake the world teeters on the brink of destruction, war is upon us, and you must get ready to meet the enemy in the south. If we do not commit to our paths, there will be no future for anyone. In a moment our guest of honour will arrive."

Prophesy
Chapter twenty three

Tor had heard stories about Kairos, ever since he was a young child. A woman who could foresee the paths of your life was a camp tale for young men. A woman who could curse you with death by simply pronouncing it. He was older now and had a better understanding of the world. This woman could give him some much-needed direction.

It had taken at least a couple of hours for Tor to navigate his way through the splendour of Kalistiel. He had not dawdled, gawked or joined in with the celebrations and revelry, however attractive some of those offers had been. He felt he was close to getting some answers.

He found his way onto the path to Ashen'Kai, the home of famed Oracle of Manthripur. He expected to see more of the Anunnaki. The populace had happily directed him when he asked. Walking across the stone causeway towards the cavernous entrance, he couldn't believe the quality of the masonry that had been used to form a giant walkway, Stones the size of houses somehow placed between the peaks.

It had been recorded some of the first Anunnaki built the walkway in tribute so that the younger races could visit more easily. It looked as if the side of the mountain had been blown away in some distant time, revealing a lost hall. As he approached, he could see strange lights illuminating the inside of the cave.

Tor stood in the mouth of the vast cavern. In front of him, he could see at least ten Anunnaki sitting in a circle around a tiny figure that he could only presume was Kairos. She was waving her arms for silence.

The entrance was blocked to Tor by one of the Anunnaki.

"I am here to see the Oracle, Kairos!" Tor announced.

*

Grey took his role as Kairos' protector and emissary very seriously and had taken a position at the entrance just as Tor arrived.

"Grey, this is not your fight. Stand down!" Kairos commanded.

"But..."

"No buts, just move it so my guest can enter!"

"How's he a Dragon? Looks more like a dragonfly." The giant laughed but moved out of the way, letting Tor enter.

"We have company!" The voice seemed to reverberate around the cave. It was a voice that demanded obedience. The cave fell silent. All eyes were on Tor.

"Come forth, Aleator Darkwing."

Tor walked forward. It was as if he were answering involuntarily to a summons. He was seventy percent certain it was of his own volition.

"Stop!"

Tor stopped at her command. In front of him, the cave dipped, forming a basin several horses wide in all directions. Stalagmites that must have been growing for thousands of years had formed in this basin. The water it held glowed.

"I seek Kairos?"

"Then, your quest is complete. I am Kairos."

"I would ask answers from you."

"And if I can only refine your questions?"

"Then I will have more than I have now."

There was silence for a moment before Kairos pointed her arms in the direction of the giant Anunnaki surrounding them.

"These are the leaders of the free people here. I have invited them to share in this, so they also understand better what is coming. I have walked many futures, and only one thing is certain, you are an axis point on which life will be balanced."

Tor looked around the room and could see disbelief in the faces of the Elders. He had always been good at reading people even the smallest expression and the slightest expression on these broad faces were as clear as a slap in the face to him.

Kairos spoke again. "I see the doubt in all your faces. The time for words has passed. Cast your eyes into the waters."

Water welled up. The natural cauldron filled and began to bubble. Tor could swear that shapes had begun to form and shift. He watched as Kairos eyes filled with light animating the shadows of the Anunnaki. Casting his eyes away from her, he looked back towards the waters, as what appeared like webs in the same light formed in the water. Seeming to connect, then expanded. He could see hundreds, no thousands, of portals to other places. The view started to move faster and faster. It felt a bit like he was flying. He felt the mountains shrink beneath him and he was travelling south, past fields and streams, cities and towns.

"Behold what comes for us all."

Tor knew he wasn't really in the Southwest. This was more like the dream of the Ib'ren Cohar. Only he could hear different thoughts. A battle of monstrous proportions was being fought in the trenches of Bastion, home of the Jaden.

Tor didn't know how he knew the names and places. He just had the memory, and he knew Uxmal had already fallen, as well as its surrounding forest, home to the Norn's who had fallen back and joined the ranks of the Jaden. They found refuge behind the walls of the fortress city of Bastion. Fiercely protecting the perimeter walls.

*

Drayson Cain was large for one of the Jaden at five foot tall. He was known for his skills in battle, a ranking member of the Storm Guard. His people were of the earth, bestowed with a strength that belied their size and handsome looks. A plaited green braid hung between his muscled shoulder blades.

The night before, one of the Sokar made it over the outer wall. Later he had found out it had been thrown over by one of the Soulless, the largest of the Va'Nahual.

His axe was heavy with their blood. Pulling back for water, it had come from nowhere all teeth and fangs. At that moment, he had thought it his last, and time slowed to a near standstill. Then the look of intent on the attacking creature changed, it was some kind of Warg on two legs, before it had been attacking. Fear now registered in those Sokar eyes. The beast was inches from Drayson's face. Putrid spittle landing on his dark brown cheeks. Jaws larger than his head snapped shut mere inches in front of him.

One of the larger male Norn's that he was fighting beside on the wall, named Ashe, had seen the Sokar bearing down on him and rushed to intervene. Catching it in mid-air as if it weighed nothing, one giant wooden hand closed around its waist. The Va'Nahual was twice the size of Drayson, but it was still no match for a Norn. His saviour threw the beast at the ground with such force the impact kicked up dirt and stones. The vibration shook the ground he stood on. It was dead on contact. Most of the bones in its body would've broken all at once. Ashe had saved his life.

Most races would feel small among the Norns. They were amazing creatures, tree spirits brought to life by an earth mother. Drayson was about as big as Ashe's leg. They had bark for skin. Asleep they closely resembled trees. He had walked through what seemed a forest on his way to meet a Maja It gave you a whole new respect for the woods, fighting side by side with living trees.

The sun was coming up, and Drayson was to meet one of the Maja to discuss strategy. The Maja hierarchy seemed a lot like insects. The females were few in comparison to the male Norns, by his estimate, around a hundred to one. Ahead of him, there was what appeared to be a giant boulder surrounded by rows of trees. As he drew closer, the sun cleared the tree line. He had met other Maja, and they still awed him.

Fifty or so Norn younglings at play stopped and looked towards him. As Drayson neared the meeting point, the outer ring of trees sprouted limbs and turned towards him. Black eyes watched him approach, but none stopped him. The rocks started to move, giant boulders coming together with dirt and grass. The young Norns that had been running about on top of the giant boulder seemed to be attached as the ground they stood on went horizontal, and the Maja pulled itself from the ground. The Maja's massive bulk cast a shadow over Drayson as she turned featureless face toward him.

The voice that issued forth was small and musical compared to the Maja's size. A smell of flowers filled the air. Some little birds landed on the earth mother's shoulder singing their song of a new day.

"So, what news, child?" The words seemed to come from all directions.

"I was going to ask the same of you, great mother."

"One of my sisters fell last night. The enemy seems to have an unlimited number of smelly biters they can throw at us. Her Norns fight on the wall, enraged with grief, they will kill many. Though I fear it will not stem the tide, but we will hold for now."

Without the Maja, the south would have been overrun by the enemy. The enemy had somehow learned the foulest of magic. These half-human chimaeras they faced once had hopes and dreams before they were captured by the enemy and twisted into the Va'nahual. Each one you killed had at some point been sentient, had a soul and even lived a normal healthy life.

It was abhorrent the things that had been done to the settlers of the south. Worst of all were the ones called the Soulless. No part of them held anything good. They were a perversion of life itself. Easily as big as a cave troll, only quicker and more lethal. The scary part was they seemed to be highly intelligent.

Drayson thought over the Maja's words. They needed help. "I will go north to seek help and bring warning as ambassador."

"One from me will go with you to represent me. I believe you have fought beside Ashe. He will join you in this."

Drayson was stunned. It was something he hadn't wanted to ask. "We would be travelling to Kishar to raise an army."

"You will stand a higher chance of success with Ashe by your side. Once you have done this, go north and seek the Anunnaki. Tell them of our enemy. Do what you must, but get help, or all will be lost. "

The Maja's words struck at his core. He watched in amazement as the great earth mother once more became a hillock of boulders and grass. Young Norns once more appearing animated and playful. He was closer now and could see the mischievous faces of the young Norns come back into view as the Maja made herself comfortable.

*

Tor was shaken and awed by what he had just seen and felt through this vision of Drayson Cain. It was like he was there.

"This is the present. You must be ready for the war Aleator. It is coming and you and mighty Argento. I see you there!"

Tor felt himself being dragged away again higher and higher until he looked upon the earth like a child's ball spinning in the vastness of space. The ethereal voice of Kairos echoed through the vision.

"Now the past, Argento protects you from."

There was a bright light, and when he opened his eyes again, Tor was back in the dungeon, slowly taking in the room beneath him. Just like before, he could only watch as events occurred. He could not interact with anything. He was stood in a dark place. Torches on the walls that barely cast enough light. Not enough to see clearly.

As he took in the room, a chill ran up and down his spine. He had been in this place before. Panic began to set in. He mentally reached for Argento and was comforted by the presence of the dragon. He moved to the corner of the room instinctually and was surprised to see someone in his place.

Tor's heart was beating so fast. It took a moment for the realization that he wasn't there, to sink in.

It was then that he heard Kairos' voice. "Do not panic

Aleator Darkwing. Nothing can hurt you here."

"Why am I here?"

"I'm sorry to curse you with this knowledge, but you cannot truly share yourself if you do not know what you have done."

Tor wasn't happy at all. Everything about this place made him feel ill. Looking around, he started to remember. He almost didn't want to see himself for the shame of what he had become.

The room was large and without windows. It was an unremarkable room except for the large fireplace and library on the far wall.

When he was released, by Bishop, he had seen creatures praying around a hole calling for something of darkness and a fire creature so terrible he had fled as fast as he could.

Walking back to where he knew he would find that relic of himself, Tor looked upon a pile of straw and faeces wrapped around the shape of a man. He wondered what else he could learn from this place except for how low he had fallen. Behind him, there was a noise at the door. He almost missed it, but his other-self looked up from his place in the grime and dirt. Mismatched eyes that were virtually feral looked right through him, one eye blue, one eye green and devoid of humanity. Only fear lived in that shell.

He hurried to the door. Mandrake entered, dragging a young female by the hair and passed right through him. She was kicking and screaming. Tor didn't want to watch and turned to face the doorway. His attention was brought to the corridor. There was a member of the People's Army there; Tor recognised the uniform. He had been a squire to one of his father's friends. He couldn't remember the name, but his father would.

The outside of the room faded away. All Tor could see now was the girl on Mandrake's rack. She was displaying the one thing he could not at that time, hope. A hope someone would hear, hope someone would help, but there was no hope in this place. The girl was dishevelled and looked as if she had been dragged from her bed, still dressed in her nightgown, a sign of wealth. Tor had to admit she was brave kicking and biting at the cloaked man. She even managed to draw blood with a, particularly vicious bite to Mandrake's hand. Her repayment was a backhand that knocked her senseless. Blood and saliva dribbled down her chin as he fastened her hands. Tor could feel his rage swell with the dragons at what he witnessed.

Once she was held in place, the cloaked figure punched her in the stomach so hard it made Tor wince. He didn't want to remember this, but he couldn't move. The cloaked figure tore her night robe from her body, tied, naked and shivering with cold. The girl had begun to sob while the man bound the deep bite mark between thumb and forefinger with a length of her shredded gown.

He watched then as Mandrake held his arms outward, and all the torches around the room suddenly burst into flame. Just for a moment, Tor was blinded by the sudden illumination. He could see his old self cower further into filth and decrepitude that surrounded him. Tor vowed that he would kill this man. He now knew who one of them was.

Mandrake finished some sort of chant which Tor could only assume was dark magic. There was a noise like the slamming of a door. He knew his shadow self would be cowering, too afraid to even look up from his sanctuary of piss and misery. Tor, however, was no longer Mandrake's creation. He was free and watched his former self with loathing.

"Dog!" Mandrake snarled.

He had cringed upon hearing his name. Tor watched his shadow self, creep from the corner and cower at Mandrake's heel. It made him feel sick to his stomach.

"Now Dog, why don't we make the lady feel at home?

Fetch the pincers."

His former-self scuttled across the room. The girl had regained some strength and began to pull at her bonds.

She yelled at Mandrake in frustration. "You won't get away with this. I will show the world who you are."

Mandrake's reply probably would have been shocking if not for the flood of memories that came back to him. "Dog, the lady believes she has something to show the world. Take the pincers and show her; her right eye."

His former self went to task without hesitation. Tor couldn't watch, but as he turned the world turned with him, he couldn't turn away. Somehow, he knew the memories would stay with him this time, a dark stain on his soul. Mandrake had broken him, and he had become his tool. The dragon's rage swelled with his own. He finally understood. He would not try and justify what he had done, but he would avenge it.

This time the memory hadn't broken him. Instead, it forced him into something stronger. Tor still did not know why he was chosen, but he would no longer be prey.

As this thought solidified in his mind, the voice of Kairos came once more, louder and louder. "The future is not written. You have been given a weapon of power."

"Argento is not a weapon. Why would you say such a thing?"

"I am not the only one listening, and some things must be said. Let us say you have been given a gift then.

You might say I have experience in receiving gifts. Let

Argento look upon me."

"You are not human Kairos!" Tor had tipped his head and was looking at Kairos sideways.

"Now you see my curse, Aleator. A lesson I learned the hard way. In some ways, I have had flashes of this moment for longer than you have lived, Aleator. Now I will show you my fear. Behold, the future."

*

Once more he was catapulted amongst the stars, but this time, he faced The Dread warlocks that had been banished, Uruku, Khnumm, Tao'nas, and Satet. They were Dragonborn, and he was stood with them, one of them. Yet somehow he knew it was not himself but Alal. He watched them Line up their Ib'ren Cohar, and they released a vortex. It was beautiful to behold. It spewed forward, then out in all directions like it had hit some unseen barrier. A moment later it was like the universe itself ripped open. A battle that ensued between the Dragonborn and what Tor could only assume were elemental gods. The battle had set fire to the world.

"This is what will happen if you are captured by the enemy, and the evil that has been lost to history is once more set free. You cannot let the dragon fall into enemy hands."

Tor was aghast. He blinked, and he was back in the cavern. Before he had a chance to speak or move, Argento pushed forward fully taking control of his body. The pool had gone dark in direct contrast to the lightening blue now clearly dancing in his eyes. Argento took a cursory look around the room and wasn't impressed. The bond between him and Aleator had become a reprieve for the dragon. For the first time in centuries, he had a human worth defending and sharing his power. Argento was able to once more feel the connection to the host. The dragon flooded forward in righteous anger, fastening his eyes on Kairos.

"What have you done insect. Speak true, or I will kill everything in this room?"

Kairos understood what she was facing probably better than anyone in High Garden. She also knew she needed to think carefully on her next words. The blades of the Ib'ren Cohar had begun dancing around the crouched figure of Aleator.

"Last chance insect what have you done?"

"It was just a vision of one of many possible futures, great Argento." The Anunnaki around the room were getting ready to protect Kairos from this upstart.

Grey was next to speak. "Watch your tone, little

Dragon."

Ignoring the giant Argento raged at Kairos again. "Insect! I would tell your servants to sit back down, or I will make them, and they may never stand ever again..."

The sheer indifference in the tone of the threat gave the Elders pause enough for Kairos to speak. Kairos put her hands up in a placating gesture as she spoke.

"Everyone back to your places. Argento, great dragon, I have done neither you nor Aleator any harm. You should feel he is back with you."

Argento looked inside and found Tor was indeed back and was shouting for Argento to stop. In the cavern, Aleator's body remained in fighting position with the blade of the Ib'ren Cohar encircling him in deadly arcs, ready to kill anything foolish enough to step within range.

Back in the soul cage, Argento could once more sense Aleator. It took only a thought, and they were once more in front of each other. Tor could sense how distraught the dragon was.

"What's wrong, old friend?"

The dragon did not speak straight away. In fact, what happened next shocked Tor, as a great tear welled up in those giant limpid pool eyes. Reaching out, he put a hand on Argento's snout. "I am here. What ails you?"

"You have been gone for so very long. I was enslaved by Alal. I thought you had died." The raw emotions rolled off Argento.

"I didn't leave Argento. We got what we hoped for.

Kairos showed me a vision."

"In my vision If you die. I will be a tool that is used to destroy the world. I cannot carry on being the plaything of whoever finds my cage next."

After spending time reassuring Argento and sharing what he had learned, Tor went back to the cavern. The blade of the Ib'ren Cohar disappeared back into the brace. Tor had heard the threats made on his behalf and was amazed at Argento's confidence that he could look at these giants as if they were no threat at all.

Bad Omens
Chapter twenty four

The grand hall in the cave had gone quiet. Kairos spoke again. Her eyes glowed the colour of the water. The dragon must have been placated as Aleator was once more in control.

"I know what you will become Aleator Darkwing. I also understand what follows you! There are many paths to defeat, and so few that hold promise! Your enemy will be in Sha'vel but, so too is one who can lend a helping hand. If you go, you will lose a part of yourself but in so doing, find a rebellion and a mighty ally.

If your companions go with you before following their own path, they will die, and Without them, all is lost! You cannot win the war alone or get revenge on your enemies. To Sha'vel, you must go alone and trust you will see each other again. Sha'vel is your first step toward finding the secret garden. There you will find the arm of Assai.

Your friends are not ready to join your fight. I have sent my son Bishop to protect them until you meet again. Now go with Grey. He will show you a different way down the mountain. "Only when you enter the secret garden alone will you strike a blow. I will tell your friends where you have gone and book them passage on a ship."

Tor didn't relish the idea of leaving his friends, but he did not doubt Kairos' words. He had seen the curse laid upon her through Argento. She was bound to the web of time and space. He turned and followed Grey out of the Hall and back across the causeway.

Grey wasn't just a member of the Elders. He was also head of technology and was overseeing many of the machines in both Kadingir and Kalistiel. His latest completed project was a water wheel that generated energy that could be used to power everything from lights to pumps for transporting water around the mountain.

A massive part of the city was dedicated to learning. Scholars and inventors came from all over High Garden, to study with the leading minds of the time. Kalistiel was where dreams were built and made into a reality. Grey was proud of his family's achievements.

Tor was by no means stupid, but some of the things the Anunnaki called science was so far beyond him they seemed like magic.

After his talk with Kairos, he finally had a direction, but he was still missing pieces of the puzzle. This next step, he would have to take alone. If there were answers in Sha'vel, he would find them. The idea of separating from Rek and Kiva left a void in his soul, but he did not doubt the word of Kairos. If leaving alone kept them safe, he would find this secret garden and then he could find his friends after.

Tor was stronger than he had ever felt before. It was like he and Argento had begun to fall in sync. They had a shared enemy, and it was time to hunt.

When they arrived at the destination, Tor watched as Grey placed an object with a strange shape in the centre of a formidable-looking wall. He heard it clunk into place followed by a whirring noise of cogs shifting and turning. Inside the wall, the wall retracted. It was an impressive Anunakki sized entrance into a room the size of several taverns.

The building was separated into sections. As they walked past the weird and the wonderful, Grey pointed out various items and projects. Tor could tell the Anunnaki was very proud, and rightly so. To say he was impressed was an understatement. He saw one woman creating sculptures with sound and picking up massive stones without even touching them. One thing that really caught his eye was electricity. He had a basic knowledge of it and had seen the lights in Kalistiel and Kadingir, but it was like lightning was being manipulated here. He watched it jump across the tops of two crystal obelisks. Tor hadn't realized he had stopped walking until Grey prodded him out of his trance.

"This next area is where we are going Aleator. If we had time, I would give you a more in-depth tour, but Kairos said not to tarry."

Tor nodded his head in acquiescence and followed the giant through a large doorway, it led them onto an open plateau, it was a clear night, and you could see the vastness and beauty of the stars from here.

Tor didn't think he'd ever seen so many stars before. They were countless and infinite, shining persistently in the heavens. A three-quarter moon hung low amongst them

"You see them with dragon eyes Aleator." The dragon answered his unasked question. Moonlight illuminated a silver ship of sorts. It was cylindrical and domed, with no obvious entry points. It was certainly eye-catching, and

Grey seemed more than proud of it. The giant Anunnaki puffed up his chest and explained, "This is my greatest treasure. Our greatest work as a species." Grey stroked the round ship with his giant hand as if it were a pet.

Argento spoke in his mind again.

"The only thing bigger than the Anunnaki is their pride." Tor just smiled.

Grey noticed Tors smirk but carried on regardless.

"You laugh at me, little man, but you simply do not understand the work that I put into this. The sheer mechanics and engineering that went into this ship almost broke everything we know about the sciences. If it were not for Kairos and insistence on your immediate departure, I would not even allow you to clamp your little eyes upon it. But, Kairos said it is urgent, so I have little choice."

"What is that, over there?" Tor interrupted, pointing towards a triangular frame, wrapped in cloth.

Grey gave him a puzzled look and replied. "I was coming to that." Grey smiled. "That is how you are getting down the mountain. Its a glider. I hope you're not scared of heights little dragon?"

Tor smiled and electricity danced within his eyes. "Not at all, and I have a friend who wants to play."

A few minutes later, Aleator stood at the precipice of the mountain with a nervous Grey strapping him to the glider. "This lever will take you left the other right."

"Any other advice for me master inventor?"

"Just let the glider do the work and don't die! If you die, Kairos will be displeased with me."

"I'll be fine, now how does this work again Grey?"

"Those levers control your movement, you're strapped in, just try and relax and let the wind carry you." Grey picked Tor and the glider up. "Are you ready?"

Kairos spoke to me of my destiny, and I will not be dying tonight. Inform Rekhaert and Kiva about my departure. Tell him that I am sorry." Grey nodded grimly and then launched Tor into the fresh night air.

Gliding across the sky a sense of freedom and exhilaration danced its way through his body, leaving his nerve endings tingling. "I hope you appreciate this, Argento?" The glider dipped, and Tor knew fear.

Argento spoke in a soothing voice. "Trust me Aleator and let me guide your movements."

Against instinct and fear, he closed his eyes and let Argento take over the glider. He could feel Argento's will exert itself upon his body, and as quickly as he had been descending, he felt the glider catch the wind and pull itself back up into the night air.

"Aleator, open your eyes and share this with me."

Tor hadn't realized he had closed them and did as asked. It was truly magnificent. Argento was filled with joy. Tor found himself gasping at the beauty of what he saw as they soared together serenely above the villages. Rivers and inlets that passed by below. To experience this and to see the world and all its beauty through the eyes of a dragon.

Knowing what was taken from Argento made the imprisonment within the Ib'ren Cohar even more vile.

"Do not dwell on the past Aleator." Argento said, sensing Tors emotions. "What was done is done. Time moves only in one direction, and we cannot change our past." And with that, Argento banked the glider to the left and let it roll into a dive. The wind rushed past Tors face again, but there was no panic this time, just pure exhilaration and joy.

Catching a warm updraft, the glider lifted skywards again. Argento spiralled the over-sized kite through a bank of clouds. As it broke through them, the glider slowly lost its momentum until it seemed to just hang in the thin air of the night. Tors heart held just as still for a second, and then the glider levelled out and caught the wind again, once again serenely floating above the clouds. As Tor looked down upon the bank of clouds, the light from the moon cast a shadow upon them. But instead of the gliders shadow, Tor saw the majestic frame of Argento, and his wings spread fully as he flew across the moonlit sky.

Argento was happy, Tor didn't know how he knew, but he was pleased to share this moment with the dragon.

"Thank you, Aleator. You truly are the finest of companions."

"You're welcome, my friend."

They had been in the air for hours before finally landing on the outskirts of Sha'vel. Not that they had noticed the time.

*

The Spider sneaked into Kalistiel under cover of night attaching himself to the bottom of the Traveller. There hadn't seemed to be anyone watching for him. How overconfident these Anunnaki were. He hadn't seen any guards at all. He had heard tales of a woman, a human woman, that could see the strands of time. His prey had no doubt come to see this oracle that sat atop the world. Stone streets and palisades obscured any possible tracks even for someone as talented as him. There was something to be said for knowing your enemy.

Once in Manthripur, it hadn't taken long to find the giant stone causeway spanning the two peaks leading to the Oracle. She would tell him where Tor was or feel excruciating pain. The Spider chuckled to himself as he realized he would inflict pain whether she knew something or not.

Kairos sat cross-legged on the floor, waiting for a shadow, not knowing the form in which her death would come, but just that evil would come to dispatch her, and she must fight it. She didn't usually feel the cold. Once she had been a simple thief that had entered the mountain in search of treasure, she hadn't found any treasure. Instead, she was bound to this place, cursed, unless she died fighting evil. Her torment could not be broken unless she went willingly. So, fight she would, addressing the shadow.

"I know you are there, Adad, Bringer of the storm. He who seeks death at the eye of the world? Come let old

Kairos see you."

"The only death will be yours. The only question is

Knock Knock?"

"Is that really what you want to ask me?"

"You're supposed to sayyyy… Whooooose there?"

Something dropped from the cave ceiling much closer than Kairos had realised. It landed with catlike grace. The creature spun around to face her. She could see the dark magic swirling around it and the mutilation this poor child had been subjected too.

It was attempting a parody of walking. Rows of eyes watched from inset sockets in its chest bones, fixed on its prey. Where the head should have features was a head shaped carapace devoid of features and as black as night, adorned in a red cloak.

"Do you have a question?"

The head-shaped shell broke open, clam-like, revealing a giant eye. A tongue lolled out, splitting the two-toned eye and displaying row upon row of incisors before snapping shut.

Kairos did not move.

"Where is the one they call Tor, his oafish friend, and snack-sized companion? I know you have seen them, old one. Do not deny it, tell me, and you may yet live!"

"Give me your real name, and I will answer your question?"

"I am The Spider."

"That is not your name... The Spider... Hahahaha! you are NO SPIDER." Kairos hunched over. Something was moving under the skin of her back writhing and pulsating. Her body had begun to convulse and arch.

The Spider was rarely shocked, but the lack of fear this woman displayed and the laughter that echoed around the cave was putting him on edge. Something was not as it seemed and yet he couldn't attack. He needed answers, or he would be the one writhing on the floor. Better to be prepared. Unsheathing his Night blades, he retreated slightly.

"I asked you a question, crone! Answer me, and I will end your pain quickly."

The voice that came forth next was no longer human, dark, venomous and laced with threat. This was something The Spider understood only too well.

"I have lived for thousands of years, insect. I have watched nations rise and fall. Yet you, a child without a name, is going to be the harbinger of my doom?

Hahahahahaha!"

The convulsing body of Kairos in front of him stopped shuddering before exploding flesh and bones in all directions. Giant black legs untangled, raising a black carapace, not unlike his own. The change was quick, and before his very eyes, a monstrous spider rose, mandibles dripping venom.

"I shall give you an answer, insect, for that is my curse, but as you have told me a lie I will tell you three prophesies. one will hide a lie, but you must decide which.

"So know the future will bring you a taste, the flesh of your prey by saving the girl in Sha-Mack in the south a week from now. Your present, if you live to see it, ends if you face the Anunnaki to the east and north.

Your past is as scattered as your soul, long lost prince and child of Uther. Your immaturity will be the reason you fail!"

The Spider barely heard a word after the name Uther. He was not this Adad. He did not carry the name Uther. As he thought the name again Images swirled through his mind, things he couldn't comprehend.

Kairos crouched momentarily readying to launch into attack. She was too slow for the enraged assassin. Barely a second had passed and he was beneath her great girth, swords lashing out at legs and abdomen.

"DIE witch! How dare you lie... Lie to meeeeee. I have no famileeeee." The last was a cry of anguish. In the violence of the attack, the Spider had landed several death strokes.

The body of the Oracle, Kairos, released of the curse that had held her for so long. Stood now as a being of light.

"I must thank you for freeing me from the web as the Adad, child of Uther it was prophesized for you to do.

The Spider slashed at her ephemeral figure to no avail. Kairos merely smiled. "You have lost once more. Aleator flies away, look." Kairos pointed, then the light dissipated, and she was gone.

The Spider ran to the entrance and watched as some strange object flew off the mountain and went down to the distant lights of Sha'vel.

"I will get you, Torrrrr!" The Spider shouted into the windy bluffs.

The Morning After
Chapter twenty five

The journey down from the mountain into Kesh had been a solemn one as the rain trickled down lightly. Rek had taken Tor's leaving badly. Kiva could feel the anger emanating from him. Watching him, she realized that he was more hurt than angry.

Rek had spent years searching for his friend, and after finally finding Tor, the man sneaked off into the night without even explaining where he was going.

Kiva's heart went out to the big man. They had been up early, and Tor was nowhere to be seen. They went to the Oracle, but the way was guarded and blocked by the Anunnaki.

Rek approached the nearest one and asked, "What's happened?"

"The Oracle has been killed."

Rek took in the news and didn't want to ask too many questions in case Tor had been the one that killed her and had to flee.

"He's probably just getting more supplies or something?" Kiva offered weakly. Even as she had said it, she knew it was not true.

Rek grunted and carried on marching without another word. And that's how the journey went until they reached the port town of Kesh.

Kiva put on her most innocent and upset face, even managing to force a tear to roll down her cheek. She began to sniffle and let out a little whimper. Rek turned to see Kiva sobbing.

"Kiva, what's wrong?" He said with genuine concern.

"It's nothing Rek. I'm just sorry I made you so mad at me." She said, wiping the tear from her cheek while trying her best not to let the smile she felt inside reach her face.

Rek let out a gentle sigh, and his face seemed to relax a little. "I'm sorry, Kiva. I don't mean to take it out on you, but I just can't believe that Tor just left without saying a word. I spent years thinking he was dead, only for him to turn up out of the blue. And now he goes and fucks off again. Goddamn ungrateful..." the tension returned to Reks face again as he walked off muttering obscenities to himself.

Kiva shrugged following the mad man mountain. She smiled as she watched how people would clear out of the way of his path. He was the most intimidating man to most, and yet it was such a contrast to who he really was.

Since they had met on that awful night in Idrienne, he had made her feel warm and safe for the first time in forever. Even when she had lived with her aunt, Kiva never really felt as if she belonged there. She had been loved and taken care of by her aunt, but something was always missing, and that was an adventure. Growing up as a street rat in the dangerous city of Sha'mack.

Kiva quickened her pace to catch up with the stampeding Rekhaert and slipped her hand into his and gave the big man her sweetest smile that she could muster. Rek looked down at Kivas butter-wouldn't-melt smile and could not help but smile in return.

"Can a man not brood in peace, you damn rascal?" Rek said with mirth as he ruffled Kivas blonde hair. "You know what? Let's get ourselves a warm bed for the night. I know of a good inn up ahead. The owner should give us a good price as we go back some." And with that, he scooped Kiva up on to his broad shoulders, making her giggle like the little girl that she should be and made their way to the inn.

Little did they realise that they were being watched from the shadows. As the pair walked on through the town, Kiva, now perched high on Reks shoulder, she could see the whole town in all its beauty.

As they neared the docks, something caught her eye. A crowd of people had circled a pair of men. The crowd were raucous and shouting at the men in the middle, who she now realized were fighting one another.

"Rek, what are those people doing over there?" She said as she pointed over towards the encircled fighters.

Rek craned his head around. "Its a prize fight, princess. Bets get placed on who will win, and whoever wins then gets a cut of the takings." Rek quickened his pace a little.

"What happens to the loser?" Kiva asked as she watched the fight unfold.

Rek didn't answer straight away, but instead grimaced and looked to the floor. "Maybe we should just get to the

Inn before it gets dark."

A few moments later, Rek and Kiva walked into The Krakens Den, a hushed whisper settled over the bar as they entered, but Rek ignored it. Kiva, however, now back on her own two feet, couldn't help but stare back at the crowd. Every face that stared back at her looked dangerous and hostile, but she knew full well not to show any fear to this pack of wolves.

Kiva looked towards Rek and realized that although he had a stern face, he wasn't worried at all. She had the odd sense that he was enjoying himself. Kiva smiled.

"Good to see you again, Felix."

The man behind the bar was smaller than Rek, but by no means was he a little man. His skin was as black as night, and his hair was braided and tied back into a tail. He rested his arms on the bar and leaned forward a little, flexing the muscles in his arms in a show of strength. When the reply came, it was said with pure menace.

"Go fuck yourself, Rekhaert Stone." Felix opened the bar hatch and squared up to Rek. They were mere inches away from one another.

"Now, now Felix. Don't be such a skunk rat for once in your miserable life. All I want is a room for the night, and we will be on our way in the morning. We don't want this getting ugly... like your mother." Rek replied with a smirk.

"Ha, you're only pissed that she wouldn't sleep with your fat ass, you turd blossom!" Felix retorted, raising his voice louder and inching ever closer.

Rek smiled and held his hands to his chest in mock shame and replied. "Well, only the gods know what she laid with to produce your forsaken features!"

Kiva fingered her knives and took a step back, expecting a fight to break out at any point when both men suddenly embraced as brothers would.

"Rek, you smelly old dog! It is good to see you again, brother." Felix laughed.

"It's good to see your ugly mug too, my old friend."

"Been almost a year since you graced us with your fat, fucking head. Where have you been? I almost went bankrupt without you to prop up my bar!" Felix let out a throaty laugh and Kiva found herself beginning to like the dark-skinned man.

"Its been a long few months, Felix. I shall tell you more later. But first, it would be nice to rest a while." "Of course, Rek. Please, come this way." Felix lead them to a room on the next floor up.

It was sparse and smelled of damp and dust, but it was better than sleeping in the rain. There was a small balcony overlooking the port and a few candles dotted around the place, and a small bathtub in the corner.

Felix patted Rek on his back and said "Its not much, old man, but the bed is sturdy, and the sheets are clean. You'll have fun tonight." Then winked and smiled at Kiva.

"It's not like that, Felix. Drag that tiny pea brain of yours from the gutter and go get me some spare blankets."

Felix seemed a little embarrassed, or shocked even, at Reks reply, and it took him a few seconds to gather himself for a response. When he did reply, it made Kiva smile a little.

"I'm sorry, Rek, I didn't realise she was your daughter. I'll go sort you out those sheets." And with that, Felix dashed from the room.

Kiva, still smiling, walked to Rek and hugged him. "You big lug, it would be an honour to be your daughter."

The smile returned to Reks face, and after a second, he returned the hug.

When Felix had returned with blankets, Rek asked if

Felix could have someone draw a bath for Kiva. A short while later some maids had appeared with buckets of steaming water. Rek left Kiva to her bath and went back down to the bar to see if any of his old friends had seen Tor, or maybe see if he could get a place on a ship going south.

When he had left, Kiva slipped from her worn and dirty clothes and sank into the warm bath. Instantly relaxing and a gentle sigh of relief escaped her lips as the water washed away the tension and dirt of her travels.

As Kiva's tension ebbed away, she felt oddly alone for the first time since Idrienne. It was more than the disappearance of Tor, but that she hadn't spoken to Argento either. The dragon had been such an amazing revelation to her, and she loved the song that Argento had taught her. With that, Kiva dipped her head under the water and got lost within the song in her mind.

*

Rek seated himself at an empty table in the corner of the bar. He smiled at the thought of Kiva enjoying her bath. Despite his anger at Tors disappearance, she had kept his spirits up and stemmed his anger somehow. But that anger was still there, simmering and stirring just below the surface.

Reks thoughts were disturbed as Felix came and sat down at the table with a flagon of wine.

"Its good to see you again, old friend. Its been too long. Last time I saw you, you were a little worse for wear. If I remember correctly, you were threatening to smash me and my bar in." Felix poured some wine into a goblet and slid it over to Rek.

"You were so drunk that I'm sure I heard your liver crying." Felix laughed loudly.

Rek chuckled himself and looked down at the drink that his old friend had passed him. It was then he realized that he had not touched a drop of alcohol since Bishop had picked him up at deaths doorstep. He could feel that the old thirst was still there, and he licked his seemingly dry lips.

"I shouldn't really, Felix. I'm trying to stay off the stuff." He said, pushing away the drink.

I don't blame you, but it's only one, and it's on the house. What d'ya say? Old times sake?" Felix replied and then drank his flagon in one.

"Go on then. One can't hurt" Rek acquiesced and drank the wine.

A few hours later, Rek could feel the wine, not as much as he pretended, but he had sung and laughed with his old friend. Felix had kept the wine flowing as they reminisced. Some of which, Rek had managed to pour away, not wanting to offend or to go back to Kiva drunk.

"It's good to see that you got yourself straight," Felix said as he pushed another wine to Rek. "I shall see you in the morning. Here finish the wine." Felix said, leaving the table.

Rek watched him leave and was surprised to see Felix escorted upstairs by what looked like pirates. Rek decided to see what was going on.

*

Felix woke with a groan, and he spluttered up a cough of blood and mucus. A look of confusion crossed his face as he looked down at the pavement from the roof of his establishment. A large man dangling him by his feet

Rek stepped onto the rooftop balcony. There were five men in all, and one held his old friend by the ankles and was dangling him over the edge of the Krackens rooftop.

"Where's the man Rekhaert, Felix?"

"Pleeease don't kill me!" Felix screamed out frantically. Why would I lie, he's downstairs."

"Doesn't matter anymore, Captain Paine said to leave no witnesses."

The men hadn't heard Rek approach, "Who's downstairs Felix, and why are they looking for me?" Rek looked about the group as he rubbed his nose with thumb and forefinger. "I'll give you one chance, and one chance only to put Felix down and walk away; can't you see we're having a conversation?" He looked around at the men and saw that no one was willing to back down. Rek smiled, "Oh well, let's get this over with then." And with that, the rooftop erupted into mad violence.

Rek shouldered into the first two men to get too close, using his massive bulk to send both men sprawling backwards. The other two circled and came at him from two sides. In one smooth movement, Rek swung right hook at the man in front, knocking teeth and blood from the mans' mouth, turning just as the other man attacked with a club levelled at his head. Rek ducked under the swing, allowing the man's momentum to throw him off balance. A shriek of pain escaped the man's lips as Rek grabbed him violently by the balls and the scruff of his neck, raised him high above his head in a show of strength. With a guttural roar, Rek threw the man from the roof.

There was just the big man left now. "Bring him in, take your friends and go or follow your friend!"

"Oh, I will go, and Captain Paine will hear of this."

Dropping Felix in front of Rek. "There are consequences,

Felix to disappointing the Captain."

Rek watched the men leave before giving Felix his full attention.

"Thank you, Rek I owe you my life!"

"Tell me what's going on?"

"There's a bounty on your head. Has been for days."

"You didn't say earlier."

"Captain Paine said he would clear my debts if I let him know if you turned up. Look, my job was just to get you drunk Rek. You and the girl were worth a hundred gold pieces each."

"Give me a reason I shouldn't throw you off this roof."

"Now I owe you my life, and my lender no longer wishes any kind of payment I wish to give."

"Wait, did you say each?"

"Yes, Rek, why?"

"They might have gone after Kiva!" And with that Rek ran down to the room. There had been a fight in the room, and Kiva was gone. Felix caught up to him, and Rek pinned him to the wall by his throat. "I am giving you the benefit of the doubt that you weren't part of her kidnapping; that way, I don't have to kill you. You say you owe me your life. Well, I'm collecting. I want whoever took her and you my friend will point the way."

Kesh
Chapter twenty six

Kiva woke with a headache that could have shaken the world apart. There was also a sharp metallic taste in her mouth, and her eyes did not appreciate the light.

When she could finally open her eyes fully, she found herself locked within a cage. She rubbed her forehead and tried to remember how she ended up in this predicament. Kiva wasn't prone to panic. Panic got you nowhere. She found, growing up on the streets of Sha'mack, a cool head and quick hands were essential to survival.

She thought of the two men who had become such a large part of her life, and it made her smile despite her situation. Looking around, she could see no way out of her cage unless it was opened. If she could get one of her kidnappers to check on her, maybe she could find an opportunity to exploit. Kiva called out. "Water, guard, I need water!"

There was no response, she tried again, but it appeared she was alone. With nothing else to do, she started to cry. Kiva thought of the song Argento had taught her, and it brought her some small comfort. Something to focus on to chase away the fear she felt. What if Rek didn't come? What if she was sold into slavery? What if... Pushing those thoughts down.

Thinking of Argento, she sang the Song of Morning.

The exact words of the song were foreign to her, but

Argento had said it was more about the implied cadence behind the words than the words themselves. The difference between seeing a morning and feeling it. Whatever that meant.

Kiva gave into the song and even got a little lost within it. The melody was intoxicating and powerful. Goosebumps popped up all over her skin, and she felt electricity spark around her. The song had a life of its own. Her head began to ache as it grew in intensity, and she was about to cry out when she saw an image of Rek.

It was as if he was part of the earth he stood on. The image wasn't very clear, but there was no mistaking that massive frame. She could see lines of power like roots, reaching down, but they were disconnected. She touched one of the many lines that radiated through the ground toward Rek while singing the song of Morning. Kiva watched as the energy found its way down new pathways and then suddenly she could feel him. Rek was coming for her.

The image blurred again, whirling and wailing inside her head colours danced. Kiva placed her hands against the side of her head as if trying to stop the dizzying effect. She concentrated hard and tried to control her breathing, just like Argento had shown her.

When her mind settled, she saw Tor. This time but, the image was grey and undefined, but she instinctively knew it was him. She felt his sadness and loneliness. There was also a little guilt that hung in the air. Whatever reason Tor had made to leave her and Rek behind, he had not taken it lightly.

Something caught her eye in the distance. It was a black void, cold and still against the swirling greyness of this place. Kiva felt a tightening in the pit of her stomach. Whatever it was, death and danger lay waiting there. Kiva felt herself being turned from the dark until once again; she was looking upon the face of Tor.

This time the image was clearer, and some colour had seeped into Tor's face. When she looked into his eyes, they danced with electric blue lightning. Kiva smiled. They were the eyes of Argento.

"Child, you learn quickly." Argento's voice was strong and majestic, yet full of warmth for her. "It is good seeing you, but this is no place for you yet. It is not safe. Why are you here?"

"I'm being held captive!" "Where's Rek?

"I think he's looking for me. Why did you leave us?" Tor's hand reached out and stroked Kiva's cheek.

She felt his fingers gently brush against her skin as if she stood in front of him. "You are dream walking, and I am too far away to be of any help little one, it is not safe for you here, and your body is vulnerable. Rek will come, Kairos told me we would all meet again in Sha'vel. What happened did you get to the ship?"

"The oracle is dead. We were ushered from the mountain. Rek thought you had killed her and disappeared."

"No, I did not kill Kairos. She did give me some answers, however. She said if we went together you would die and that in Sha'vel I could find answers if I came alone. There has been passage booked. You must escape and make your way to the docks.

And with that, Kiva felt herself being pushed back to her body. When she opened her eyes, she was back in her cage.

BANG! A loud crash shook Kiva from her singing, and she saw a large man standing in the doorway to the room.

"Shut that noise up, or I'll put ya to sleep again!" He snarled, sounding a little drunk and dazed as if he had just woken from sleep. He was a rotund man with big, black curly hair and his beard was braided. After a moment, the man seemed satisfied that he had shut her up, turned a little drunkenly, and mumbled under his breath as he skulked off.

Kiva tutted and folded her arms in a sulk. "Arse!"

She cursed under her breath.

"What did you call me?" The drunken man had appeared at the door again looking more than a little angry and flushed.

Kiva was shocked at the man's sudden reappearance, but she wasn't afraid. Instead, a plan formed quickly in her mind. She smiled.

"I called you an arse. However, that's an insult to all the arses in the world. I mean you're so stupid that you couldn't pour water from a jug with the instructions on the bottom of it. And as for that smell!" Kiva feigned being sick from his smell.

Her insults had the desired effect on him, and he stormed towards her cage. He grabbed her through the bars and lifted her from her feet. Now that he was this close, Kiva noticed that his eyes were red and glazed over. She smelled his fetid breath which did make her want to puke.

"How about I skin you a little, huh? We could still sell your scrawny arse with a patch missing on it. I don't imagine it would put too many buyers off you, not with yer pretty face and blonde hair." The drunken guard laughed to himself, pulling Kiva closer with one arm as he drawn a knife from his belt with the other.

Kiva took advantage of his drunken grip and kicked out at him between the bars, catching him square in the groin. The drunk released her from his grasp as he fell to the floor. He rolled around there for a while until he regained a little composure. He eventually got up into a kneeling position. His face was contorted in pure rage as he held his now bruised groin area.

"Why you little bitch!" The drunk ran at Kiva, his arm shooting through the bars of the cage as he tried to grab her again. This time she was ready for him. She had taken a step back so that he had to stretch further into the cage. Swiftly, Kiva pirouetted under his outstretched arm, locking her arm over the drunken guard's elbow. She then pulled with all her weight so that his arm bent the wrong way against the bars until she heard a loud snap, which was very shortly followed by a satisfying scream of pain.

The arm was now a bloody mess, with bone protruding skin at a sickening angle.

"Now, you arse, I would appreciate it if you could pass me the keys to this damn cage and I will be on my way." Kiva smiled at the injured man.

"Please, I can't. They'll kill me," sputtered the drunk, tears rolling down his cheeks, his mangled arm on the floor of her cage.

"Well, why didn't you say?" Kiva laced every word with an exaggerated, sarcastic tone. "Tut, tut. There's me, worrying about myself being sold as some sort of slave or having you skin my arse. There I go, totally ignoring your need to breathe." She then stomped on the drunk's arm for good measure, making him scream once again.

"Keys! Now!"

The guard quickly searched for the keys with his free arm. Kiva took the keys and opened the cage door.

*

Rek's panic was palpable. It had been several hours now since Kiva went missing. Felix had known of several of the pirates' hideouts, which Rek tore through as if he were fighting children, but to no avail. Despite knocking the seven hells out of every pirate they found, none of them knew anything of Kiva or where she might be.

Exhausted and frustrated, Rek sat down upon a bench and stared out towards the sea. Rubbing his fore and middle finger back and forth across his forehead, he tried in vain to release the tension stored there. With a sigh, he watched the waves crash into the shore. "There must be some other hovel that you've not thought about, Felix," each word laced with accusation. Rek was on edge, and his temper was fraying.

"I'm sorry, Rek, but we've checked every place I know. I have pulled in every favour too. If she is still in Kesh, then she is somewhere that only the leaders of the pirates know." Felix paused and sighed deeply. "If she has left Kesh, then... then, I am sorry." Felix seemed to want to say more, but words failed him.

Rek hated to believe that either scenario was true. He would rather have fought a thousand enemies than feel the pain and helplessness that he was feeling. He knew that Kiva was in real danger.

Suddenly, Rek felt a strange sensation flow through him. An image of Kiva sat in front of him, crossed legged and humming some strange song. He tried to place his hand on her, but it just passed through. Kiva's image then dissipated like smoke in the wind. He couldn't see her anymore, but when he closed his eyes, he instinctively knew where she was. Not the street or building, but he had a direction.

"Rek! Rek! What's going on? You look spooked," Felix said, also looking around to try and see what Rek was looking at.

Rek stopped where he was and tilted his head to one side as if listening to something. "Felix, do you hear that?

It's Kiva. Rek set off in the direction that the song was leading him leaving Felix to play catch-up.

*

Kiva, now released from her cage, dragged the unconscious guard into the cage and locked it. She turned and looked around the room. It was plain with no windows and just one door, which led into the room in which her guard had been drinking. She assumed there must have only been one guard since no others had come to their fellow's aid as he lay screaming on the floor. Either way, Kiva would have to venture forth with caution as she crept into the next room.

She found a table and chair with a half-empty bottle of whiskey on top. Behind the table was a heavy door. She slinked over to it quietly, trying the handle and found it locked. Kiva cursed until she realized that she still had the guard's keys.

After going through several keys unsuccessfully, relief washed over her as the lock clunked open. She slowly opened the door. Every little squeak and creek thundered through her senses. She expected every guard in the building to pounce on her. Luckily, the Thieves guild of Sha'mack had taught her well. She knew that this effect was just from the adrenaline running through her body.

So, she breathed in deeply, and slowly calmed her rapidly beating heart.

Peeking around the door, it led to a sparsely lit corridor. Kiva smiled. The shadows were her friend, and she would use them to help her escape.

She surreptitiously walked along the corridor, pressing herself against the wall so that she was all but one with the shadows. The corridor eventually led to a landing that encircled a large room. There were a number of other corridors leading off the landing, which made Kiva guess that this was a rather large complex. There was quite a lot of noise coming from down below, and she dared herself to peek over the railing to see what was happening. What she saw made her gasp and tremble for it confirmed what kind of place she was in.

In the room below were dozens of men. They were all men of wealth, evidenced by the way they were dressed and adorned themselves in jewellery. They all sat round tables, talking excitedly and laughing at each other's jokes. Her attention was drawn to the far end of the room, where a naked girl stood upon the stage. She looked as if she was drugged out of her mind, barely even able to stand. Kiva shuttered. The girl on stage was of a similar age to her.

Anger now rose in her chest. This was a skin auction where girls of all ages were sold into sex and slavery. It took all of Kiva's control to stop her from jumping down and trying to save the girl from her ordeal, but she knew that it was fruitless.

The room was protected by twenty or so guards, dressed in black steel and chainmail, their faces covered by plain black masks. Each held long staffs with rather large and sharp blades placed on top. Her only hope to stop this was to find a window to escape from and then tell Rek about this place.

Kiva knew that Rek was only one man, but he would know what to do to save this girl and any others that may be in the compound. Just then, she heard a floorboard creak behind her. She turned in time to see two big hands grab for her. Kiva tried to fight back, but the man was too quick and too strong. His hand covered her mouth and pinched her nose at the same time, cruelly suffocating her.

Kiva desperately kicked out, but to no avail. Her lungs burned and begged for oxygen. She tried to scream, but there was no air for her to scream with. Very slowly, her vision began to blur, and her world slipped into a black void.

Kiva's Escape
Chapter twenty seven

Rek raced through Kesh. It was like he could feel her heartbeat through the ground leading him to wherever she was. Felix was barely keeping up with Rek's pace, lagging a good ten paces behind and gasping wildly.

"Rek, you mad bastard. Slow down just a little, will you?" Felix leaned heavily against the wall, trying without success to catch his breath. "I'm not quite as fit as I once was."

Rek stopped and looked at his friend and grimaced. "If anything happens to that little girl while you're catching your fucking breath, I swear I will turn you inside into your outside. Now, fucking move it!" And with that, Rek tossed Felix forward, giving his arse a kick.

Felix picked up the pace with renewed vigour.

Rek smiled to himself as he caught up. He had always been a good motivator. He moved ahead, allowing Kiva's song to lead him. He didn't quite understand how but he could feel her through the ground, and he could sense her getting closer. The further he went, the stronger the feeling became.

After a short while, they arrived at a massive warehouse situated upon the docks of Kesh. It was an ostentatious building, and it stood out like a sore thumb compared to the surrounding buildings, which were shabby, and run down. The warehouse was painted bright white. It had narrow, tinted windows that were barred and what seemed to be a solid oak door perched between two sturdy columns.

Guards were placed on either column to the entrance. Rek turned to Felix and gestured to the building. "She's in there, I can feel it. Do you know what that building is?"

Felix, still panting, was crouched beside Rek. "Well, its Paine's auction house. It's very hush, hush. All I know about it is that you've got to be a member and extremely wealthy. And I'm neither, unfortunately."

Rek studied the building and rubbed his chin. He knew Kiva was there and he needed to find a way in. The question was, how subtle did he want to be? That question was answered as he threw one of the guards, through the solid oak doors. Motivator: yes. Strategist: definitely not.

Unhooking his throwing axes from his thighs, he stepped into the reception area of the auction house. Inside stood a well-dressed man, whose face was in such a state of shock, that his eyebrows almost reached the top of his receding hairline.

Rek calmly walked over to the well-dressed man until he was towering over him. "Last night, you or your associates kidnapped a young blonde girl." Rek gave a deliberate pause to roll his neck until it made a cracking noise. Head tilted slightly backward, looking down his nose at the puffed-up clerk.

"If you do not fetch her to me right away, then you and your associates are going to learn that I have a specific set of skills, of which I am more than willing to use on anyone in this fetid cesspool. This will be your only warning."

The clerk's face was now covered in his sweat, and he had begun to tremble violently, gripped by indecision. His eyes were wide and darting to and froe. Finally, he came to a decision. He slowly backed away from Rek towards a bell.

The well-dressed man's breathing was ragged, but a stubbornness was now etched upon his face. His shaking hand slowly raised itself towards the alarm bell.

Rek raised an eyebrow. "You really, really don't want to do that." He warned, ever so calmly. But the welldressed man did not heed the warning. His arm shot out and rang the bell as he screamed out "Guuaards!".

His scream was cut short by Rek's fist connecting with his chin, with what Rek would describe as a very satisfying crunch. The well-dressed cleric crumpled to the floor. Within moments, a dozen or so black-clad guards appeared to face Rek.

Felix had caught up to him by this point and slid his sword from its sheath. "You'll owe me after this," Felix stated with a smile on his face.

Rek nodded. "Just stay behind me."

And with that, the violence erupted. Rek slung his two axes, which slammed heavily into the masked faces of two of the guards, knocking them dead. He then unclasped his hammer. Rek wielded the massive two-handed weapon in one hand as if it weighed no more then a feather.

The hammer swung viciously through the air, anything that got in its way was devastated. In his first swing alone, Rek had taken out three guards.

Alongside Rek, Felix had slashed, parried and countered furiously. The warrior had lost none of his fighting skills. Within moments, they had cleared the room with minimal fuss.

"Well, that was a bit too easy. They really don't make guards like they used to, old friend," remarked Felix chuckling sliding his sword back into its sheath.

Rek nodded in agreement, retrieved his axes, and the two men walked through into the next room.

"Ahhh shit. Why do I hang around with you? It always ends the same way," Felix moaned.

Rek just smiled as he looked at the thirty or so guards staring back at him and replied to his old friend, "Felix, you can leave if you want, but you know you've missed this."

"Well, shall we get on with it?"

"Aye."

With that, the two men charged at the remaining guards.

*

Felix's world became a sea of silver and red as he danced through the thrusts and parries of the guards. He had missed this feeling, and he realized as he dodged the gleaming edge of a sword that was aimed for his throat. He hadn't known until this moment why his life had felt so empty and sedate. Nothing could replace the feeling as your world slowed down, and you felt the adrenaline pump through your body because your life was at risk. He blocked a spear thrust and fired in a riposte that sliced through his attackers jugular, releasing a crimson spray across the room.

He breathed deeply, it felt like the first real breath he had taken in years. When he exhaled, his body felt primed and invincible. He was a man reborn, a man of purpose and direction. The steel blade in his hands sang loud and proud now. It cut a bloody path through his foes. Twisting and turning like a dancer amongst the steel, his counters always seeming to find their target.

Every so often, he would steal a glance at Rek as he swung his massive war hammer around him like it was made of air. The hammer's arc was so great that not even the guards with spears could get within striking distance of him. If any guard was unfortunate enough to get within that arc, they were quickly dispatched with glorious violence.

Suddenly, there seemed to be a respite to the fighting. The last few guards had backed off from the two formidable attackers. They were beaten and bloody. Several guards lay unmoving on the ground in front of them.

Felix could see the doubt that had seeped into their stances. He made a move to attack them while they were at their weakest, finish them off before they recovered their bravery. But he was stopped by Rek's meaty hand as it shot across his chest. He gave Felix a shake of his head.

He then turned to the remaining guards and threatened, "Leave now, and you'll see tomorrow. Stay, and you will not see nightfall. Your choice, lads."

It was plainly said. A simple statement, but it had the desired effect. The guards took all of a second to decide to drop their weapons and leave. Felix watched them warily as they passed him, his blade at the ready just in case one of them decided to change their minds.

When they had gone, Felix turned to his friend shocked with disbelief. "What the bloody hell was that?

We could have had them all!"

"We're not here to kill, Felix. We're here for Kiva!" Rek stared intently towards Felix until he conceded and backed down.

"Come on! We need to get her and get out of here." Rek set off in a determined fashion.

*

Kiva slowly woke and realized that her hands and feet were tied. She let out a muffled moan through her gagged mouth. Looking around, she found herself in a dark and dingy room, much worse than the first room she had woken up in. The stench of mildew, damp and decay hung heavy in the air. There were no windows, and the only light source was from a candle which sat upon a small, round table. Around that table sat three men, who seemed to be arguing.

Kiva recognized one as her original guard, the drunk whose arm she broke. She did not like her chances now and began to wriggle in an attempt to loosen her bonds. It was then the drunk saw she was awake. A sadistic and cruel smile appeared on his face.

"Come on, boys. The little bitch is awake." The guard moved forward with grim intent, his arm splintered and placed in a sling.

The other two men were of the same age and ilk as the drunk, and all three men had a dark and dangerous look upon their faces.

Despite the three men leering over her, she refused to give in to the fear she felt in the pit of her stomach. Kicking out, catching the drunk on his broken arm, she made him squeal like a pig. He wheeled away in pain, landing awkwardly on the floor.

A flurry of blows rained down on her from the drunk's companions. Kiva curled into a protective ball, trying to shield herself from their blows.

A loud crash put a stop to Kiva's pain. As the two attackers turned towards the noise, whatever it was, it had snuffed out the candlelight and sent the room into pitch black. A shallow light came from the corridor outside of the room, illuminated the immense frame of a man. His shoulders hunched, and his fists clenched.

It was Rek, he had come for her, and her heart soared. He charged into the room like a raging bull. The first guy tried to block, but it was already over as Rek's axe thunked into his forehead.

The second man dropped to his knees and pointed at the man with a splint. "It was his idea, just a little fun, he said!"

"And you were going to join in?" Rek replied, closing the distance between them. He grabbed the kneeling man by the jaw. The man barely struggled as Rek snapped his neck; it was all so quick.

Kiva screamed a muted warning through her gag as she watched the final deviant guard dash towards Rek with a knife in his good hand. Rek turned in time to catch the guards arm, which he twisted sharply backwards, forcing the man to release the blade he held. Rek then drove his weight into the twisted arm, making it snap grotesquely.

Kiva watched on in shock as Rek slammed the drunk's head into the wall four times, punctuating each slam with a word, "Don't! Hurt! My! Kiva!" The man was probably dead after the first hit.

Rek ran over to Kiva, untied her and removed her gag. "I'm so sorry, Kiva. Please forgive me. I'll never let you down again. I promise." Tears ran down Rek's cheeks as his emotions spilled out of him. The tears dripped down onto Kiva's face, leaving dirty streaks as they streamed along the bruises and welts.

At that moment, Kiva seemed so vulnerable and weak, until she smiled and released a tiny, pain-filled laugh. "Rek, it's okay. They barely scratched me. I would have been in more danger if they set a pack of kittens upon me. Now, can we get outta here?"

Rek could not help but laugh loudly. For some strange, unexplainable reason, he had never felt prouder than in this moment with this amazing little girl.

"Come on then, Princess. Let's leave this shithole." Rek gave Kiva a hand up and headed for the door.

As they left the darkened room, Kiva saw Felix, who had been standing guard. There seemed to be a hint of guilt about him, but she couldn't figure out why. She let it slip from her mind, for she had much larger concerns to deal with.

Kiva turned to Rek and pleaded, "We can't leave this building standing. They sell kids here Rek. It needs to burn."

Rek had never before heard Kiva speak with this sort of tone, but he understood the pain and anger behind it.

"Okay, little one. It'll burn, don't you worry.

Felix, lanterns."

Felix understood. He slid his sword from its sheath and smashed every lantern that he passed, letting flaming oil leak down the wooden walls and pool upon the floors. Before long, flames licked the ceilings and plumes of thick, acrid smoke rolled through the building.

By the time the trio had made their way down the stairs and exited into the main yard, the whole building was aflame. Alarms rang out throughout the docks, as dockworkers and guards ran about with buckets trying to extinguish the fires as the rest of the inhabitants fled the scene.

Rek walked with Kiva by his side and Felix a few steps behind. They walked calmly through the panic and chaos that now engulfed the docks. Fire bells rang as the fire spread. Back on the street, they disappeared in the chaos.

Felix turned to Rek and asked, "So, what now?"

"We leave town before they come looking for us. Do you know of any ship captains that will take us?"

"Aye, maybe? Let's go... oh shit!" Felix exclaimed.

"What is it?"

"It's Paine!" Felix discreetly nodded to where a giant of a man stood.

As Rek took in the huge man, it occurred to him that he had a similar physique to himself. If not for the big, flame-red beard, Rek would have sworn he was looking at a reflection.

It was then that the two men locked eyes, and even across the madness of the crowd swarming around them, By reputation, Rek knew the man known as Paine, and he could see the

man had recognized them. Rek watched as

Paine signalled to several different spots on the docks, and just like ants emerging from nests, dozens of men appeared from seemingly nowhere and started to make their way towards the trio.

Rek calmly turned to Felix and proposed, "They've spotted us, Felix. There's too many to fight this time, and I won't risk Kiva again." He glanced around quickly as the approaching men neared them with every second that passed. "We need to split up, old friend. Else we are all done for."

Felix just smiled and nodded. The two men embraced arms like the warriors they were.

"It's been great seeing you again, but the man who wants to kill me is over there. Let me be clear, though. Our debt is settled, may the Gods be with you both!"

Before Rek could stop him, Felix had sped off in the direction of Captain Paine, his sword held high above his head. Rek stood stock still for a second before realization hit him. He was half tempted to chase Felix, but he knew better. This was Felix's choice, and it would give Rek and Kiva a chance to escape. Rek began to run.

Two of Paine's men appeared in front of Rek and tried to grapple him to the ground. He dipped his shoulder and charged them, sending the two men sprawling. Another dived at his legs and received a brutal knee to the face, smashing his cheekbone. Rek continued to forward like an enraged bull, barging people out of his way. He couldn't afford to look back except to make sure Kiva was at his side. There were dozens of Paine's men behind him, hunting them down like a pack of wolves. His only chance of escape would be to lose them amongst the crowd, so he ducked down into the flow of the people on the docks as best he could.

Kiva pulled on his arm. "The docks Tor said we had passage on a boat."

Rek had questions, but he was out of options, and he could see some ships at the docks. It was better than where he was, taking Kivas hand and keeping his head low and following the crowd until they began to thin and disperse. Finally, he stood upright, his back aching, and looked around for any trouble that may have been heading his way. They had somehow made it to the docks safely at least for now.

Turning to run again, he stopped in his tracks as he saw more men blocking off all other exits from the docks. Lead amongst them was the pirate Captain Paine signalling Reks location. Backing down a pier, as their escape roots continued to be cut off, the pirates closed in on Rek and Kiva.

Rek's heart sank. He knew that he couldn't fight his way out this time; there were too many. He would be damned if he was to go down without a fight, though. His only worry was how to get Kiva to safety. A whimsical and familiar voice sang out above him.

"Are ye gonna stand there all day, laddie? Or are ye gonna shufty your arse up here?" Rek turned and looked up to see Bishop throwing down a ladder from the side of a ship. "Come on, will ye! We hav'nee got all day now." Rek smiled and helped Kiva up the ladder before following her. He heard Bishop shout some orders on deck. The ship's large sails unfurled and took wind. A dozen or so men with large poles appeared from nowhere and began to push the boat away from the pier. Before long, the ship was away and leaving Rek's pursuers quickly behind.

As Rek climbed aboard, he was greeted by a smiling Bishop. He gave the little man a huge hug.

"Bishop, you're a beautiful little bastard! I thought you weren't coming or that you disappeared with Tor."

"What? And miss all the fun?" Bishop asked through a toothy grin.

Voyage
Chapter twenty eight

Kiva and Rek had been on the high sea now for a couple of days. Their getaway vessel was a merchant ship called Howl. Kiva instinctively knew there was more to Bishop than he was revealing, but she could never get a serious answer out of him. Well to be fair, he had tried to answer her questions seriously, but every time he opened his mouth and spoke, she would burst out in a fit of laughter. His accent was so cute. It annoyed Bishop no end, but her glee brought cheer to the rest of the crew and even the indomitable Rek.

Today Kiva was entertaining herself talking to the masthead of the ship. Upon boarding the ship, she drifted to the prow, never having been on a boat. Before Rek could do, or say, anything she had cut her palm with one of her throwing knives and placed it on the giant wolf's head. Rek ran over and grabbed her hand. He was about to ask what she thought she was doing, but as he inspected her hand, there was no blood, and neither was there on the masthead. Rubbing his eyes, Rek decided he must be tired. It'd been a long week.

"You can let go of my hand, Rek!"

"Sorry, I thought you cut yourself."

"Don't worry. I'm not hurt."

"I think I need to find a drink and somewhere to rest." Rek left Kiva at the prow, unsure of what he saw as he walked away. When he looked back, Kiva appeared to be talking to the huge wolf masthead. He decided to let it be. He would ask her later.

Kiva was fascinated to learn that the carving was in fact, alive. She had heard the captain say to Bishop that to see the ship you must bleed on it, she didn't know why but she knew it to be true. As Rek walked away, In front of her eyes, it looked like the layers of the hard-worn exterior paint began to crack and break off, floating away on the breeze like embers from a fire, disappearing leaving only the ocean that was breaking on the prow. Slowly the carving started to come to life, fur, muscles, and even a wet nose sniffing the sea breeze. The most surprising thing was the eyes. A light steel blue like Tor's and right now they were watching her. The giant wolves head turned slightly in acknowledgement as it sniffed the air. Kiva's face lit up at the transformation. No longer some slow merchant's trawler, this ship was alive.

Running her hand through its fur, Kiva asked, "What's your name?"

"I am Howl, named for the warning in the dark."

"Well, Howl, the warning in the dark, what do you bring warning of?"

"Bad seas and anything else I can sniff out little one."

"My name is Kiva not, little one!"

The conversation between Howl and Kiva continued in this manner for days, and she learned a lot about him.

Cargo ships like Howl, roughly fifty-foot long Ta'luburun ship was carrying exotic cargo; Raw copper, jars, glass, ivory, gold and spices.

Howl was one of twelve ships made by the Fenn to help the side of light in the days of the Chaos war, but most of these crafts were destroyed as abominations, created from untouched souls of baby boys.

Howl had told her in a manner-of-factly way how the ships had been made. Howl didn't seem to understand why she was so upset

"It hadn't hurt, and there was a great need." Howl had told her when he saw how upset she was.

Kiva had cried late into the night at what she had been told. She hadn't been asleep long when the crew had been rudely awakened by the noise of the ship's masthead. Howl was calling its crew to arms. Something was wrong! A mist had settled in around Howl, and the ocean threw the craft this way and that. The fog was so thick you could barely see through it, as it settled on the deck.

Sailors ran furiously about looking for the cause of the disturbance. The whole ship had slowly started to tip. Sailors grabbed rigging or anything else available as the ship rolled precariously to one side, then all of a sudden, rocked violently back into an upright position. Whatever force had hit the craft, it had taken them perilously close to capsizing. A shadow to port was getting larger and larger hidden by the mist. Whatever it was it lifted the ship's bow out of the water, then disappeared again leaving the vessel to crash back into the waves.

Kiva, Bishop, and Rek emerged on deck to find the craft buffeted by waves. Kiva could see the captain at the front of the ship talking to Howl and made her way towards them. Rek and Bishop were arguing about whether or not there was a howling noise at all. Rek was not a seafaring sole and had kept to himself on the voyage hidden away below decks. He had only risen from his selfpity due to the raucous noise of the crew. His mood wasn't improved as he was rudely awoken and thrown from his place of rest onto the hard floor.

Rek looked over the railing as something of monstrous proportions raised from the depths. If it weren't for the imminent threat, it would be a creature of wonder, one giant eye flanked by two smaller. The creature's limbs looked a bit like the Ashiri's fans used for seduction. However, these barn sized appendages held only the allure of destruction. Amidst the different blue colourings lines of ice-white seemed to emit the fog that was surrounding the vessel. This thing from the deep looked like it could eat the ship in two bites

*

Bishop ran to the stern of the boat removing his clothes as he went. No one was looking in his direction. Their attention fully engaged with getting them as far away from this behemoth of death as quickly as possible.

Bishop began his transformation. Hands turned to claws, and skin turned to fur. Muscles rippled under tearing skin as wings of purest white pushed out from his body and arched outwards catching the wind like mighty sails. Unlike the boat held in the thrall of the fog pouring off of the creature, Bishop, unperturbed, launched his feline bulk into the air and flew straight at the sea monster. He took only a moment to throw a cursory glance at the deck of the ship and the mayhem below.

Bishop had never seen one up close before, but he had read about them in the great library of Kishar. The Sea Dragons were survivors of the great freeze that lived on the ocean floor. They were a relic of another age, bred for destruction by a long-dead race called the Gobi. They were rare and deadly.

Unable to think what would make it venture from its home, Bishop knew he needed to distract the creature, or his mission would be doomed. Above water, it was vulnerable, and with little choice in what he must do next, he needed to attack the creature head-on.

*

On the ship, Rek could see Kiva talking with the captain near that damn wolf masthead. He wasn't happy about Kiva being above decks at all. After Kesh, he was just glad she was holding it together and if talking to the masthead helped her, well so be it but, It wasn't the time to be talking to an imaginary bloody wolf or getting in the way of the captain. As he got nearer, he could hear them yelling something about someone not being blooded yet! Rek couldn't believe the captain was playing along with Kiva's game. He even looked to be talking to the masthead as well.

"Kiva get off the deck. This is no time for silly beggars."

"Have you bled on the ship yet?"

"I may not have bled, but if you don't get to safety below deck, you're not too old to go over my knee!"

The captain with a knife in hand went to grab Rek over Kiva's head. It was a mistake he would not make twice. Rek blocked with his right and landed a left cross that sent the captain two feet in the air before landing him dazed on the deck.

Pulling Kiva behind him, Rek yelled, "What in seven hells do you think you're doing?"

He felt Kiva drag on his arm, then a sharp pain. Rek growled looking down. Kiva had cut his hand. She dropped the knife, and her hands came up in a calming gesture.

Rek looked at his hand and watched in slow motion as a drip of his blood dropped towards the deck. He watched as it disappeared into the wood. He blinked, and when he opened his eyes again, his head was clearer than it had been in days. What had been a battered merchant ship became something more. Finally, he understood the ship was alive just as Kiva told him.

"Rek?" Kiva ventured. "Rek, I had to do it. I'm sorry." Kiva had to shout over the commotion on the deck. The captain was shaking himself off. Kiva had positioned herself between the captain and the big man. "He wasn't going to hurt you; he was just trying to make you see."

"He should have bloody said so!"

Some of the ship's crew were yelling and pointing at another mythical creature from legend. A Griffin had appeared and was attacking their foe.

The fog the creature was emitting remained just above water level except for occasional wisps, which Bishop whipped up as he flew at the behemoth. Bishop felt almost sorry for what he must do to the beast; it was probably just hungry. Claws flexed in his giant paws as he attacked clawing at the creature's eyes.

Against him, the Sea dragon had no defence. It opened its maw and released a harrowing sound of pain and defeat. The smell of whatever it had been eating was almost enough to knock Bishop out of the sky. Pumping his wings a couple of times, he lifted himself above the stench, noting that the ship had somehow broken free. He made one more pass. The Sea Dragon seemed to have gone, retreated to its home in the deep. Its foggy emanation dissipated on the wind.

Bishop was about to catch up to the ship when he noticed the ocean below him start to climb into the air.

The crew on the ship watched as a Griffin, a creature from a children's bedtime story, pounded its wings climbing higher and higher as the Sea Dragon exploded from the ocean beneath it as it rose into the air. The sea dragon propelled itself closer and closer, opening its gigantic maw as it propelled itself into the air. It looked for a second as though the beast of the deep blue had its prey, but something much older and more powerful exerted its power; gravity.

Bishop was looking down into the abyss. His heart pounded in his ears as he climbed with all his might. Jaws of death had momentarily surrounded him and begun to close. He thought about how ironic his death would be. After all the cat usually eats the fish, but before he was crushed in the creature's maw, it started to fall away, and his momentum carried him to safety.

Howl, in the meantime, had managed to pull away from the creature's fog. The behemoth crashed back into the ocean with such force the wave it created picked up Howl hurling the merchant ship in the direction of a small island.

*

Rek and Kiva made their way to the stern of the ship. They watched in wonder at the epic fight off the prow, and when the ocean picked them up, he had held on to Kiva and the guard rail for all he was worth. As the craft splashed back, down Howl used the momentum to take them to safety.

It looked to Rek as though they would escape to safety until the massive flying feline headed their way. He started to pull out his trusty hammer while attempting to push Kiva behind him.

She sidestepped his hand and yelled, "It's Bishop!"

"What do you mean, it's Bishop?"

The crew froze as the Griffin landed amidship and started to shrink before their very eyes. Wings now covered its body as it shrank even further until leaving a buck naked child-sized form of Bishop. There was absolute silence for a moment, and then a cheer went up from the crew.

Rek was reeling at what he just saw, and as he stepped back towards the masthead, the now visible Howl turned to him ever so slightly and smiled.

Howl remarked, "Now there's something you don't see every day!"

Island
Chapter twenty nine

Bishop watched as Rek took Kiva below deck. A smile touched his face. When he had first met Rekhaert, he had been a broken shell of a man. It was hard for him to see what relevance this man could have in the fight to come. The man's soul had a sickness leaving him cold and empty. What he saw now was a different man altogether. Now strength resonated from Rek and Bishop understood that Kiva had played a large part in that.

The captain approached the now diminutive Bishop. Still unsure of what he had seen, yet grateful for the intervention. He coughed lightly before stammering, "Y-YYour clothes, Master Bishop." He held out the clothes Bishop had left on deck.

Bishop took them gratefully and began dressing. "Dinnee call me master. Ye need not fear me, captain. Now tell me what's the state of yer ship?"

"Not good, sir. Howl took some damage during the attack. We're seaworthy but only just. If that monster decides to come at us again, we'd be easy pickings."

"I see," Bishop responded simply as he finished dressing. "Can ye ship sense the beast?"

The captain replied, "If it is close Howl will alert us."

Howl was anxiously scanning the water's surface as the two men approached the masthead. As they got closer, they could hear Howl was making a keening noise.

"What's wrong boy?" The captain scratched behind the massive wolf head's ear, which seemed to calm the ship slightly. "Howl, where's the Sea Dragon?"

"Somewhere between us and High Garden, Captain."

"Then we cannee go back, and we cannee stay on the open sea. Captain, do ye have a telescope." Bishop placed the scope to his eye and scanned the horizon. "When I was fighting the beast, I saw a chain of wee islands. There, to the east of us." Handing the captain his telescope back, Bishop pointed him towards the islands.

The captain gave a disapproving click through his teeth. "We can't dock there, sir! That's Mors'Terrem."

"And what pray tell does that mean, Captain?"

"Those islands are cursed. A place of the dead."

For a spymaster of Bishop's calibre, it was a pleasant surprise to hear of something completely new to him and curiosity piqued in his mind. He could see, however, that the captain did not share in his curiosity. The captain's brow furrowed with concern. He ran his eye over his crew, seemingly worried that any of them may have noticed their topic of conversation.

"No ship in three hundred years has docked there and sailed to tell the tale. It is said to be where the gods imprisoned all the evils of humankind. A forsaken place."

"I can see ye fear the unknown, Captain. How long would the repairs take?"

"The damage is significant but is easily fixed. Maybe a day at the most."

Bishop was about to press the matter when Howl began keening again. In the distance, a bellowing moan could be heard. The Sea Dragon was still stalking them.

Bishop turned to the captain. "Can we outrun the beast?"

"Howl?"

"No, Captain, I'm already taking on water."

"It seems te me our choices are limited, and if we cannee outrun that monster or survive a second attack, then we dinnee have a choice, laddie. Set a course for Mors'Terrem. In my experience, possible death is a world better than definite death."

The captain hesitated briefly looking to the islands making a warding symbol with his hands and saying a prayer of some kind. Bishop only just caught some of the words on the wind. Something about, "Blessed be the Riverking." and "watch over them," then "the crew ain't gonna like this," before the captain turned meeting his gaze with a determined look.

"So be it! Howl set sail." The captain grumbled as he walked off to give the orders to the crew. "Hoist the mast and raise the sail."

Bishop decided he may as well join Rek and Kiva below decks. He needed to know what Rek knew about Tor's whereabouts and now was as good a time as any to face him.

Climbing the ladder below deck, he was surprised to see Rek was sat alone in the mess next to the galley, seemingly lost in thought gazing at the dining table. Kiva must be in the hold. Before making himself known, he grabbed a gourd of wine and took a swig. The change always made him thirsty.

Rek looked up as Bishop as he slumped into one of the chairs opposite him at the table. "What are you, you're not human?" Rek stated bluntly.

"It's complicated, laddie."

"Well, un-fucking complicate it!" Rek demanded, spittle flying from his mouth.

Bishop wiped his face dry and sighed deeply. "Okay, you deserve the truth, but it is long and complicated. In its simplest form, I am a Griffin. As far as I know, I am the only one left of my kind."

"When we first met, how did you know where Tor was or his connection to me?"

"If I said prophesy I dinnee think you'd believe me, but dinnee forget I am the Hand of the King. I had been tracking a dark cult called the Fidelus on behalf of the King. My investigations have led me te believe they have infiltrated at the highest levels. I needed someone capable who was no longer in the Kings service, and then I found ye, fevered, half-starved out of yer mind. I needed an ally and a capable one. You had been a legend in the

Athanatos until Aleator disappeared, but you had been out long enough that I felt you could be trusted.

"Okay so finding me was just luck but what about

Tor?"

"I dinnee know Tor was there but, Kairos had told me I must free whoever was imprisoned, then clear the way for them and leave someone I trust to help once the prisoner was free. You seemed perfect for the job. I plan on having the Athanatos wipe the accursed church from the face of High Garden."

"Why not help him yourself?"

"Te say people tend to be scared of Griffins would be an understatement, but for the dark one's emissaries, we have an almost instinctive hatred of one another. I dinnee want to alert our enemies to mi involvement so they could change their base. A fight to the death would provide no substantial gain. My mission was to gather information, and at Kairos' bidding, I was to help the prisoner no more than setting him free. So I sneaked inside the building, finding Tor was the prisoner was a surprise te me."

"So, you released him, then left him to escape or die."

"The idea was to kill any that got too close as he escaped from the air without alerting the temple to my assistance or giving away my true form." "What happened?"

"Something I did not expect. You see me in this form.

I am not agile or strong. I would have been a hindrance. Also, I need to stay in the shadows. I had to try and conceal my involvement in this. It was to appear the prisoner escaped on his own as Kairos said if he could not, we would all be doomed. I was flying high above ready to aid if attacked, just as I killed the Va'nahual pack that chased you off the cliff near Idrienne. Unfortunately, some horrid little thing got the better of me or else I would have been there with you."

Bishop sighed once more and scooped a short stick from the floor. Using it as a cane, he hobbled over to a sack of grain and sat down. This image of a small, feeble middle-aged man was a sharp contrast from the beast that Rek had witnessed just a short time ago.

"Unfortunately, I underestimated our enemies' strength, and it nearly cost us our lives back in the forest.

For that, I apologize. It was foolish and arrogant of me."

Rek still didn't fully trust the man, but he conceded that Bishop had always been there to help when it was needed. Rek had enough enemies to choose from at this moment, and with friends in short supply, he knew he needed Bishop on his side. "Okay, Bishop. I will trust you. But do not think for one second that I don't know that you're holding something back from me."

The conversation was interrupted by the sound of shouting and fighting above deck. Rek and Bishop glanced at each other. "What's going on up there?" Asked Rek.

"It may be a small mutiny." Bishop quickly explained their situation and the island of Mors'Terrem. "Rekhaert, we need to stop this mutiny before it gets out of hand."

Rek stood up, stooping under the low ceiling. With his fists clenched and his jaw tight with built-up tension, he walked to the door of the cabin. Kiva started to join the two men above deck, but Rek turned to her and apologised, "I'm sorry, Kiva, but things are gonna get rough up above and I need you to stay down here."

She began to argue that she'd been through worse in the last few days, but then she saw the sadness in Rek's eyes.

"Please, Kiva. Just this once, let me keep you safe."

Kiva harrumphed and sulked her way back to the bunks. "You better not enjoy yourself up there then; otherwise, you owe me."

Rek smiled. Even when she sulked and was angry at him, Kiva always seemed endearing to him. "I won't." And with that, Rek and Bishop moved to go above deck.

As Bishop and Rekhaert got to the deck, they found the captain surrounded by his angry crew. Insults and slurs were being shouted alongside threats of violence. Rek noticed that some of the crew's hands had found their way to the handles of cutlasses and daggers and decided immediate action was needed.

The big man stormed his way into the crowd of sailors, knocking them out of his way until he reached the captain at the centre of the melee. "What the fuck is going on here?"

The sheer size and presence of Rek made the crew back away, but he still felt the captain's tension.

One of the sailors gathered the courage to speak up. "It's you and your friends. You're cursed." A chorus of cheers and murmurings reinforced one of the sailor's confidence into continuing. "I've been on this ship five years now, and have we been attacked like that... by fucking monsters? Never! And now the captain says you want us to sail to Mors'terrem of all the fucking places. Well you, that fucking midget, and your little slut can..."

The sailor's tirade was interrupted as Rek's mammoth hand clamped down on his shoulder and collar bone pinching hard upon the nerves bundled under the skin. The sailor buckled to the floor his face contorted with pain. Rek applied a little more pressure until he felt the sailor's collarbone crack. The sailor cried in pain as he folded up on the deck.

Rek addressed the crew in a deep, fearsome grumble.

"Anyone else? Any of you shit bags disagree with the good Captain's orders? If you do, I suggest you jump overboard and start swimming. Now, get back to your jobs!" Rek commanded, with maybe a little more aggression than was needed, but he was tired, and his patience was worn thin.

The crew backed off in the face of the angry giant and slowly went back to their business. The captain thanked Rek and asked if he had ever considered becoming a Captain. He grunted grumpily in reply and headed back below deck. He caught Bishop smiling to himself. "What you smiling at?"

Bishop turned his smile to Rek and observed, "You wonder why I wanted you along for the journey? I think that situation explained beautifully.

A couple of hours later Rek came topside to check on the crew and was surprised to find Howl had navigated them to the coast of Mors'terrem. The still waters had a haunted feeling, hulls of ships protruded from the waves like some sea graveyard. Rek couldn't decide if it was the ghosts of the dead seamen that were giving him the chills, or the light breeze pushing them along.

The crew were clearly on edge, and he knew why. The place had a certain foreboding feeling about it. There was a feeling they were being watched. Rek had spent many years in the field travelled a lot of High Garden, and the one thing he had learned to trust was his instincts. "What do you make of this place, Bishop?"

"I'm unsure; there is a certain familiarity to some of the damage I can see."

"What do you mean?"

"You see there." They had sailed further inland, and rotting husks of once-great ships were now clearly visible.

"The gouges in the hulls?"

"Yes."

"They are claw marks. Howl, do you sense anything in the waters?"

The masthead was making a quiet keening noise, clearly unhappy with their predicament.

"No, I sense nothing alive, just hundreds of ships sunk beneath the waves."

"I dinnee wish to come to shore here, Howl. Are there any inlets or coves ye can sense?"

"Around that outcropping, Master Bishop." The masthead's fur stood up in fear and anger.

"Dinnee worry, Howl, I'm more powerful than I look.

I'll protect ye."

Howl seemed happy with this and stopped keening. "What about the marks?" asked the Captain.

"Sea creatures don't usually have claws. Once at the inlet have yer men make camp. I am gonna scout ahead and make sure we ain't heading into a trap."

Bishop made his way through the scared crew. Once at the raised stern area to the back of the ship, he faced the crew while undoing his shirt, he raised his voice so all could hear. "Dinnee fear the unknown, shipmates. I am with you." His shirt hit the floor. "I will keep ye safe and scout ahead." As Bishop dropped his pants, a stunning pair of beautiful white wings shot out from his back, wrapping Bishop's diminutive figure. A moment later, they separated, revealing a creature of power and grace. Bishop roared at the sky as if in a challenge to whatever evil force that may be watching. Stretching newly formed muscles and with that, he leapt to the air, his giant wings carrying him higher and higher.

The boat rocked at the departure of the griffin's great bulk. The display seemed to have raised the spirits of the crew, who had lost their daunted looks and found a look of determination.

Bishop circled the area and saw no immediate threats. From what he saw, Mors'Terrem was devoid of life. He did not know what had happened here, but at one point, it must have had a broad culture as he had seen the remains of what must once have been a larger civilization. Bishop still could not shake the feeling of having been here before. Or the more unsettling feeling of being watched.

He was about to make his way back when he saw the remains of what once would have been a grand building. It was overgrown but may have some clues as to what happened to the ships and society. He decided to take a closer look as he flew nearer he could see a single solitary figure stood watching him from the buildings grand foyer. He would have been hidden from most within the shadow, but Bishop's eyesight as a griffin allowed him to pick out the detail easily.

Bishop swept down, assaulting the earth as he landed. The figure had stepped back inside the building. There was a power here, but he was not afraid. If anything, he had an odd sense of home. There was a scent that took him back to a to long-forgotten memories. Any hesitation he may typically have had seemed to have disappeared as he padded into the building.

*

Back at the inlet, Kiva and Rek were helping make camp just off the shore with a few of the crew members. The rest of the crew had been set about tasks to repair Howl. There had been no word or sighting of Bishop for an hour now. The crew began talking about omens and a need to be away from the island.

There was a fair amount of talk about not needing to set camp as they didn't need to stay that long. Kiva had been listening to the sailors and was worried they might just leave if Bishop wasn't back.

She decided to approach Rek. "Rek?"

"Yes, princess?"

"You know that thing you did to find me? Can you sense if Bishop's okay?"

"I don't know how I did it. It was like I heard you singing, and then I could just feel where you were?"

"Will you try for me?"

Rek nodded and closed his eyes. A moment later, he opened them again. "I'm not getting anything."

Kiva was squinting at him. "It didn't look like you tried very hard. You barely closed your eyes," she scolded.

"That's all I did last time."

"What did you actually do last time? Step-by-step."

"Well, I was about to punch every sailor in that port like a drum until they talked. I needed a place to start. Then it just happened. As I blinked, my eyes locked shut, and it was like I was floating down streets and alleys. It almost felt like I was propelled by the earth itself."

"Were you scared?"

"No, I was just worried about that nosey little monkey that had been following Tor and me around."

Kiva stuck her tongue out at him. "I'll give you a monkey." She started climbing and tickling Rek. The pair rolled around for a moment laughing, the worries of the journey fading away if only briefly. "Are you going to try properly, or do I need to tickle you some more?"

"Okay... okay, but I'm not promising anything. He's probably fine." Rek sat on the floor. He closed his eyes once more.

After a couple of minutes, Kiva asked, "so do you know where he is then?"

"No."

That's when the pair noticed raised voices from the crew. "Look Cap'n we will have the repairs done in the next couple of hours and intend to be gone not long after. These people are not our concern, and to stay is death!"

"Master Bishop is making sure we're fine, Silas."

"You say that Cap'n, but he's not been seen in an hour. The curse as ad im!"

Rek and Kiva had made their way over. Rek spoke first. "Had who?"

"Yer flying friend. The islands cursed, I tell you." The Sailor in an act of bravery shouted the words in his captain's and Rek's face, either of which could probably snap him in two. "If yer not on the ship when the repairs are complete, the crew have agreed we'll leave anyone not aboard here." The man seemed to realize who he was being so direct with and added in a quieter voice. "And no amount of thumping from either of you is going to change that; Cap'n, Sir." The sailor gave a cursory nod at the last and stormed off.

*

Bishop walked into the ruins of what would once have been a stunning temple. Above the door carved in the old tongue, a language mostly dead in High Garden, it read 'Temple Of The Winds where those with Faith can ride the skies'. Pushing forward, he entered what appeared to be the main hall. That was when he saw them, two massive yet beautifully carved griffins with the appearance of being in flight and circling each other. He was unsure how these majestic sculptures were suspended. The wings met at the centre of the room.

There were walkways that had been constructed over and around this masterpiece of engineering. Light broke through gaps in the ceiling dancing on dust motes in the air. Whatever this place was, it must have been a sight to behold in its day. It must have been neglected for centuries. Crawling plants had grown up the walls. A couple of potted trees had escaped their confines to reach out of the building into the light of day.

As he padded closer to the centre of the temple, a voice broke Bishop from his awe.

"Come closer, mi eyes are not what they once were."

Bishop's eyes followed the sound to a large shape just outside of the falling light at the back of the room. What he saw there took his breath away, stopping him dead in his tracks.

"Dinnee fear me. I willne harm ye."

"I do not fear you!" replied Bishop enunciating every word shocked to have his own accent parroted back to him.

"Then come closer, that I might see ye."

A shape stepped out of the shadow, just far enough that the light would illuminate his form before lying down once more. A form Bishop was only too familiar with. Bishop couldn't believe his eyes. The Anunnaki had very few records of the Griffin. The Oracle had been one of few with any idea of his heritage, but like all things she prophesized, they were vague like the visions she shared.

"Welcome youngling. I imagine ye have questions. I had begun to think the prophesy lies and that I was the last of the Griffin."

The old griffin remained motionless as Bishop came closer.

"You're a Griffin?"

"Glad te see our legendary eyesight isn't failing one so young, even if yer mind doesn't seem as sharp!"

"I'm nearly three hundred years old."

"Is that two hundred and a half? For a Griffin that makes you a teenager. I am coming up to five thousand years of age, and I can feel my time is nigh. I have a great many things to tell ye about who we are and what our place has been in the world."

"I have people waiting for me. They could be in danger."

"I am the only danger here, and I will not attack yer ship."

"So, all the sunken ships... the death... that was you?"

"In mi prime, yes, and in years gone by this island held many of our race who protected this island with our lives."

Bishop was unsure what to make of the response. He certainly didn't want to believe he was kin to killers.

"I see some doubt in your eyes, youngling."

"The slaughter committed on those bays, tis reprehensible. I am not like you!"

"Do not judge what ye dinnee understand. All sailors know not te sail to Mors'Terrem. In the distant past, there was no need to kill. The island was protected by our great civilization, but our ranks have slowly diminished until we could no longer protect our borders. Those of us that were left had to make it clear to pirates and thieves; their presence was not welcome. It was a necessary evil."

"Necessary, a word I have heard bandied about by many a killer."

"ENOUGH! If you wish to judge us, fine, but save your petulance until you know the whole story. You should have more faith in your own kind!"

"Faith is in short supply at the moment, and I have never known any others, old one. I will hear ye out. Shall we start with names? I am Bishop."

"A great name! I am Orion the last custodian of this island. Let us take our human forms and take refreshments. You are safe here." Orion sniffed at the air. "Two of your companions are making their way here."

Bishop hadn't noticed until Orion stood and the light caught his side, that one of his wings was broken and his side was severely scarred. His eyes had whitened considerably leading Bishop to believe Orion was blind. The old Griffin gathered his strength and transformed his body back to that of a small white-haired balding old man. Bishop had never witnessed the transformation before. "What happened to your side?"

"I'm not as strong as I once was, and the enemy fought with a fire elemental by his side. Once they had the Sun Disc, they disappeared into a wall of fire but not before the djinn gave me the damage you see."

"The Sun Disc was taken?"

"It will forever be my shame that it was taken on my watch. Come, I have much to tell you and your friends will be here soon."

*

"Yes, Kiva, I can sense Bishop is that way." Rek still didn't understand how he knew. It was almost instinctual. He waved his arm in the general direction of Bishop.

"Then let's go and find him!" Kiva was already jumping up and down with excitement.

Rek wasn't about to leave Bishop behind or leave Kiva with the sailors. Letting out a deep breath, he grabbed a few things from the makeshift camp, and he set off into the jungle with Kiva.

It hadn't taken more than a couple of hours for them to find the ruins and within them Orion and Bishop. The two men stood in matching floral cotton, and gold robes neither had pants or shoes on. The stranger was the first to speak.

"Welcome... I am Orion the last guardian of this island."

The two men had a surprising resemblance to each other. Rek protectively draped his arm around Kiva. "Bishop, who is this man to you?"

"Although it tis strange for me te say, he is a griffin, like me. I thought I was the last of my kind until now. Rek, he says he's got something for us."

"I am dying, and when I do, this island will sink once more. It was prophesized that you would all come. It is not by chance we meet here. This temple was built a millennia ago by our creator, the Goddess of Faith. Once we were of the Fenn and when all is against you, you will find the Fenn a powerful allied, just tell Lyssa you are the wards of Orion.

"What do you mean we were once Fenn?" Asked Bishop

"At the end of The Age of Wonders, the Creator tasked the Fenn with the task of keeping man from anything to do with the seventh god and to cleanse the land of any of his creations. In this task, the largest and strongest of us were chosen "

Looking at the diminutive pair Rek couldn't help laughing at least he started until Orion silenced him. The snarl that came from the small man belied his size, but it was more than a sound it was like the ground shook and Orion radiated threat.

"Careful child of earth lest ye make me angry!"

"Sorry please continue great Orion," Rek responded reproachfully.

Orion took a deep breath, and the menace left the hall. "No I am sorry, you must understand we are a proud people. What you see was the intention. A way for us to infiltrate and hide our true form as a griffin and for millennia we have destroyed all that have stood against us and collected knowledge humankind is not ready for. I am afraid I dinnee have time to teach you more my time is upon me but know that if you are true to yourselves, you will overcome the darkness that falls upon the land. In this task, the three of you each have a gift to choose, choose wisely, and you will each gain a gift from the goddess to aid you on your journey."

"And if we choose wrong?" Rek asked respectfully.

"Then you will die…" The old man's voice hung eerily in the air.

"Bishop, it's time to go!" Rek commanded.

Orion pointed at the doorway they had entered through, and giant slabs of stone moved and blocked the entrance. The entire building shook. Rek told Kiva to find a doorway to stand in as he drew his hammer and faced Orion. When Rek turned back from Kiva, he was face-toface with Orion the Griffin.

"The hammer will do you no good." The ground had stopped shaking, but Orion's voice rumbled through the hall. "Look around this hall. You may take one item each, choose carefully."

Bishop was still taking in that the only other of his kind was dying. "Yer sure there is no other way Orion."

"There is always another way, young blood, but there is rarely more than one right way!" Orion laid down, and Bishop walked over to sit by him.

When the room sealed, every wall, pillar and obelisk hung with treasures from the age of wonders. Tome filled bookshelves and statues of long-forgotten heroes. Most of the items held elemental magic.

The Griffin had been tasked to collect these items so the Thall would not use them. The Thall's were what was left for the most part after the Creators rage separated man from his ability to create magic with thought alone.

The magic had been given to the elements to hold until humanity had evolved and was worthy of such power. The removal of magic rendered all curses or magical weapons inert for the most part. Very few elemental weapons existed in High Garden.

Rek had been in the Athanatos long enough to recognize this room held enough power to crush nations. He was awestruck as everything appeared seemingly out of thin air.

Kiva's voice echoed down the hall, "We can have anything?" Her voice came from somewhere above.

Everyone was looking up now, as Kiva ran along the outstretched wing of one of the circling Griffin statues and jumped a meter gap onto the other rotating statue. Running across the breadth of the other griffin up the outer raised wing, she jumped to a platform.

Rek shouted, "Kiva, what are you doing? I told you to find a doorway."

"But there is a doorway," Kiva shouted back.

On the other side of the door was a matching earring and necklace with the most beautiful blue jewel she had ever seen. They were on a plinth in an open box. Kiva closed the box and tucked it under her arm. Then waited for just the right moment to jump onto the giant circling wing as it passed. Then as it circled back onto the first obelisk, she had climbed to gain access. Her small fingers found easy purchase on the old stone, climbing down until she was confident enough to jump the rest of the way.

Rek stood tapping his foot, a stern look on his craggy features.

Kiva ran straight at him and gave him a massive hug. "I'm sorry, Rek. You know I just kinda get curious. You forgive me, right?"

How could he say no? "We will talk some more on this another time."

She gave him a squeeze. "Thanks, Rek!" No sooner had the words left her mouth, then Kiva circled him and sat with Bishop in front of Orion. She had the box out in front of them. "Do these count as one thing?"

"Yes, little one. They are more than what they seem though. The earrings will allow you to hear the rhythm and song of the element of water. It was Faith's favourite piece of jewellery. It is said she even crafted them herself. The necklace holds a tear of our Goddess Faith, and it will heal any illness or injury. A good choice, although your friend just looks and does not choose!"

"C'mon, Rek. Something must have caught your eye?" Kiva asked excitedly.

Rek walked across the room to a statue of a warrior maiden carrying a shield, but the shield was not part of the statue just mounted on it. Rek didn't know why, but it was almost like he had felt this shield as soon as it appeared. Pulling it from the statue and putting it on his arm, he tried a few moves with it. He had never seen such a shield. It was pronged like a split butterfly axe on the bottom, and the points had been sharpened. He didn't recognise the metal, but it was so light he could barely tell he was wearing it and more than that. The shield had somehow connected him to the earth filling him with strength. Rek walked back over to Orion with the shield.

"A great choice, my mountainous friend. The shield is called The Ocean Break. It is a fighting shield and dependant on the strength of the bearer it can draw strength from earth and water. And you, my... Bishop, you choose nothing?"

"Are you dying?"

"I will fulfil my destiny. Now choose yours!" commanded Orion.

One of the other statues that had appeared was that of an armoured Griffin with a couple of Fenn archers riding on its back. In front of this impressive sculpture was a small pillar holding a belt. There was a plaque. It read: Orion's belt. He was unsure why he wanted the belt. It wasn't particularly ornate.

"Then I will take your belt."

"I am glad you made that choice. So I will answer your question. We, Griffin, don't die, we simply become part of the universe. You see those three stars?"

Bishop hadn't noticed before the vaulted ceilings glowed with a perfect representation of the stars.

"We call those three stars the Griffin's Belt and it's where I must go, but before I go let me see you wear my belt!"

Bishop put the belt on over his robe as he walked back over.

"Now change into your true form as a mighty

Gryphon. Dinnee worry about the robe."

Bishop did as he was bid, but something strange was happening. His robe had grown with him. It was like the robe became liquid. As he finished his metamorphosis, he was head to toe in armour. It was strange the armour fit him perfectly and seemed to move with him. He suddenly felt powerful and let out a roar, but something about the helm made it come out like a screech.

"That's it. The belt will mimic any clothes you want in your human form but as a Griffin. This belt creates a battle armour called the Gryphon that will make you near invulnerable. Your tail now carries a club. Your claws are protected and enhanced.

Most importantly, your wings can also now be used as weapons. The eagle helm is more than just decoration. Ye will now have magnified sight and yer roar a call to fight by the light and a piercing weapon against the dark.

Go to the carving of a door in the wall at the back of this hall. It will open for you now to another place. The island already begins to sink, and your boat has left you behind. You must be on your quest and save the Dragonborn.

His enemy is the one who broke my wing. They must be stopped at all costs. Do not be sad for I go back to my goddess and my family."

Standing up, Orion was a sight to behold. His giant head rubbed Bishop's, and then he seemed to change into a blue light that disappeared in the direction of The constellation of the Griffin's Belt.

Rek could feel the land sinking. "It's time to go!" Grabbing Kiva, they ran to the back of the hall. As they approached, runes around the doorway danced and shifted, until the opening filled with blue light, then disappeared. It was a doorway into the sky over eastern High Garden.

Rek stepped back. "Fuck that!" he protested fearfully.

Bishop turned to Kiva and Rek. "Get on."

Kiva was only too happy to oblige and was upon Bishop's back in seconds. It had taken water entering the hall for Rek to work up the courage. No sooner was he aboard than Bishop soared through the doorway.

When Rek and Kiva looked down over Sha-vel, it seemed so small from the back of the Griffin. Rek was still unsure how he felt about Bishop being able to manifest into such a creature. He was, however, a pragmatist and however, he looked at it, this journey would've taken a lot longer by boat. He also reminded himself that Bishop had nursed him back from death's door and given him a purpose. He was passing through some low hanging clouds he had to admit it had been a pleasant journey. Rek had never been good with change, and at the moment, his whole life seemed in flux. Looking at the city below them, he didn't know how, but he felt Tor was down there someplace.

Reaching around Kiva and stroking the side of Bishop's giant feline neck to get his attention, Rek pointed down at Sha'vel

"TORS, THERE!" He shouted into the wind by the side of Bishop's ear. Down, down, down they went in a slow spiral.

Kingslayer
Chapter thirty

Achill manifested in Blaquart's office. He watched from the shadows for a moment. Blaquart had gained a new member of staff, a young woman. Blaquart smiled as she batted her eyelids at him. Achill watched as she played Blaquart, pretending that her breast touching his arm as she put his drink on the table was unintentional. Now was not the time for stupidity. It was time for the general to receive a lesson.

As Damaris was on the way out of his office, she turned to face him and winked before disappearing down the corridor. Blaquart was happy. He didn't know when he had been happier. He exhaled a contented breath. Taking in the surrounding his power had afforded him. He watched the coalescence of Achill, claws growing from the hands, fire red eyes, and a smile filled with dagger-like teeth spread ear to ear.

Achill eyed up the newly appointed Lord Commander. "This is not the time to be oafing around with some milkmaid. You will be able to have anything you want once we take power."

For a moment Blaquart looked as though he was going to protest, but Achill continued anyway.

"Gabriel is on his way to the king after a long talk with one of the librarians. They were gone for some time before reappearing, and Gabriel seemed to leave with a sense of purpose."

"What do you need of me, Achill?"

"It is time to neutralise the threat. You wanted a distraction, I have burned down the librarian chapter house."

"You can't just slaughter all the librarians!

"I have proof to the contrary. Can't you hear the fire bells? If nothing else, this is a perfect distraction for you to enact your plan."

"Gabriel?"

"He is heading to the king. Whatever you are planning, it needs to happen now. If you cannot get control of this situation, I will find someone who can." With that Achill faded back into whatever dark place he came from leaving Blaquart to ponder his future.

It was time for the Lord Commander to put his plan into action before it was too late. Grabbing a few things, he left his offices behind hopefully for the last time.

*

It was getting late. The sun hung lazily in the sky. Leander the King was reflecting on the day. Reports from the south had him worried, and there had been a lot more tension in the council meetings. He looked about the great hall. Six of the Athanatos, three aside, stood guard one at each pillar down the large walkway to the throne. These were his personal guard, his elite. He recognized each one of them and even knew their names. The outer ring of the room, including the two standing to attention at the door, were members of the Peoples army. Gabriel had argued vehemently that the throne room should be only be guarded by the Athanatos, but politics had allowed for a small contingent in the palace.

The majestic doors to the throne room opened. Inside the grand awning stood Blaquart of all people. As Gabriel would say "A man whose stature is only rivalled by the heels on his shoes." Leander smiled at the memory.

Blaquart issued some command to the men at arms on the door, then approached the aisle leading to the King.

The first two Athanatos stepped forward to search Blaquart from their places either side of the aisle. He kneeled, making their search a little more complicated.

For Blaquart, it was now or never. He would have to hope that his planning would be enough to get him through what must come next. He had always hated kneeling, but now it had a purpose, flanked by two of the Athanatos his heart was beating fast now, and a bead of sweat rolled down his brow. He looked around. The other Athanatos seemed almost asleep at their posts.

Leander watched Blaquart kneel. The little man seemed unsettled and whatever the man's issue Leander would rather scrub the floors in silence than listen to him prattle on about some imagined inconvenience.

As Blaquart stood, he took a blade from each of his boots. Quickly burying them deep into the necks of the Athanatos searching him on either side. Blood gushed from the open arteries giving the little general a monstrous look as he was showered with their blood.

The remaining four stepped forward, weapons drawn, ready to defend the King, but Blaquart had managed the unthinkable, he had infiltrated the Athanatos. The four remaining Athanatos looked at him like he was a halfeaten worm in an apple, something insignificant that needed removing.

For a moment, he was unsure of himself. That moment was as short-lived as the two Athanatos he faced looked shocked. Blaquart had managed to buy the loyalty of two of the men, who had just driven their swords through the other Athanatos midsections and were now twisting the blades.

*

Gabriel had hurried back to the palace from the library. He needed to bring his suspicions to the King. As he arrived at the entrance to the throne room, his way was blocked by soldiers of the People's Army. The gall of these runts to block his passage.

"The King is indisposed."

"Not from me, he isn't. If you do not remove yourselves from this doorway, I will be forced to remove you."

The following scuffle was brief, Gabriel stepped forward and punched the first one that had spoken in the throat. The man dropped to the floor, gasping for air. The second had gone for his weapon, which had pleased and shocked him. After all, their job was to protect the king. So in one way, he was glad, but for them to attack him was outright madness.

"I am the Hand of the King. How dare you pull your weapon on me?"

The man continued to draw his sword with no reproach, a mistake he would not make again. Stepping into his space, Gabriel covered the hand, removing the sword with his hand and brought his other hand over and down on the guard's forearm with savage force. The snap of bone could be heard, even over the scream of the guard who fell to the floor clutching the wreckage of his arm. Stepping over the bodies of the injured guards, he reached out to open the large ornate doors which seemed to give way just before his hand got there. One of the Athanatos, a big man, named Raif had come.

"What goes on here?"

"Raif, will you get these malcontents from my sight before I do something they will regret."

"Yes, sir." The big man moved to the side to let the Lord commander through.

Gabriel stepped past Raif into the throne room. What he saw next shook him to his core.

Dead members of the Athanatos littered the floor. At the other end of the room, another one of his Athanatos held the king in a neck lock crushing the air from him. The King reached in his direction, a plea for help in his eyes. In less than a second Gabriel had drawn his elemental sword Ninti and gone into fighting position.

A voice echoed through the throne room with the ringing of swords being drawn around the room.

"Hello, Gabriel. I wouldn't do anything silly if I were you or I will order Leander's neck snapped!"

"Show yourself, Blaquart. You coward."

Blaquart walked into the central chamber from behind one of the colonnades.

"If you harm the King, Blaquart, I will cut you in half."

"Big words. Pass your sword to Raif."

Gabriel still couldn't believe Raif had turned on him. What could Blaquart possibly have offered them? The big man came around him.

"Now don't do anything silly, Gabriel. Just give me the sword."

Ninti had no blade as it was made of wind and air, but without Gabriel's tie to the elements, it was nothing more than a fancy handguard. He threw the handle in Blaquart's direction. "If you dar..."

"Stop with the empty threats. Raif, tie his hands."

"You'll never get away with this Blaquart."

"But I already have and with your help!" "My help?" Gabriel spluttered.

"Yes, if not for you pushing our beloved King into sending out the Athanatos to find news and support the south I couldn't have done this. With Raif picking who stays and goes, I was able to ensure only the ones loyal to me remained at the palace - Well nearly all." Blaquart jibed gesturing to the dead Athanatos as he picked up Gabriel's sword."

"So, let me get this right; everyone knows only you can wield this blade... Correct?"

Gabriel ignored Blaquart and looked to Raif who was tying his hands.

"How could you betray the king? Your brothers? Hell, me?"

Raif looked at his old commander in the eyes. "I follow who I must to get what I need. I will be wealthy under my new King, as will my brother and the others who have changed allegiances."

"You're not Athanatos. You're all whores, taking

Blaquart's small cock and lapping up his promi..."

Raif punched Gabriel hard in the jaw. It felt like he had been kicked in the face by a horse. Dropping to one knee Gabriel spat blood on the floor. He nearly fell over without his hands for balance.

Blaquart had started again. "So back to my original question, only you can use this sword?"

"You know that you stinking cowa..." Before he could finish the statement, Raif hit him again, this time knocking him over.

Blaquart had started walking to where the king was being held. Once he was within striking distance, he turned back to face his nemesis.

He wore a satisfied smile at seeing the great Gabriel humbled and bleeding on the floor.

"I'll kill you for this," swore Gabriel. "You sons of whores." Gabriel waited for another blow from Raif. A painful betrayal from a man he had trusted above all others.

"Poor, poor, Gabriel. What will you do if the king dies?"

"You'll never get away with it, Blaquart."

"You see, that's where you're wrong." Blaquart nodded in Raif's direction, and pain exploded across Gabriel's cheek. It took a moment for his head to stop spinning. He saw Blaquart was next to the King, and it would seem he had one more surprise for him.

Blaquart put his hand on Ninti's hilt.

"Good, you're back with us, now you can watch. I'm glad only you can do this!" A blade of black smoke coalesced from the hilt in Blaquart's hand, unlike when Gabriel held Ninti.

"You people and your superstitions. The sword may not yield all its secrets to me, but you are not the only one who has elemental energy, behold the dark wind."

Blaquart was in striking range of King Leander. Gabriel watched in horror as the dark blade clove the king clean in half. Raif's little brother who had been holding the king also appeared to have been cut in half at the mid-section, blood, guts, and bile hit the floor. Oddly the legs remained standing for a moment, one last defiant stand. Then they fell too. In those few seconds, Raif had left Gabriel with his hands tied on the floor and was halfway to Blaquart. "You have killed my brother!"

"Raif it was an accident. C'mon you can't think I meant to do this," squealed Blaquart.

"I'm gonna tear out your eyes!"

"Raif," Blaquart pleaded "Raif... what do you want? Just tell me, and it's yours?"

The big man thought of the most outlandish thing he could "I want Sha-vel."

"It's a deal. You will be Lord of Sha-vel!"

"And one more thing."

"What?"

Raif punched Blaquart so hard he spun like a top. To Blaquart's credit, he managed to stay conscious. Blaquart made a mental note to have Raif killed some time in the near future. Taking a moment to gather his wits, he said, "Right, help me with the body, Raif. Your brother was a hero, cut in half while defending the king from the Mad Hand." Blaquart entreated to Raif. The last was meant as a jibe for Gabriel, but as he looked at the spot where he was, and Gabriel was gone.

*

Gabriel had taken advantage of the brief distraction. He knew if he did nothing, he was dead. He must presume that those left of the Athanatos had also been bought off.

He needed to get away so he could plan. Breaking his thumb, he had managed to free his hands. Bishop had assured him he could trust Emmel and so he would. He just needed to make his way to the little man's home unseen.

There were secret tunnels throughout the complex known only to the King and his royal Hand. Gabriel would need to make use of these now.

He could hear the alarm go up in the palace. How had Blaquart used Ninti? Whatever he did, he broke his connection to the weapon. It had shocked him. He had no memory of anyone being able to do that. In any case, debating whether a thing could, or couldn't, be done when he had borne witness to it was a waste of energy.

Gabriel was starting to feel the withdrawal from Ninti. He felt a sharp abdominal tearing. He wretched, emptying his stomach. He hadn't noticed the blood before.

The whole city seemed somehow louder. The librarian chapter house was on fire, surrounded by people furiously trying to put it out. He couldn't see Emmel in the crowd. Every fibre of his being wanted to sit down and rest a moment, but he knew if he stopped, he would probably die. He had one last hope... That he could find sanctuary in the library.

At this stage, he was unsure of his thoughts. He stuck to the basics, one foot in front of the other. After what felt like an age, he made it, and he could swear he saw Emmel.

He called out, or he thought he did. Gabriel hit the floor hard, and his breathing slowed, skin pale. The last thing he remembered was Emmel chastising him for smoking in the library. He smiled, and the world went black.

*

Flames roared amongst the buildings. Emmel had been helping to put out the fire at the chapter house and was heading back to inform the other librarians of the tragedy at the chapter house when he saw Gabrel stumbling in his direction.

Emmel managed to help Gabriel to the library, but Lord Marshall was bleeding badly and was on the verge of passing out. Half dragging his old friend, They made their way into the library.

Dead bodies of the remaining apprentices lay strewn across the main hall. Their bodies ripped and torn as if some wild creature had attacked them. Smoke filled the room as several small fires burned. Emmel looked away. He could not bear the sight. Whatever visited the chapter house was here. Emmel only had to get them to the portal stone.

It was a struggle half carrying, half dragging a catatonic Gabriel through the blaze "Not long now,

Gabriel. Stay with me. Nearly there."

At the end a large corridor that went past several more rooms, each containing a horrific scene of death and fire. Emmel was on the verge of breakdown with his loss, but Gabriel needed him, so he focused on getting them out of there. Laying him against the wall hidden behind a large statue, Emmel began tapping individual bricks with his ring. The wall started to ripple and disappear, opening to the King's Vault.

He was just about to drag Gabriel through when a voice caught Emmel's attention coming from the closest hall on the left. It was one of his students, Able. The voice seemed so close it stopped him in his tracks. Walking to the entrance, he could see a creature made of shadow and flame hulked over Able. Emmel recognised it as a Djinn.

"Where is he?" it hissed menacingly.

Wide-eyed, Emmel watched the beast slash at Able. Panic set in, and it was like the thing sensed his fear.

Horror filled his soul when the creature looked right at

him. Emmel began backed away, and the Djinn started toward him.

Grabbing the Lord Marshal's prone body and dragging him to the portal stone.

"Well, what have we got here?" The Djinn hissed from the entranceway Emmel had just been stood. "Nowhere left to run!" Its dagger-like talons were scratching the walls as it made its way towards them.

"You'll get nothing from me!" Emmel responded, stepping through the portal with Gabriel. Looking back through the gateway, the vile creature nearly had them. Its raised taloned hand was ready to strike. Emmel hit the wall and closed the portal.

The Djinn's arm connected with was stone, a blue wall of flame erupted on its arm momentarily engulfing it. The Djinn cried out in surprise and pain.

The silence was the first thing he noticed, then his own breathing so loud in this secret place. Absent the fire bells and death.

Mathias Assai himself had passed down the secret of travelling through these stones, or at least the ring he wore carried the memory. The stone accessed several locations, but at the end of the Chaos War Assai closed down the network. The ring he wore, as far as Emmel knew was the only way to use the stones. The vault was secure, located hundreds of miles away in the belly of the mountains of Manthripur. His order was forbidden to explore outside this vault and had been tasked with securing dangerous items here. He would have to be careful. The creature was a Djinn.

Emmel was a keeper of the hidden histories and the protector of the greatest treasure nobody had ever heard of. If Kishar was ever compromised, he was under strict orders to destroy the ring and with it any easy access to this vault.

It didn't take Emmel long to realize Gabriel was without his sword. If his bond was severed, the man would likely go insane or die, neither of which was an outcome Emmel could afford. Taking a pendant from his neck, he fastened it around Gabriel's neck.

"This is the charm of Illya. It was created to heal magical wounds, even those we cannot see. Can you understand me, Gabriel?"

"Waaater?"

"Yes, of course." Emmel scurried off to return a few moments later with a gourd of water.

"What happened?" asked the little man passing Gabriel the water.

"Blaquart happened. The little shit! I will gut him and show him his insides. He got to the Athanatos, and they have killed the king. He has taken control."

"Blaquart killed the king... How?"

"Yes... Leander was cut in half, and somehow he used my sword to do it!"

"Was the blade dark and smoky?"

"Yes, how did you know?"

"It's worse than I thought. Blaquart has made a pact with an ancient and fearsome creature called a Djinn. There are very powerful pieces in play here Gabriel. A game where the board is obscured so you cannot tell which side is which."

"Then we need to make the game come to us, where our pieces allegiances are assured."

"How would you do that?"

"I would find those that were sent out. I will create rebellion and take back the palace."

Emmel appeared thoughtful for the moment. Gabriel's head had cleared enough that he knew he must be back in the secret catacombs. Realizing he was still lying down, he tried to sit up, but Emmel's hand pushed him back to lying down. He felt as weak as a day old puppy. "And where would you go to accomplish this?"

"South... I need to catch up to the real Athanatos if we're to stand any chance of taking back the throne from the usurper."

"Do you crave the throne for yourself?"

"No, but Blaquart cannot be left in charge."

You cannot defeat him alone, and I must insist you rest." Emmel knew Gabriel's lucidity was an initial reaction to the charm and would soon pass. Emmel poured some tea in Gabriel's mouth. "Sleep, and I will get us out of here."

Sha'vel
Chapter thirty one

Sha'vel was a grand city and home to a large compliment of the People's Army. Tor had even seen members of the Athanatos patrolling. He had kept his head down. Some called this the frontier as it was the closest city to the Thall homeland and was considered a staging point for many of the patrols. It was a place to re-stock and rest before once more entering the flatlands.

Rain poured down as Tor entered the inner city of Sha'vel. The dark gloom of the night reflected his mood. He had understood the need to leave Rek and Kiva, but it still did not feel right. They had been through too much together, and now he felt alone. Kairos told him that he must find the man that time forgot and something about a secret garden, she insisted he be alone, or his friends would die.

A smell of cheap perfume and some kind of stew wafted down the street toward him. His stomach growled. He decided he would have some stew. Tonight could be a long night if he found what he was looking for.

Argento had been silent, hidden away within his dreams. It was probably a good thing, as Tor did not feel like talking to anyone, such was his mood. It had been a couple of weeks, and he still didn't feel he had made any progress.

Tor followed the smell to the Inn. A pleasant escape from the rain which had been off and on for a few nights now. The Inn was poorly lit, a strong aroma of stale mead and roasting meat permeated the place. Something caught Aleator's eye as he reached the bar. A wanted poster behind the bar, and it had Rek's face on it.

Wanted for High crimes against the Crown, treason and murder.

Rekhaert Stone

Bounty offered, Dead or Alive.

Emotions swelled up inside Tor. Anger, fear, confusion. It took a few seconds to notice the wanted poster next to Rek's had his face upon it.

"What the f..." Tor felt eyes upon him everywhere now.

"What can I get yer?" asked an unkempt barkeep.

If he just left without ordering it would look strange. "I'll have some stew, bread, some of that roast meat and have you got any fruit juice?"

"Just the wives mixed berry?"

"Fantastic!" Tor dropped a silver on the bar. "I'll sit at that table in the corner." He had been sleeping rough and grown a decent beard while searching for the secret garden. He had learned a long time ago that the best disguise was confidence. As his food arrived, he pointed at the poster of himself behind the bar and asked the barmaid, "what are they wanted for? Does that say dead or alive? Can I see them?"

"I'll fetch them for you for a copper."

Tor downed the juice. It was light and refreshing "Get me another juice as well, and I'll give you a silver coin." A moment later she was back with the posters, a large bowl of stew, and some healthy slices of roast meat. She had a skip in her step. Paying her, she smiled at him.

"For another silver, I'll pour you a bath and give you something soft to sleep on tonight." The thought of a bath was intoxicating. Then he remembered his commander's lessons 'Dirt is the best disguise!'

Coming back to the moment, the barmaid had presented Tor with two great reasons to stay. She leaned provocatively over the table, pretending to clean. Maybe he'd come back if all went well tonight. "I'm afraid I'm promised elsewhere, or I would. Maybe later or another time."

The barmaid left him to his meal which he devoured with vigour. It was a surprisingly good stew, with chunky vegetables, beef and a rich gravy. He stuffed a couple of roast meat into some of the bread and slipped it into his pocket. He had befriended a crazy old one-armed man on the street, and it would be a pleasant surprise for him.

Tor had noticed the bar starting to fill up. He listened to several conversations. A merchant was talking about the fall of the royal house and the man who would lead them to the future, Blaquart. The merchant had drunk one too many in Tor's opinion. Biting into a piece of roast meat, he cast his attention to the next table, just farmers talking about the harvest and complaining about raised taxes. Near the entrance was a game table, four people were playing cards. He had eaten all the food quicker than he thought possible. Argento had shared experience and enjoyment. Tor could feel the dragon's contentment.

Drinking some of the juice, he looked over the posters. Thankfully his description still had him with one blue eye and one green. His eyes were both blue since the melding with the Ib'ren Cohar. This had been his saving grace with the patrols that stopped him. He had to give credit to the artist that had captured his likeness and thanks to whoever had thought to add his old eye colour. It had allowed him a certain anonymity.

The Inn had filled up since he started his meal. Rising smoothly from the table, it was time to leave. Making his way to the exit, he felt eyes watching him. A pair of big, burly men blocked his path.

"Where do you think you're going?" roared one of the brutes, as he reached out to grab Tor.

He sidestepped the clumsy grab easily. "Lay a hand on me, and I will break one of your bones!"

Aleator felt Argento awaken. The dragon was excited at the prospect of combat. Tor felt his senses increase. The dimly lit room was now bathed in colour. The scents of the room now separated into distinct, individual smells. Tor felt the warm airflow over his skin. Electricity now danced around his eyes and time slowed. Tor watched as the brute's arm slowly snaked out towards him again, totally ignoring his warning. Dodging with consummate ease, Aleator raised his arm to block the blow. Using his attacker's momentum, a quick twist and he'd snapped his opponent's arm and moved past him toward the door.

A roar of pain erupted from the brute he left on the floor, drawing the attention of every other drinker within the Inn. Ducking under an incoming right from the second man Tor continued to move toward the exit. Turning into his attacker, he pushed the big man off-balance, or so he thought. This one kept his balance and was clearly no ordinary reveller. Most likely a bounty hunter with some training in grappling.

Tor admired the man's tenacity as a knife appeared in his hand, and he flew at Tor again. Against most people, this man was probably a formidable foe, but Tor and Argento were no ordinary foe. He delivered a punch to his opponent's chin, snapping his head back, sending him flying back into the table of card players.

The thug landed hard, and violence erupted throughout the inn. This time it wasn't directed at Tor himself. The patrons of the inn attacked one another, giving Tor the chance to slip out the door and into the night.

Within just a few moments, Tor's reality had been flipped. He had thought Rek and Kiva would be safe, but now he knew he had left them alone and hunted. Bounty hunters would be tracking them down for crimes against the King. Tor didn't even have to think about it. He made his way to exit the city.

"Stop, Aleator," came the voice of Argento. "You cannot leave here."

"The hell I can't, Dragon! We can't leave them behind.

Rek and Kiva are in danger!"

"If we do not complete the task set out in front of us, The Dread will return each with one of my kind at their wrist. If they do, what do you imagine will happen to Rek and Kiva then?"

Tor clenched his fists tight. He knew the dragon was right.

"This is our priority, Aleator. If we leave now, we are all doomed. We have no choice."

Lightning flashed across the sky. A squadron of the

People's Army flooded into the inn that Tor had just left.

He would have to move before they came looking for him. Running through the shadows and back streets.

Not wanting to draw any attention to himself Tor had been sleeping on the streets since arriving at the city. He had made friends with a crazy old man, who seemed to know his way around all the best spots and abandoned buildings. He hoped that the man would eventually lead him to the secret garden.

Tor had tried asking the man his name, but he became agitated, making loud noises which drew the attention of the guard. After that, he decided to search by himself in the day, and find the old man at night. Tor brought the man food in the evening. People ignored the destitute, and he hoped to endear the man to him.

Tor had taken to calling the old man, Mathias, after a legendary, one-armed warrior blacksmith from childhood stories.

Tor had been dodging the People's Guard for weeks, and it had been no simple task. Sha'vel was indeed a bustling city, built on the ruins of a fortified city from The Age of Wonders. The only plus side was that it was home to fifty thousand inhabitants. It was an easy place to dodge the searching eyes of his enemies.

The Oracle had been right; if Rek and Kiva had come with him, they would most certainly be captured. The poster said he and Rek had been accused of conspiracy and aiding in the murder of King Leander.

Sha'vel seemed to be in mourning for the now-dead king. Tor struggled to understand why he and Rek had been implicated in his murder. They had been nowhere near the capital, and he was still considered dead. That is by all except whatever was chasing him. It meant the enemy was much more organised than he had imagined.

After acquiring a hooded robe, Tor spent most of his time stalking the People's Army, who had to be some of the worst gossipers in any army. He had overheard them talking about the new King. They named him as a Thaddius Blaquart, and he remembered that was the name of the soldier outside the door. One thing he knew for sure, Blaquart knew who Mandrake was, and once he found the Garden, he was going to pay him a visit.

Reunion
Chapter thirty two

When Tor got hold of Blaquart, he would have pointed questions for him. Putting it all aside, He could not solve that particular problem within the old walls of Sha'vel. He had to complete his mission here first.

Tor's troubled mind stirred Argento.

The dragon's deep voice echoed through his mind.

"What is wrong?"

"Nothing."

"I can tell it's not, nothing."

"You're in my head. You tell me."

"No need to be rude, Aleator Darkwing!"

Tor could feel he had hurt the Dragon's feelings. It was night time, and he had found a lead, a rumour of a blacksmith's that had been converted. He found the records in the city archives. Lathes of payment for some of the best masons of the age and yet the maps showed simple structures.

This was the area on the map that he was walking around. Argento felt some kind of magic and flooded Tor with adrenalin. His eyes slit, and Tor could see the light emanating from behind a hedge surrounding a large section of the wall.

"What is it?" he whispered in words of wonder across his mind.

"It is magic!"

It looked like the hedge was afire. As he got closer, he could see a symbol emblazoned on the wall shining through the hedge. This was the entrance. At last, his long search was complete. He was just about to reach out and touch the seal when he heard a familiar voice.

Looking up, the sky was obscured by the majestic wingspan of an armoured Gryphon. Riding atop the great beast was an elated Kiva and a pale yet happy looking Rek. As Bishop landed, Kiva pirouetted from his back landed gracefully on the ground. She ran over enveloping Tor in a hug. Rek was less graceful. His body turned as he dismounted, but you would not call it a pirouette. The more wondrous sight was watching as the Gryphon and its intricate armour shapeshifted into a rather elegantly dressed Bishop. He would look almost a commanding man if not for his stature and bright windswept red hair.

Argento couldn't help laughing in his mind. To him, Bishop was a wonder.

Before he could get another thought, Kiva said, "look at that pointing at the Sigel." She ran to the hedge and reached out.

Tor interceded, grabbing her hand before she could touch the Sigel. Argento was with him.

"Let me." Tor touched several points on the Sigel. The ground felt like it was rumbling under their feet.

Kiva had run back to Rek who seemed to be still getting his legs.

A large section of the hedged wall turned to create an opening. Crystal streetlights began to glow. That's when they heard it.

"Hahahaha, did kitty lose its teeth?"

Tor's face went ashen Rek and Kiva were there! The Oracle had foretold one of them would die if he didn't find the garden alone. In his panic, he called forth Argento. Whatever happened, neither of their friends would die.

Bishop placed a hand on Tor's chest. "This one is mine!" His tone brooked no argument "Protect them!" And with that he turned, his body growing and shifting into the dominant form of the Gryphon. Armour glistening in the moonlight. Bishop let out a ferocious screech filled with menace.

*

The Spider watched the transformation. "You should fly away kitty-kitty before..." The Spider turned his back to the Griffin with a flourish, red cape danced through the air, one of his top arms lifting the hood. The other had taken a sword out as well as his abdominal arm on the other side. He turned to face a charging Bishop. "My capes better than yours!" He jumped at a wall away from the oncoming Bishop, then pushed off that wall in a spinning mass of arms, blades and teeth.

Tor and Argento watched the first part of the confrontation in awe. Marching footsteps echoed around the street. Looking to the exits, they were boxed in. A thirty strong contingent had turned the corner blocking Kiva and Rek's escape, at both ends of the street.

Tor and Argento released a deep breath as one and walked toward the oncoming hoard. He could see every face, every expression on the faces of his foes. Their confidence in their numbers melted away as he closed his hand and released the blade of the Ib'ren Cohar. It extended like a whip. The blades a windmill of death, ripping at the ground and throwing chunks of earth into the air as he approached.

Tor turned to Rek and Kiva. "Rek protect Kiva! Go to the garden."

The People's Army had stopped their advance completely blocking the street. Tor could see someone passing through the ranks. It was… He couldn't believe his eyes. The man that had tortured him for three years had walked forward from the ranks as if to parley.

Opening his hand, the blade retracted whip-like back into the brace. There was a tremor in his voice as he yelled, "why are you here, Mandrake?"

"And I thought that was obvious. I'm here for what you stole from me!"

"Small price after what you stole from me," Tor remembered now.

He thought he'd kept the tremor from his voice, but Mandrake sneered. "Oh, of course, dog!" Mandrake laughed. "That's it... now you're figuring it out. The Ib'ren Cohar is mine. The power of the dragon was promised to me."

"Why did you take me?" No sooner had he asked the question he realized it didn't matter. This man would die by his hand. This man would die now!

Argento spoke in his mind. "Together." He released control to Argento.

Mandrake yelled, "Attack!" and stepped back into his ranks that swarmed forward.

It was like a meat grinder. Argento and Tor fought as one. Filled with rage, they practically flew at the oncoming men. Moving amongst them at an unnatural speed. The soldiers were no match for him.

Aleator and the dragon swerved in and out of the men with the grace of a dancer. Pointing his fist at the neck of a man in front of him, the scale-like blades speared the man's neck like it was cutting butter, then it extended almost instinctually another foot into the next soldier's neck. Opening his hand, the blades whipped back severing both heads as Tor ducked under a clumsy overhead swing. As Tor stood, he turned his body jumping and landed a powerful spinning kick to the man's ribs. Bones crunched as Tor's foot impacted the soldier's midsection, launching him backwards into surprised looking conscripts.

There was an unearthly quality that radiated from Mandrake as he stepped forward again. Bodies Tor had just killed started to twitch and move. Somehow this was no longer just Mandrake; it was Alal they faced. By his side was a creature of fire and smoke.

Tor and Argento thought in unison, "Kill him!" But they were caught off-guard as Alal attacked at an incredible speed.

*

On the other side of the compound, Mathias had been sleeping in a doorway when the walls had opened onto the courtyard of his smithy. It all came back to him, losing his apprentice to the Dread. Khnumm's betrayal and subsequent banishment that had broken his heart. It would be three hundred years in one more year. The prophecy had said "When you look upon the blood moon, the dragon is reborn. The battle is just beginning and give a helping hand. The man that time forgot will arm the revolution as his last stand. Make haste the Secret Courtyard is open, say your name and remember!"

To be honest, prophesy had never made much sense until right now as unbidden, he proclaimed, "I am Mathias Assai." No sooner had the name left his lips, he remembered; his name was Mathias Assai. His wards had been broken. He wasn't a perfect man, and he had lived longer than any since the age of wonders. This was his redemption. He could feel all the elements around him pulsing with life. The strength he had long forgotten flowed through him. The old one-armed man set off at a sprint

*

Back in the street Bishop was fighting for all he was worth. The People's guard appearing had been a surprise, but not so much of a hindrance as the creature in the red cape that always seemed to be two seconds away from Bishop's razor-sharp claws. The thing had killed almost as many of the enemy troops as he had. The thing may have had the ability to foresee his attacks, but the soldiers hadn't been as nimble. They had been rent in two, guts spilt, steaming onto the road. Some of the men began to run away. Bishop spun around looking for the creature, the club on his tail smashing several men from their feet. Then pouncing on the men in front of him, two swipes from Bishop's newly armoured claws cut chunks from their bodies.

The few remaining soldiers had backed off from the destruction these creatures of legend wrought on their surroundings. The two circled each other over the bodies of the dead. Something changed.

"Here... Kitty, Kitty!"

Bishop spun his armoured shell damp from the light rain now falling. The ground was slippery from blood and rain, and the dead were rising. This shouldn't be possible.

The bug-eyed creature had jumped out of the way of their grasping hands like an acrobat and climbed the massive Gryphon.

The Spider was enjoying himself immensely finding a perch atop Bishop. He was laughing and smacking Bishop's armoured rump with the blade. "Too late to run Kitty. He comes... Wheeeeeeeee!"

Bishop pounced into the air with The Spider clinging to his back. He needed to block the entrance to the courtyard. Bishop was holding his own but had been pushed back to the opening. He would squash this insect against the wall like a bug.

"I wonder, Kitty, are your eyes armoured?" The spider appeared to be thinking over his own question.

Bishop had gained some height, while the maniacal creature was still whooping on his back. He furled his wings and dove directly at the wall.

*

Kiva and Rek had backed into this newly lit courtyard. A large working fountain with water cascading into a wide basin was a central feature. Seeing what was coming for them, they strategically put a wall between them and the oncoming enemy by climbing into the fountain.

Kiva was scared, but she was with Rek, who appeared to bat away a relentless stream of what she could best describe as fireballs launched by a man-made of fire. Kiva didn't think she'd ever been so glad of the rain. Hissing as it touched the beings shell, she could tell it pained it. It looked to Kiva like it had a cloak of steam or smoke as it approached.

Kiva could also see Tor was being pushed back towards them. The monster of fire and smoke launched a blistering attack. To Kiva it looked like Rek was carrying the sun. She had to help, but she didn't know-how.

Orion had told her that her song had power and so she sang of the ocean's power to Rek's back. It raised the water in the fountain as a shield wall. Her voice echoed through the courtyard.

Achill, cloaked in his armour of fire, seemed visibly shaken if that was possible.

Tor was desperately trying to get back toward his friends. Thanks to Alal's onslaught, he had gotten to the courtyard entrance. The ground felt like it shook for a moment as Bishop crashed to the ground behind him. The Spider had launched himself from Bishop flying over the wall with both swords drawn. For Tor, it was as if time had slowed down.

"Stoooooooooooop Siiiiiiiingiiiing!" The Spiders harsh cry tore through the cold night air.

Tor had no time to think he jumped and kicked Alal square in the face launching himself at The Spider, the arm holding the Ib'ren Cohar extended reaching for his target. The blades of the Ib'ren Cohar closed the distance in seconds dissecting two of the Spider's sword arms from its body and knocking the foul creature away from Kiva and Rek.

Behind him, he heard Alal shout, "Now!"

Tor could see the dead entering the courtyard behind Alal following him in. He did not, however, see Achill's attack. An obsidian blade as dark as night and twice as sharp took Tor's arm clean off at the elbow. He heard it more than felt it collapsing into a ball as his momentum carried him into the fountain with Kiva and Rek away from his arm and the Ib'ren Cohar, which was now lying a few feet outside the fountain wall.

The pain in his arm was immense. Rek was catching his breath while Achill's attention was elsewhere happy to let the dead take their fill. Kiva had a look of determination that wasn't there before, stabbing a dead soldier in the face as it tried to climb the fountain wall.

Tor watched through a pain-induced haze as

Mandrake, and apparently, Alal's host picked up the Ib'ren Cohar, pulled Tor's arm from it, and disdainfully threw the unwanted limb to the ground. It was then he realized he could no longer hear Argento. He suddenly felt bereft. His eyelids had become heavy. He could not focus. He must be dreaming. It was like the dead had stopped to watch as Mandrake thrust the serpentine blade of the Ib'ren Cohar into the air in celebration. Then all went black.

All was lost. Kiva was holding him now. She was singing softly when she unscrewed her pendant and gave Tor the healing tear of the goddess.

Rek was doing what he was born for. He was holding the line against impossible odds. All seemed lost.

*

That was when the strangest thing happened, and a familiar voice echoed around the yard.

"The dead have no power here!"

Tor could not believe his eyes. The runes lit up along every wall. Then there was a blinding flash. Looking away, he watched as the attacking dead were turned to dust and fell to the ground.

The crazy one-armed man he'd made friends with when he'd had to sleep rough, Mathias. It was strange Tor could swear the man had an arm of pure light.

That was the last thing Tor saw as he passed out from blood loss.

Somehow this new arrival had banished the dead, but The Djinn had opened a portal and left with Mandrake taking the Ib'ren Cohar. They disappeared just as the massive bolt of white energy crackled across the yard, discharging on the building where they had been.

Rek and Kiva were dumbstruck.

*

Assai walked over and tapped the shield Rek was still holding up. "Can use your shield to carry your friend inside."

"Who are you?" Rek asked eyeing the new man in their midst.

"I am Mathias Assai." As he spoke, he waved his hand at the closest wall to the fountain. It sank into the ground, revealing windows and doors. "This is my home, and you are safe now bring Tor in I will clean and bandage his wound."

"You just lead the way. I'll get Tor." He threw his shield back over his shoulder and picked his friend up.

Tor seemed delirious with pain.

Assai looked at Kiva. "We need to search for all the uniforms and hide them. Who knows what you might find?" And winked at her conspiratorially

Kiva was in shock but being from the street, she understood the value of a thorough search. "And all I have to do is collect everything from the road?"

"From the road first, bring it all into the compound, as quick as you can!"

"What about the bodies?"

"All the bodies will be nothing but ash. We must retrieve all the weapons and uniforms, though. Bring them into the courtyard so I can close the way in again and reset the wards."

Rek was relieved she had something to do. "Kiva stay within shouting distance."

Assai had opened a door into a modestly sized but decoratively dressed inn. He led Rek to a backroom pointing him toward a bed where Rek laid Tor.

"Now let me attend your friend's wound. If you would help the girl?"

"Will he be okay?"

Assai just smiled. "Go… help the girl. I need to examine him before I can say how he is!"

Rek did as he was told, which even surprised him. Outside Kiva was poking at the remains of The Spider.

"Kiva! What are you doing?" she jumped. "It's not like the others!" she blurted.

As Rek got closer, he could see she was right. This was more like a spider shedding its skin. The creature was nowhere to be seen. "Come away from there, Kiva. We need to check the road."

"Okay."

Rek caught her up in a big hug. "I'm just glad you're okay... You are okay?"

"Did you see any food in there?"

The big man smiled. Even the recent battle had not dulled the girl's appetite. "I don't know. There must be something, we'll do this quick, and we can search for some."

He put her down, but she didn't let go straight away. They walked to the corner hand in hand and were confronted with the catatonic Gryphon Bishop.

"Quick Kiva get that man."

A few moments later came out of the building mumbling something under his breath. Moving Rek out of the way he looked over their friend, "Impressive armour!" then with a quick motion, pulled a snapped blade from Bishop's eye. No sooner had he removed the blade. Bishop shifted back into his human form.

"I think that's everything. Can you carry your friend inside? I'm sure you're both hungry."

Kiva and Rek looked at each other and smiled. Rek picked up Bishop, who was a lot heavier than he looked. As they entered the lodging, they could hear Tor talking in his sleep. It sounded like he was having nightmares.

He said, "You cannot have my friends. I will find the garden alone!" Again, and again, he repeated it.

Assai brought him a cold, wet towel. "Calm yourself.

Your friends are alive and safe."

Tor's eyes shot open, and he grabbed Assai by the shirt. "They cannot find the secret garden with me, or they will die, Kairos said only I could survive the garden."

"That's alright then. This isn't the secret garden; it's my courtyard. The secret garden is in Sha'mack."

Tor visibly relaxed. Then sat bolt upright "Wait... I brought you something in my coat!"

"Thank you, Aleator. Sleep now, you need your rest." Assai pushed him down, and Tor was out cold. He should have died from losing his wounds. Momentarily curious Assai checked Tors Jacket, he found the roast sandwich. So you are him Assai thought as he reminisced on a prophesy he had forgotten. Taking a bite of the sandwich, maybe all was not lost just yet.

The End of Book 1 in The Forgotten Trilogy

Coming soon Book 2 Rebellion

Epilogue

Emmel didn't fancy his chances in Kishar, mostly as Gabriel was down and would be for some time. The last thing he said was that they needed to go south. One thing was for sure if they had any hope of survival, they needed to be far away from Kishar. One more trip through the portal stone and he would destroy his ring.

His current problem was that he could only carry so much and with so many choices it made gathering as many items as he could a complicated affair. Filling a shoulder bag, he made his way back to the unconscious Gabriel.

Drinking one of several rare potions he had collected. He said a quick prayer to the goddess of earth, Gaia. There was a ten percent chance it would kill him, but he had no other choices. It felt like he was drinking lava as it went down and ripped through his small frame like a firestorm. I was a Jaden strength potion made to enhance children of Gaia.

Pain like nothing he had ever felt wracked his body, his eyes blackened and new muscles formed under his once baggy clothing. Cracks appeared in his skin, blood and tendons glowing in between the cracks in his skin. The change felt like an eternity but arise he did. Grabbing his pack and throwing the unconscious Gabriel over his shoulder, he headed for the portal stone.

Opening a gateway to Sha'mack the wall rippled and faded into a darkened hall. Once through he broke his ring. Now the only way into this trove would be through the mountain of Kidinger and no-one had entered that way in millennia.

At this time of an evening, the royal box for the games was vacant. Emmel knew he could not stay here. No, he needed to go further if they were to build a rebellion. He would get them passage to Sha'vel. He could not afford to be seen by any of the People's Army.

Thankfully this city was full of secret passages. One, in particular, was just down the corridor from this very room.

Laying Gabriel down, Emmel walked to the entrance, where he could see two guards. He already regretted what he must do next. These soldiers probably had families and loved ones, but the potion he had taken would wear off soon, and he could not risk witnesses. He prayed it would get them where they needed to go. Stepping from the doorway, he was at the first guard in seconds. On any other day, the soldier's armoured shoulder would protect him from most blows, but in Emmel's current state, he simply crushed the metal plate and bone between his fingers. The man momentarily let out a strangled cry before being slammed into the wall with such force his skull was instantly crushed on impact.

The second guard managed to draw his weapon; it would do him no good. Emmel caught the mans arms as he attacked, closing his eyes he didn't want to see the fear in the guard's face. No man should have this kind of power. It was as simple as tearing a piece of paper; ripping this man in half. Blood sprayed the walls, and guts pooled on the floor. Turning away from the carnage he had wrought he went back for Gabriel.

Grabbing his things and throwing his best hope at forming a rebellion back over his shoulder, Emmel ran back down the corridor, avoiding the blood so as not to leave any boot prints to show his passing. Pushing on a stone in the wall it gave way, and a large section lowered into the ground revealing a long dusty tunnel.

A spasm wracked Emmel's body dropping him to one knee. The potion was wearing off quicker than anticipated. Closing the secret entrance, he set off at a run. He ran until his tendons burned. Emmel felt like he'd ripped every muscle in his body as he arrived at the secret entrance to the cellar in his nephew Arden's Inn, The Silver Dame.

Arden had never really been accepted in Kishar due to his affinity for wearing women's clothes. Unlike Emmel, his nephew was a fighter and above average in size, but eventually, even Arden grew weary of the city of light and made his home further south in Sha'mack. Emmel had put his nephew in touch with Brea Darkwing who had helped find Arden a place he could be free. Of course, he still ran into fools, but he finally had the freedom to be who he wanted, and as such owed Emmel a favour and it was time to call in the debt.

With the last of his strength, Emmel carried Gabriel into The cellar to the silver Dame and collapsed from exertion. It was strange just before the world went black; he could swear he heard voices in the room with him.

*

It had been a slow night in The Silver Dame which annoyed Arden profusely. There just wasn't any appreciation for the arts anymore. Thankfully his girls still kept the dullards of Sha'mack coming back.

Arden had been singing a favourite shanty on stage when he noticed one of his patrons was getting handsy with one of the girls without paying for the privilege. Arden finished the song stepping from the stage, and the situation was escalating. These things always seemed to happen when he was wearing his best dresses.

The man was fumbling up Miriel's under-dress, and her distress was clear. No one mistreated Arden's girls and the backhand the man delivered to quiet the girl was the last straw. "Miriel back to the changing rooms girl!"

"She's going nowhere you ugly bitch." The drunk foolishly responded.

Arden threw the man to the floor. "Go now, Miriel!"

"Now I'm going to cut you whore!" The drunk pulled a wicked-looking knife. The bar had gone quiet, and the tension in the room was palpable. Arden had spent his whole life dealing with fools such as this and had taken the knife off him in seconds and was astride him on the floor and beating the man bloody. Arden's barkeep was shouting his name. Always something when your busy teaching a lesson. "Well I guess no one is going to call you my lovely ever again and normally pulling a knife is death!"

"Arden It's important!"

"In a minute!" Arden yelled at the keep before leaning back over the fool and whispering. "If I ever see you again, I will bury this knife where you most like to scratch." Arden grabbed the limp mans hand placed it on the wooden chair he had been sat on and rammed his knife into his hand. The man screamed. Arden's security had come over and taken over the removal of the piece of shit form his establishment. Arden looked around the room "The next drinks on me." A cheer went up as Arden went to see what was wrong at the bar.

"Someones entered through the cellar!" said the barkeep in hushed tones.

"Okay I'll see to it, you see to them." Arden nodded at the bar where a queue was building for their free drink and with that Arden ran down to the cellar.

Arden was worried as this entrance was only known to a few and a disturbance on this night imparticular was cause for alarm as well as hosting upstairs there had been a secret meeting called downstairs by none other than the leader of the crows' a spy network. Brea Darkwing himself. Arden wasn't worried about any immediate trouble as the men and women downstairs could look after themselves, but the possible ramifications of being found out didn't bear thinking about.

Two Ashiri warriors guarded the cellar door and moved to let Arden pass. Entering the cellar, he could see two men laid on tables. The first was none other than the Lord Marshal of the Athanatos. The second, Arden couldn't believe his eyes it was Emmel, his uncle, and he was covered in blood. Running to his uncle's side, he began checking for wounds and saying his name trying to rouse him "Emmel, Emmel."

"He is alive and from what I can tell the blood is not his, Arden. I have ordered the men to seal the entrance from the sewer tunnels." Came the deep baritone of Brea.

"Who has done this?" Arden's voice was filled with menace."

"That I do not know, and it would seem we will not find out until they have rested." Brea was a man who spoke little, but when he did, his voice rang with authority. "You must go back upstairs and keep appearances; we will tend to them. A woman from Ripstones manor had brought some wine and trickled some into each of the men's mouths. "I will send word up when and if they wake."

Arden wasn't happy being told what to do, but this wasn't a man you made ask you twice. "Fine, I will send some food down, and the moment he's awake you send for me!" he responded frustrated.

"I will."

Somewhat placated Arden stroked his uncle's cheek and whispered in his ear "You are safe now, dear uncle, rest." And with that, he went back to running the Inn.

*

A few hours had passed before Emmel awoke and his head was pounding "Water."

Brea fetched his old friend some water and helped him to a sitting position so he could drink. Looking to one of the Athanatos "Go fetch Arden."

"So I made it then, wasn't sure I could."

"What has happened, Emmel?"

"The king is dead, and the usurper has blamed Gabriel and taken the throne. Gabriel, where is Gabriel?"

"He is here." Brea stepped aside so he could see the unconscious Lord Marshal. "For the life of me, I do not know how you got him here, but you are both safe now." "Nowhere is safe Brea." Emmel's eyes fluttered, and his head spun "We cannot stay here! We must go to Sha'vel…" The little man's words trailed off.

Brea gently laid him down to rest once more. "Gain your strength old friend, your safe now, and there is time for talk of rebellion in the morning."

Glossary

Achill pronounced A-kill

An elemental being of smoke and fire. Once a King among his kind. Can travel through fire or shadows. Makes a pact with the Dragonborn to aide in their release and they would end the ice age

Anunnaki pronounced A-nun-aki

Giants, children of the god of knowledge

Assai pronounced Ass-eye

A master geomancer wizard/blacksmith missing for centuries. Creator of weapons of legend, All-Father. He disappeared from the face of the earth. His forges went with the knowledge.

Athanatos pronounced Ath-an-at-oss

Immortals. The king's warriors, assassins, judges, ambassadors. Trained to be his voice in peacetime and his fist in war.

Bishop

He is a Griffin displaying a large feline body suspended by wings of white feathers. In human form, his other half, he is Bishop. The Kings left hand. Small in stature at 4 foot 6" with some elemental magic. Comical yet devious and crafty.

Blaquart pronounced Black-art

Lord Commander of the People's Army.

Dread Dragonborn

Five Ibren'Cohar were crafted, and four of the five had become Dragonborn.

Khnumm - Fire dragon Huabolis.

Satet - Water dragon Khawn.

Tao'nas - Earth dragon Typhos

Uruku - Air dragon Malius

The fifth member of the Dread walks the halls of the dead as a Licht.

Alal - Searching for a way back to the realms of man – Spirit dragon Argento would have been his.

Fenn

The Fenn have a long history. They are bipedal but have feline features.

Fidelus pronounced Fid - dell - us

The faithful evil human minions of the Dragonborn. Will do anything asked by their gods in the belief of being raised up above all others.

Ib'ren Cohar pronounced Ib - ren Co - har

Made from dragon bones tougher than metal. The blade is made of dragon wings and can extend or retract, giving the blade the ability to be used as a razor-sharp whip. Forged by capturing a dragon, chopping off the legs and wings and using magic to melt the Adamite bones to forge the blade. The dragon had to still be alive to merge its elemental life force.

It was made in the elemental age by Khnumm to force a bond with the bearer, creating an unparalleled assassin to take out wizards, demigods and heroes. Five were made by Khnumm using the techniques stolen from Assai. The ultimate weapon, the Ib'ren Cohar.

Jaden pronounced Jay-Den

A small yet physically strong people, they are the miners and stonemasons, tied to the element of earth. Finely chiselled features and athletically built, averaging between three and a half feet and five feet in height. Fiercely courageous.

Laforte pronounced La – for - tay

Lord Commander of the Peoples guard

Licht pronounced Licked

A dead warlock. Able to walk the halls of hell and earth. General abilities – possession, necromancy, persuasion, fire.

Mandrake

Tor's torturer and teacher of things he never wanted to learn.

Nightkin

A flesh-eating goblin. Able to release a noise that inspires panic and fear.

Ninti

A sword of the element wind. It was made by Assai. Retains the memories of any surviving the tests to become a bearer.

Norn's

Elemental tree creatures, many shapes and sizes. Wardens of the south and friends with the Jaden. They live long lives getting larger as they get older. At around four hundred, they fade and become trees.

Orions belt

A relic from the Age of Wonders. It is made from metamorphic material by a god to protect the Griffin. The belt would give the bearer an almost impenetrable armour in feline form and back to formal clothes when human.

Portal stones

A way to travel. Created from the same stone by Mathias Assai, the stones shared quantum entanglement over great distances. This allows for instant travel through any of the stone monoliths scattered about High Garden. It was said they were shut down sometime during the Chaos War of 300 AG.

Warg

Pony sized wolves

Va'Nahual pronounced Va na-who-al.

A human being who has the power to magically turn himself, or herself into any animal form. The Va'nahual however a twisted thing of evil, a human forced into blending by dark arts. They come in many shapes and sizes. They are the Va'nahual.

Dren

Like the Sokar but smaller and due to a child's innocence, the more dark magicians can feed if they can taint the child's soul. The result was a child-sized creature of evil intent, blended with multiple animals of all kinds.

Sokar pronounced So-car

Predatorily chimaera, humans turned into killing, eating, and fucking machines. A powerful witch or warlock forces the bond.

Soulless

Human and Sokar half breed children. Touched by demonic powers in the womb. Some elemental magic. Giants among the Va'nahual

Elemental Gods and their children

Gaia pronounced Guy-A

Earth goddess

Maja pronounced My-A

Elemental creatures of earth and stone. They are a hive mind and as such, have no names. They are Maja. Norns grow on the back of them until they are strong enough to be separated.

Ostara pronounced Oh-star-a

Fire. Goddess

DJinn pronounced Jin

Lords of the lower planes of reality able to possess other creatures, shadow beings of fire and smoke. Consumers.

Raijin pronounced Rye – Jin

Spirit. God

Suijin pronounced Sue - Jin A

Water. God. The river king.

Stribog pronounced stry-bog

Air. God

Printed in Great Britain
by Amazon